Doctor Zipp's Amazing Octo-Com

AND OTHER LONDON STORIES

Dan Carrier

LONDON BOOKS BRITISH FICTION

LONDON BOOKS
39 Lavender Gardens
London SW11 1DJ
www.london-books.co.uk

A catalogue record for this book
is available from the British Library

ISBN 978-0-9957217-0-8

Printed and bound in Great Britain by
CPI Antony Rowe

Typeset by Octavo Smith Publishing Services
www.octavosmith.com

All events and persons in these stories are entirely fictional
and are in no way based on real events.
Please remember: you can't believe everything you read…

For Richard Osley and Tom Foot

CONTENTS

THE *EUPHRATES* KARAOKE BARGE

THE *EUPHRATES* KARAOKE Barge was moored up in Camden Town almost every weekend. It was run by Eddie Roll and I'd long been fascinated by him. I wasn't just attracted by his extraordinary business – and it was a sight to behold, a bloke who had a karaoke bar on a boat and filled it out with people and drink and songs and singing – but the way he'd converted a seventy-year-old timber cargo vessel into something else completely, and all done by his large, rough hands. It made me suspect there was genius lurking in this scruffy-looking character.

I'd first met Eddie when I staggered past his boat one night after a few after-work drinks and heard raucous voices. They seeped out from beneath a closed door, which was also giving off a warm, enticing light. It was a tuneless and drunk rendition of The Kingston Trio's 'Where Have All The Flowers Gone?' and it made me laugh so much – particularly the gusto with which the chorus was sung by everyone inside – that I couldn't help but stop and go in.

I am a fairly nosey person. I'm a newspaper reporter, so I kind of have to be. I spend my days chasing stories and then heading back to a newsroom to hunker down in front of a computer screen and bash away at a keyboard. The newsroom is a messy, noisy and stimulating place full of laughter and argument, politics and posturing, the stirring of trouble and caring for those who need a champion.

I work at *The London Evening Press And Star*. It is one of a dying breed – an independently owned local that aims to do news properly, with a group of reporters who generally enjoy their beats and don't consider their job to be a mere stepping-stone to a national. It helps that we are lucky enough to have a great area to cover – Central London and its surrounds – and an editor who was schooled in the news-gathering techniques of the past, which means he expects you to shift your arse from your seat, unglue your eyeballs from the internet and go out and meet real people.

Quoting Mark Twain (but pretending it's a line of his own), he would shout he wanted copy that was 'peppery and to the point, not this milk and mush you've given me' and that he needed 'bare-knuckle copy, get-to-the-meat, jump-to-the-marrow' stories, not 'this flimsy say-nothing'. His was a stereotypical editor's approach to management, as if he'd read too many novels about newspapers, seen too many films based in newsrooms and modelled himself on a gruff, silver-haired, cigar-chomping overlord of tomorrow's fish-and-chip wrappings.

It's never openly said by the reporters at *The Evening Press And Star* – it would be getting above ourselves – but I consider us to be social historians, chroniclers of the immediate world around us, telling the stories of our readers, campaigning on things that matter, tickling the public with things that don't, and trying, in this quick, shouty, crunched-down world of modern communication, to make sense of it all through the traditional medium of a weekly printed newspaper.

Someone once said to me how they liked the way we focused on 'everyday folk', a condescending phrase but recognition all the same that the *Press And Star* didn't just write pathetic half-truths about famous people as a form of newsprint escapism for the readership. We worked on the premise that everyone had an amazing story to tell: everyone had broken a heart or had a heart broken. People had committed fantastic crimes and had sins foisted upon them. Every-one had a tragedy and a miracle to share, and we tried to fill the *Press And Star*'s smudgy pages with such stories each week. It was my job to hunt them down, to hear people out and try to make some readable sense of fantastic yarns in a few hundred words that would get past the critical eye of our old-school editor.

Eddie's barge seemed just the place to pick up a tale or tip, land a lead, follow a thought, and I gradually became accepted by Eddie and the bloodshot regulars who leant against the bar or slumped back in the various broken-down armchairs on board.

I would discover that his clients included curious day-trippers, parties of drunk students, gangs of scruffs and herds of hipsters. But he had also earned the daily custom of the market traders, the flower men, the fruit-and-vegetable sellers who saw through the attractive kookiness of the barge's bar and simply knew Eddie – liked him and wanted to give him business while enjoying his company.

Every night Stephen, who ran the second-hand bookshop, would come in for a beer before heading home. There was Rick The Jeweller, who would close his small workshop in the Lock every day at 4pm and drop by before the place got busy. Rick knew everyone and everything that was going on, and he and Eddie would trade information and gossip. They'd discuss the day's sales with stall-holders from the more touristy bit of the market, and their cash-in-hand staff – the people who flogged T-shirts, old Adidas tracksuit tops, records, homemade clocks and second-hand cameras. Later, they would be followed by the barmen from Camden Town's pubs who fancied a change of scene and didn't want to give their wages back to their bosses.

There were three Greek Cypriot bakers, who'd spend all day making things out of filo pastry and vine leaves, had flour dust in their hair and smelt wonderful. Staff from Camden Town tube station, a couple of road sweepers and trainers from the St Pancras Boxing Club all considered it home from home. There were musicians and actors – some well-known, others unhappily anonymous – and they also deserved to be regarded as *Euphrates* regulars, whose favoured tipples Eddie knew to pour without asking.

While it was these low-paid workers who kept it afloat, they were frequently joined by high-earning media types whose firms had taken over the canal-side warehouses and came in on a 'night out', acting as if they owned the joint. Dark looks would be cast in their direction when the cramped interior got too hot and stuffy, but it didn't matter to Eddie. He had that knack of making everyone feel at home. It was another talent of the many he possessed.

*

Eddie did a line in ill-fitting clothes when he wasn't entertaining: old chequered shirts, baggy, grubby jeans and sagging, shapeless, over-large T-shirts, plus either old hiking-boots or scuffed trainers.

More often than not he wore a woolly hat with the Rasta colours going round in a band. It had been knitted with dreadlocks in mind, but he was virtually bald, so it sagged down the back of his head and drifted sullenly towards his neck.

He was thin, tight-cheeked, bony-faced. It looked like his head had been held in a vice and squished. It was long, went on for a bit and then for a bit more, before being offset by a massive pair of pointed ears.

His mouth gawped open when he sang, showing a broken and blackened interior, and he had a habit of peering down his nose when he spoke to you, and this gave him a strange air of constantly weighing things up.

You might say he was rat-like if you had to describe Eddie to a stranger, but knowing Eddie like I did, I'd say his character was more like Mole from *The Wind In The Willows* – his buck teeth and elongated face did not remind me of a rodent, as he was just too kind in his habits, although I'd been told it did for others.

His face also bore the marks of a life well-lived. Physical exercise and outdoor living would have given him a polished hue in different circumstances, but he was racked with the ageing signs caused by tobacco, ganja and rum. Yet his eyes told of the delight he felt in all he saw around him. They were sparkling, alive, vibrant, even when stoned, reflecting a character that found joy in simple things. He had spent a lifetime behaving pretty disgracefully and had enjoyed every minute of it, and it showed.

Eddie had a soft voice, but the words it contained were often fierce. He would spit and chew and damn everything that came near if he was in that type of mood. But sometimes he would speak elo-quently, particularly about literature and the books he had read, and after knowing him for a year or so he told me he used to teach English at a comprehensive school, and that made sense. He could tell you something about the poetry of Thomas Hardy and the Edwardian response to grief, love and sex and DH Lawrence, the comparisons between *Goodbye To All That* and *All Quiet On The Western Front* as examples of English and German reactions to the Great War and other topics on early-20th-century literature, which he had studied and enjoyed.

His other passion was music. He had always been absolutely mad about record collecting, and that was the reason he ran such a unique business. He'd played guitar in a skiffle band as a kid – 'I wanted to be Lonnie Donegan at first, and then Hank Marvin,' he told me – and could pick up just about any stringed instrument and bash out a passable tune. He loved turning on his stereo, and he loved having people in who wanted to see if they could hold a note and have a stab at their favourite song.

*

Eddie told me he had bought the *Euphrates* when he was teaching, and saw it at first as a holiday thing, a weekend project.

'It was just a shell,' he said.

'I got it from a boatyard near Rugby and then brought it in stretches down the Grand Union, a few miles every weekend, till I reached Camden Town. It took me about two years to get the inside in any way acceptable to live in, but when I had, I realised it was crazy on my small teaching salary to have a house and a boat. I built a bunk and have been living on board ever since.'

Perhaps, I wondered, it was this that had led to the split with his wife. He'd mentioned in passing he'd once been married – 'Wasn't much good at it,' he'd added – and he also had a son.

Perhaps she didn't like life on the canal and that had caused the schism. I didn't pry.

The interior of the *Euphrates* was remarkably spacious. Everything had a place and had been carefully designed to make the most of the room available.

A bar ran along one side and tapered off into a nook before you reached a door that led to a toilet. The back of the boat housed a kitchen and a bunk-room, and then you got to the stern, which you accessed through a set of double doors with stained-glass windows. It led to an outdoor deck area, with a seat for the pilot next to the tiller. In its floor was a hatch to access the huge, asthmatic diesel engine, and more space to stash things.

The trick of living and working on board was, he told me, to store things carefully: it meant everywhere you looked there were nooks and crannies, hatches to lift up, drawers to open out. Every built-in seat had a cavity beneath. His bed had a huge gully beneath the mattress. It was like a Tardis. Not one inch was wasted.

'At first I looked at the shell of the *Euphrates* and thought to myself that it would be easy to get everything in. It seemed so very big,' he said. 'But then I started writing a list of all the stuff I needed for a bar – the pipes and hoses and a place to store the kegs, and a little space for the singer to stand, and a spotlight in the roof to shine on them, and the speakers… there was just so much to fit in. My mate Jim helped me out – he's a chippy, excellent at making cupboards, foldaway tables, that sort of thing – and we kept joking: "We're gonna need a bigger boat."'

The bar comfortably held twenty people, including Eddie, who would work the stereo and serve drinks. He had designed it so he could pour beer, administer shorts and operate the karaoke machine all at the same time.

He had a shelf with a mixer and decks, and a telly mounted on the wall that the lyrics would scroll across. It turned into a mirror by day. A sofa ran down the port side with a fold-up table in front of it, and at the end of the bar on the starboard side was further seating.

I loved the little attentions to detail Eddie had included. In the centre of the boat was a two-foot-square board set in the floor. It had two brass rings Eddie would flip up and use to hoick it out from its spot. Turning it over, four small legs could be unhooked from their position strapped across the back. He would then pop the legs up, put it back in its slot, and it gave the singer a three-inch-high stage to stand on. A tiny glitter ball hung from the ceiling and a pair of spotlights hit the stage from behind Eddie's serving area.

While to my eyes the *Euphrates* was basically perfect – a work of art – Eddie always seemed to have a project on the go. I'd sometimes pop in during the day if I had managed to find him moored within walking distance of the office, and more often than not he'd be wearing a tool belt and contorting his body into a strange shape as he wriggled himself into a cranny to fix something, or be stood on the towpath with his old, paint-splattered Black and Decker Workmate out and a bit of wood at his mercy. When he had a job on, he got a perverse pleasure out of wearing the grubbiest blue overalls you could possibly imagine, as if the oil and grease stains were badges of hard work, every paint splat a motif of how much time he had invested in the *Euphrates*.

The exterior of the boat was painted beautifully. It had a black hull, then a two-foot strip of bright red as a Plimsoll line, followed by a two-foot strip of dark green. It was topped off with a sunshine-yellow roof that had portholes cut in to it and a line of window boxes growing herbs and tomatoes. Extra light was provided along both the port and starboard sides where Eddie had cut large windows. He'd built in wooden shutters to give him some privacy when he wasn't open.

The name '*Euphrates*' was picked out in fancy letters of his own design across both sides of the prow, and then written larger in the same font along the back of the stern. He had brightly coloured car tyres hanging low in the water at the bow of the boat and more at the stern. He told me that few other barges bothered with proper tenders.

'After all, they say barging is exactly that: barging,' said Eddie. 'It's a contact sport – they drive their boats into the locks and use the walls as guides, so there are always scrapes. They don't mind a little bump either when they're heading in the opposite direction as you. But I used to cringe every time the *Euphrates* struck anything – really made my teeth hurt, and sent a shiver down my spine – so I thought I'd stick the car tyres down the sides. I don't know why other people on the canal don't have them. It makes it barely any wider.'

*

When Eddie wasn't entertaining or tinkering about with his odd jobs, he would kick back on the sofa and play his favourite music through the boat's home-built sound system.

As I spent more time with him, I began to recognise his fads and moods. On Sunday morning, he'd listen to gospel, soul and Motown. He'd play Nina Simone's spirituals and Toots And The Maytals doing reggae'd-up covers of Southern classics as if he were celebrating the music created for the Sabbath, if not the Sabbath itself.

When he had work to do, he liked Led Zep cranked right up: Jimmy Page's power chords and Robert Plant's warbling vocals, crashing their way through 'Ramble On', 'You Shook Me' and 'Heartbreaker'.

Before he went to bed, he'd dust off a Yehudi Menuhin LP or something by the Berlin Philharmonic. He loved Shostakovich, Beethoven, Bach, Handel. He had a fat collection of old LPs he'd harvested over the years and was always adding to it by visits to charity shops. He liked to give discarded vinyl a loving home. I often wondered how the *Euphrates* managed to stay afloat with Eddie's hoarding.

It also showed how wide his taste in music was: ELO and Free sat beside folky stuff and trad jazz, punk and eighties synth pop nestled next to techno and doo-wop. He loved everything – and I mean everything. He had a polyamorous approach to music, and his karaoke song listings were as wide and vast as his record collection. It was an added attraction to the *Euphrates*. No one who chose a track to sing was ever made to feel silly by the proprietor. He loved cueing the song up, introducing the singer and giving it some spiel about what they'd chosen. ('Did you know that Crosby, Stills, Nash and Young were asked to write the theme tune for *Easy Rider*, but when they offered the film studio the tune "Find The Cost Of Freedom", found on the B-side of their hit protest song "Ohio", it was turned down... and now here is Benjy from Chalk Farm giving us his own, no doubt beautiful, rendition of it.')

*

He had no opening hours he strictly adhered to. It depended where he found himself on the London canal network. Between Monday and Thursday, when there was no curtain call, he would chug east or west, and at quiet moorings do remarkable things to the *Euphrates*. He'd paint, polish, improve, customise. The first time I stepped on board 'out of hours', he greeted me so warmly it was as if he had been waiting for me to appear. I was immediately charmed.

The smell inside – a mixture of wood smoke, coffee, warm liquors and a faint hint of marijuana – seemed to seep out of the warm golden wood that he had used to panel the walls with, and that was charming, too. He had a cloth in his hand and a pot of Brasso – no doubt yet another layer of the fragrance I was smelling – and was furiously buffing up the metal rims of the portholes, the beer taps and the incidental brass he had tacked to door panels.

I liked the idea of him working away on his home and business, and I found watching him tinker about fairly mesmerising.

When he was in an expansive mood, and wanted to talk about his life and times, he'd put Burning Spear or Macka B on the stereo. I'd sit back on the most comfortable chair in the place and, as he worked, I gleaned more about his background.

He was a good storyteller. Eddie would talk of how moving barge-pace gave him extra time to think about the world around him – 'like Thoreau', he said without any air of pretension – and he'd litter his conversations with observations.

'I know every coot and moorhen from Paddington to King's Cross,' he told me.

'I know every swan and every drake, every heron and all that's in between. I know the fishermen. I know what they wish they'd catch and what they actually get hold of. I know the days of the week they don't work and the days they do.

'I know which trees shed their leaves first each autumn, and which bud first in spring. I know where the water is so still it'll ice up each winter as soon as the thermometer drops below zero.

'I know where every summer the duckweed blooms. I love watching the prow of the boat push through it like an Arctic icebreaker. Makes for good fertiliser for the tomatoes on the roof.'

He said that all these things made the canal feel alive, not an industrial highway but a meandering route through a hidden, special Neverland of London.

Eddie enjoyed life on board all year round, and would find something beautiful in every season. Perhaps he needed to. Living on a boat made him very aware of what the weather was doing.

'I love it when it rains and you hear it on the cabin's roof and the portholes trickle with silver,' he told me. 'I love it when it is sunny and the light comes in through the door and the portholes become spotlights.'

It might have been pissing down, but, as Eddie pointed out, he couldn't do anything about it, so he tried to enjoy the experience. If he felt the cold, or disliked the wet days, I don't think he could have enjoyed the canal life.

We'd been friendly for a while, and after he revealed he had worked in a school teaching English in the days before the *Euphrates*, he also told me he had a son called Joe who would sometimes pop on board, say hello and check up on his dad.

'He is a part-time Hare Krishna,' Eddie said.

'He has this job during the week and seems straight as a die, and then when Friday comes it is all Hare Krishna this, Hare Krishna that, Hare Krishna the other... he is a weekend Vishnu-botherer...'

I wondered aloud how that worked, and asked if he had a Krishna haircut that looked weird during the week.

'The hair's no problem,' he said. 'He is even balder than I am. And the other Krishnas do not seem to mind. He chants along with them like it was a 24/7 thing and helps cook for their free-food van. He says they've given up trying to convert him properly, and I think they like the fact he has a job and gives them his money. It was the food thing that drew him, you see... he's a dinner lady... cooks grub at a primary school, working in the kitchens, making buckets of spaghetti bolognese and big trays of jam roly-polies, and then goes out at the weekend on the food vans and does it all over again, serves up food for the down and outs. All quite admirable really, though I don't understand the God thing, and the chanting and stuff.

'We never had any religion at home when he was growing up, but the feed-the-world aspect, well, it's hard to argue with that.'

I wanted to ask about life before the *Euphrates*, and about his partner, his son's mum, but sensed that there was a tragedy relating to her. A shadow crept across the brightness in his eyes when he mentioned her in passing, as he told me about their offspring. I didn't pry, but I did wonder. Had she left him? Had she died? Something had happened, as she clearly wasn't part of his life now, and I sensed it was related to him leaving the teaching profession and coming to live on board the *Euphrates*.

*

In the evenings, when the bar was open, Eddie would change into a pair of worn Levis and put on one of his 'entertaining' shirts. They all had the same vibe, bought from one of the second-hand stalls in the Lock, and boasted patterns of varying garishness – cowboy on acid, Hawaiian beach bum, Italian mobster, African leader. He wore all sorts of patterned outfits with a swagger, and no matter how grubby or ill-fitting they were, he carried it off and looked just how the host of such a unique venue should appear.

His evenings would take on two forms. He tried to open on a Thursday for people who he knew and wanted a beer in relaxed surroundings, maybe only firing up the karaoke if a couple of them had drunk more than they planned. It would also rely on him making the run up from wherever he was – Maida Vale, Paddington, Lisson Grove in the west, or around King's Cross eastwards – during the Thursday afternoon to get to a berth in Camden Lock. There were limited mooring-rings by the old Ice Wharf, and he liked to use the same one each week, believing it was good for business to be tied up in the same place, so customers would know where they could find him.

On Fridays he often had a booking – a group of people who liked the idea of going on the water, getting sloshed and raising voices to the night skies. On Saturdays it would often take till lunchtime to recover and clear up. Once he had done his chores he'd open for business, hoping for passing trade, let the tourists pop in for a cold lager as they wandered through the famous markets, welcoming aboard those intrigued by this piece of Londonabilia, and then people would get comfortable, like the music on the stereo and hunker down for the evening.

Sundays had originally been a day of rest, when he kept the shutters shut and the batons down and the curtains drawn and would take his time to clear up the bar and stick a record on and light up and kick back. But he gradually noticed how many people were poking their noses up against the window, attracted by the colourful, hand-painted sign advertising the business of the *Euphrates*, and he realised that this was easy money walking by. He could hang out at the bar, drink tea, coffee or beer, depending on how much he'd had the night before, and sell his beverages all afternoon. So he began to open on Sundays, too, and in some ways he liked it best. The drink, drink, drink culture that gripped the groups who came in to sing and get pissed and then sing some more on other nights was less pronounced on a Sunday: people were happier to savour what he was flogging, admire his craftsmanship and not get up and go all rah-rah-rah.

*

For someone whose livelihood partly depended on strangers coming on to a boat that was also his home, getting inebriated, losing their shyness and belting out Whitney Houston, James Brown, Dean Martin, Sandie Shaw and Ian Dury, judging by what he said he seemed happiest when he was alone. He liked nothing better than chugging gently through the watery, industrial hinterlands of North, West and East London, playing Steely Dan and Bob Dylan, Gwen McCrae and Pink Floyd, Sly And The Family Stone and Creedence Clearwater Revival at a volume high enough to counteract the throb of the engine beneath his feet.

Once in a while, he'd do what was called the London Loop, which meant getting on the Thames down at Limehouse and then going upstream until he met the junction leading to Uxbridge, then getting back off the river and on to the canal again. He told me he liked nothing more than to be on the move, and would aim to take one weekend off out of every four, simply for a cruise out of town – or so I at first thought.

I was later to discover these excursions had a hidden motive.

*

Eddie found that the licensing laws for the barge were hideously complicated – or at least for him to deal with – as he would be moving about so much and couldn't face applying to the seven or eight different councils for a bar licence. He was never asked about it, so he simply didn't bother. He also lacked a mooring certificate, which was needed if you were stopping on a residential mooring, but his policy of ignoring officialdom seemed to work okay. Combined with his hatred of paperwork, a hand-to-mouth cash flow and his deeper-rooted need to be able to up sticks when the mood grabbed him, he'd avoided anything that involved filling in a form, paying a fee, using a 'hotline' or 0800 number, going online. It meant he was regularly on the move by necessity as well as choice.

'With the old British Waterways, you'd have to be on the go all the time anyway. They offered twenty-four-hour, maybe forty-eight-hour pitches, and checked you didn't stay too long,' he said. 'But it suited me. What was the point of staying still if you could fire up the engine and spend a couple of hours a day chugging about? I could start my day in Greenford or Uxbridge and make my way right along through the Grand Union and the Regent's Canal, and then after I'd go down to Victoria Park and turn up the Hertford Cut and go along it until you meet the Lea Navigation... and then take that up through Walthamstow, and on out of London. I would reach those little towns in the countryside, my house with me. The new Canal & River Trust seems more interested in selling as many licences as they can to people who want to live on the canals because of the silly money you have to pay for a house these days, but they don't seem to bother checking boats once the paperwork is done. It suits me just fine.'

He told me he liked to make the most of the summer to earn all he could for the leaner winter months, would take a holiday in the barge in late autumn or early spring: go back up the Grand Union, towards the Napton Cut where he originally bought the *Euphrates*, and head towards the River Avon, on to Bath, Worcester and the River Severn. Sometimes he would head up the Lea Valley, park himself in the town of Ware or Hertford, and spend a week or two working on the boat. He'd use the holiday to brew his own beer and rediscover his land legs with long country walks.

One afternoon, as I sat on board and ate cake and drank mint tea – he used the herbs on the roof for cocktails – there was a knock, and a young man stuck his head through the door. He gave us both a big grin and asked how we were doing.

'Ah, Abdi, come in, come in,' said Eddie, and introduced us.

*

Abdi The Micro, as Eddie called him, had gradually become a fixture on the *Euphrates*, and one day I asked Eddie to tell me his story.

Abdi was about eighteen and lived on the estate by the market. He was born in London, but his family was from Somalia. They had fled the war that had wrecked their country around twenty years previously and eventually settled in the Camden area.

He told me Abdi was a friend who did some work with him, and went on to explain what he meant by that.

'He and his mates are always after earning some spending money,' said Eddie, 'but they face problems. People have such an ingrained racism towards the young Somali men around here. They think they are always up to no good. They think they are in gangs, mugging people, fighting, all sorts. It is very, very sad. Abdi tells me he has tried to find work in shops, bars, cafés, all sorts of places. And he is a such a bright lad. He is a handy mechanic. He knows his way around the *Euphrates* engine, and has tried to find work in garages while he studies, but doesn't get the breaks. None of his mates do.

'He's a whizz on computers, too: that's his real skill. That's why I call him Micro. He knocked me up a website for the *Euphrates* in about twenty minutes flat. There's nothing he doesn't know about computer technology, about coding, about web design. Should be heading to college to study it, really, but didn't get five GCSEs to go on and do his A-levels. Sad really. Can't afford an access course right now. I was thinking of sponsoring him, but I'm skint as well. If his mates get jobs, it's working in a family cab firm, cleaning out cars or washing them, doing simple servicing, answering calls. He sometimes gets to put his real talents to use, doing stuff like making his friends and family websites, but there's no money in doing people favours, is there?

'He told me sometimes his crew get a few hours at the halal butcher's in Greenwood Place unloading meat when there's something big going on. But the chance to earn a few quid spending money regularly is small, so a load of them stand on the bridge over the canal on the high street and sell bags of weed to tourists at silly prices. Their customers seem to be mainly young Italian students, who they'll never see again, so the quality of the deal isn't exactly a priority. The bridge, they say, is a good spot: not just for passing trade, but if they should get collared, they have a moment to dump their stash over the side and into the canal.

'Abdi's parents have no idea. He is a straight-up bloke, plays a full role in his family's life and rituals. He goes to prayers, is home for dinner, understands the importance of the Somalian celebrations that dot the calendar, looks after his younger siblings. His parents have no reason to overly complain about the friends he runs about with. A thoroughly nice young man.'

Over time, Abdi began to trust me, and I heard his story myself. Gradually we became friends, and I could understand why Abdi and Eddie enjoyed each other's company, despite the difference in age and backgrounds.

*

'Breakfast...' said Eddie, as he stood in the galley and used a spatula to flick hot oil on two eggs he was frying in a pan '...is my favourite meal of the day. I love the feeling of getting myself a large munch together. A proper breakfast sets the tone for the type of day you will have, don't you think? No other meal satisfies like it.'

It was a few months after I had first met Abdi on board the *Euphrates*, and I'd planned to have a gossip with Eddie that morning on my way into work about some trouble that had occurred over the weekend around the Lock. I thought Eddie would be able to give me a better steer on a mass brawl that had taken place outside one of the nearby pubs than the lines the police had issued.

The smell of toast under the grill was getting me hungry, and

Eddie noticed, told me to pull up a chair, said he'd make me a portion.

As he relaxed over the fry-up, our conversation became expansive. He mentioned how the fight had involved a few of the youngsters who milled about selling puff, and it wasn't half as bad as the police were making out. I asked him if Abdi or his mates were involved, and he said there was some politics in the puff trade, but thankfully Abdi generally managed to keep clear of it. Another group of street dealers employed by the same mob who supplied Abdi had been throwing their weight about as they peddled gear, and it had caused a bit of grief. It got us on to the subject of Abdi, and Eddie told me a bit more about him.

Abdi, Eddie said, had an ingrained mistrust of middle-aged white men – they were a group who had so often paraded a deep-seated racism towards him and his friends. Teachers, police officers, shopkeepers – all too often people who looked like Eddie had given Abdi a hard time. But Eddie was different, and made Abdi feel at home, and they'd sit on the *Euphrates*, Abdi showing Eddie crazy computer graphics he'd designed. They would drink mint tea together and eat digestive biscuits, and it was as their friendship grew that the following episode panned out.

Abdi and his mates sold bags of skunk weed provided by a gang of unscrupulous drug dealers with fingers in various unsavoury pies. They also ripped them off. They gave them underweight bags of weed to sell, and Abdi and his friends would find themselves in debt and tied to working for their dealers very quickly. The temptation to smoke the stash they were meant to sell was great, and they'd quickly make their way through any slim profits. Eddie had heard all about this from Abdi, who watched his friends fall further and further into debt.

'The gang he is working for sounds terrible,' said Eddie. He was distressed by the trouble his young friend was courting. 'They aren't small time. Nasty bunch. Proper East London big boys. Abdi says they have these dope factories out on the Isle of Dogs. Grow tons of the stuff. He says it is called English Cheese. It fucking stinks. Says they have links with all sorts. It's not just drugs. They're gang masters who run slave-labour rings, fruit pickers, cockle gatherers and those blokes who go around the pubs with the dodgy DVDs. Abdi doesn't like them. Not one bit. And neither do I.'

Eddie had tried Abdi's skunk and told him he didn't like that either. Eddie had given Abdi some Moroccan hashish and Jamaican bush, and the pair had closed the doors, slumped on the sofa and spent an afternoon rolling joints, comparing what Abdi sold and what Eddie enjoyed getting high on.

'Smoke this,' Eddie had said to him. 'It'll make you giggle, it'll give you proper munchies. I'll make you the nicest cheese-and-pickle sandwich you've ever had, five minutes after you've had a go on this little number. Leave that skunk alone. That stuff – all it does is make you think the Prophet is after you for doing bad shit.'

They smoked his resin, smoked his weed and filled the *Euphrates* with a thick, heady scent of ganja. Abdi played Eddie some grime and dubstep and recited Somalian poetry his gran had taught him, and Eddie played Abdi Weather Report and Love and told him about 1960s West Coast jazz and spaced-out rock, and they began to hatch a plan.

Now, while Eddie had very few overheads running the boat, it was around this time that things on the canal had begun to change.

'What looks like progress isn't always progressive for everyone,' Eddie told Abdi one day. 'Take my situation. Look around this canal. Look at these buildings alongside it. Now, when I built the *Euphrates*, these old warehouses and pumping-stations were either empty or cheap to rent. All sorts lived and worked here. It was where *The Muppets* was first made, you know. You could afford to invent Kermit The Frog here. Now you've got to be a seriously big company to work anywhere in this postcode.

'Multinational media businesses, design agencies, internet start-ups with big-time serious backers, TV channels… and the blocks which aren't open-plan offices have become flats, posh flats. The lock-keepers' cottages have gone, too – people used to live in them because they worked on the canal. Not any more. Now they've been turned into fucking Starbucks. It's called asset stripping. They have been sold off – and what for? The bottom figure on an accountant's spreadsheet.

'The canal is nothing more than an asset now, too. I used to be able to chug happily about for a few hundred a year. Have the freedom to go this way or that. But everything is now all about the money. For this bit of London, the mooring fees and the licences have gone through the damn roof – they are threatening the old community – you know, us lot who've lived here for years and years – making it the preserve of the rich, the weekend boaters, the Saturday bargers, and soon it will be gone. It means I need a new revenue stream, just to keep floating. I can't only rely on the karaoke and selling a few beers.'

Eddie said to me that hearing Abdi tell him about who he was selling dope for, and his own straitened finances, got him thinking.

'With Abdi and his mates always in debt, always having these tough guys causing them untold stress, I wondered if there was some way we could come to an arrangement,' he said. 'I wondered if I could help them out.'

*

Now, as I said, Eddie was a genius: he came up with solutions to problems and he put his mind to the conundrum of needing to find a few extra quid, of helping his mate Abdi out, and also trying to wean him and his friends off the skunk weed they were smoking, which wasn't doing any of them any good.

It was during one of his post-Christmas trips eastwards out towards Hertfordshire, using up the dog days of late January when the bar trade was at its worst, that he chugged along a deserted stretch of the Lea and a project began to form in his mind.

'I first came up with the idea on a cold, foggy afternoon as I went up the east,' he confided in me. 'I'd seen Abdi on the canal bridge as I went underneath it, and as I started my journey we'd waved at each other, and it just played on my mind that there he was, taking risks, and for what? Some scumbag gangster. It really got to me.

'Anyway, when you get out to Hertfordshire, it's like the land that time forgot. It is no longer industrial, no longer full of small workshops where they used to make stuff, but it isn't rural either. Right along that stretch nature is slowly reclaiming the land, with trees poking up through concrete and buddleia and ivy and grasses creeping back across the abandoned quays.

'You notice this all too easily driving a canal boat,' he said. 'It puts you in a different space to just about everyone else. You go at a speed that the post-canal world has forgotten exists. It is conducive to taking in your surroundings, a pace where you notice the little things, and it gives you time for wondering, pondering and dreaming.

'And it was on a gentle run along the Lea that I decided I had an answer and got my plan started.

'I'd noticed all the way up and down the Lea these old abandoned huts and little warehouses, workshops... places you could only get to in a boat. They were old storage shelters, boatmen's woodsheds and coal dumps. There was no gentrification out this way.

'It got me thinking. Who built these little structures, who owned them, and what were they for? They were in fields ringed with barbed-wire fences, and overgrown with brambles and all sorts. It's where TV cops find dead bodies. But you could, using a dinghy or kayak, get to these banks from the canal. It got me wondering.'

Eddie described how up the Lea there was one ivy-coated hut he passed and peered at. It had a damson tree in front of it and was hidden in undergrowth. Behind it was a decrepit, twelve-foot-high fence with chain-link wire and rusted barbs, sagging between concrete fence posts. Behind that were acres and acres of scrubland.

'I had noticed it a couple of times before,' he said. 'It had a pitched roof and looked like it had been built with an unusual degree of care. It was one of those landmarks outside the town of Ware I would use to tell me how far I had to go before a good mooring.'

And then he revealed his secret.

'I thought to myself: what could those huts have been used for when they were first built – and what could they be used for today?

'It occurred to me that this particular shed could be the perfect place to grow a big crop of ganja. And once the idea was in my head, I couldn't put it away, couldn't stop pondering on whether it was possible. I could chug up there once a month, wait till dusk and then slip ashore and look after the plants. I could rig up a battery on a timer so they could get a good burst of extra light from some lamps, and, if they were found, there was nothing there to link them with me. I could smuggle my crop down the canal into the heart of Camden once it was ready.'

He kept his eye on the hut for around six months before one early-summer's evening he motored slowly through the green water, pulled up on the opposite bank and waited for the lengthening summer's day to slip into darkness.

Eddie had a small canoe strapped to the roof of the *Euphrates*. He took it down, stuck it in the dark water and lowered himself into it. Armed with a torch, shears, secateurs and garden gloves, he paddled across to the opposite bank and pushed the boat over reed beds. He was wearing boots, and the water at the canal edge was shallow. He stepped on to the bank, dragged the canoe after him and hid it in the bushes. He climbed carefully over a few tree branches, stumbled through grasses and slipped on wet clay. He shined his torch on the hut, wriggled the wooden door open and went inside.

And what he found was better than he could have possibly hoped for.

'All the way up the Lea, during the 1930s and '40s, were munitions factories, aircraft factories, army bases, all sorts of things to do with the war effort,' he explained. 'All those light-industrial estates you get up there now – they were started from the war days, when farm-lands and paddocks and fields were taken by the government and built on by the military.

'Now here is my theory: the land where this one hut was had been used for army bases. I looked it up on an old Ordnance Survey map and it said "restricted area"… that meant there was an MOD depot there, and I bet it was used to billet troops – rows of Nissen huts, full of conscripts doing their basic training… This block I'd found was put up by the army, probably as a guardhouse.'

Once he had jemmied the door, which ached open slowly on a set of rusting hinges, and stepped inside, he found an interior perfect for his plans.

At first glance, it had a wooden floor and one window, with a board nailed to the frame blocking it up. Eddie shone the torch around, and decided it was about the right size for what he wanted to do, but he wasn't totally convinced. While hard to reach from anywhere but the canal, he did have misgivings as other bargers would be able to see it as well as he had, especially as he would have to leave lights on for cultivating purposes. He fretted that it might attract unwanted attention.

Then, as he was about to leave, a hatch in the floor in the far corner caught his eye. He forced it open and found a trapdoor and a ladder leading down into a cellar.

'I got a bit spooked as I opened it up,' he admitted. 'I shone my torch down there, lay on my belly and peered in… It seemed pretty big, and I got a bit of a feeling that I was disturbing something I shouldn't really be disturbing, y'know? It was all a bit *Blair Witch*, like no one had been there since the end of the war. But then I told myself to get it together and to stop being such a fool, to get on with it.

'I lowered myself on to an iron ladder that was bolted to the wall – it was pretty sturdy, considering its age – and I climbed down. I reckoned I'd found an air-raid shelter for the guards on duty.'

He reached a stone-flagged floor. The shelter smelt damp and had nothing in it but sets of rusting bunk-bed frames. It was perfect.

'I worked most of that night,' Eddie said. 'I ferried over a series of planks to build shelves using the old bunk beds, and reams of foil blankets, the type they give you if you've got hypothermia. I'd bought a job lot of them. I had three car batteries and three big lights. My first task was to completely black out the place: not a chink of light must be visible from the outside.'

He measured up the trapdoor, and decided to make another one from a single, complete piece of wood rather than planks, and got a ragged, thick woollen rug to pull over it.

Downstairs in the shelter, he took a heap of old blankets made of heavy-duty felt cloth. He attached wooden batons at yard-long intervals along the wall and then got a staple gun and tacked the material to the ceilings and walls.

He then doubled it up, with the centres of the sheets covering the edges of the first layer. He did this three times, and the triple-thick material – like a huge coat on the inside – made sure no tell-tale lights could be seen through the floorboards but also had the added bonus of making the damp cellar feel instantly warmer. His final touch to this part of his project was to staple the foil blankets on top.

Eddie had visited City Farm near the canal in Hackney a few days earlier, and asked his friend Rick the stockman for some sacks of chicken dung. He'd read it was great fertiliser, and Rick was only too happy to allow him to help clear out the coops and take the mess away.

Eddie wanted to be able to leave the plants for as long as possible without having to visit them. He ran the car batteries on a relay system so they wouldn't drain too quickly. Ever resourceful, his next clever trick was to take a watertight plastic crate and place it on brackets on the upper part of the cellar's walls. He had cut a small hole at the bottom and forced a piece of hosepipe into it, then sealed the edges with glue. In the end of the hose he shoved a length of sponge, pushing it down into the pipe. It would mean water could dribble through at a slow rate. Finally, he pierced the hose with a sewing needle, making minute holes along its length. He buried it in the trays. It took three more trips with a heavily laden canoe to bring over the bags of compost, and he sat on the floor and filled the trays with this and earth.

He had bought a big bag of High Grade Kush cannabis seeds from a Rasta called Trevor who lived near the canal in Tottenham. He took the seeds from his jacket pocket and carefully tucked them, one at a time, a thumb's depth into the soil.

He had a water carrier with him – the type you take camping, with a little plastic sprocket tap – and he watered the seeds carefully.

Then he plugged the lighting cables into the car batteries, and watched with satisfaction as his dope factory was bathed in light.

Before leaving for the *Euphrates* and a well-earned cup of tea, Eddie filled the crate with water, and his makeshift irrigation scheme was set to go. He estimated he would have to come back every six weeks to fill the tank or recharge the batteries, while the crop he had chosen would take around three months to grow to a respectable size and create large buds. He would have a harvest four times a year.

He admitted that he wasn't quite prepared for the amount he would grow, hoping for enough to quench his own thirst for a spliff and provide Abdi with enough to sell with his friends at the weekends to get them away from the gangs previously supplying them. But, as he put it, the first crop took on the size of a 'sodding bale of gorgeous, high-grade weed...'

Suddenly he was in the big time, and Abdi had a huge quantity of dirt-cheap ganja to sell.

*

A few months later I found myself in Camden Town on a nice sunny morning and, with no pressing work to do, I thought I'd take a wander along the towpath and see if Eddie was about. We hadn't caught up with each other for a while. I imagined the *Euphrates* had been out of the area, somewhere else on the waterways, with a red-eyed skipper at the helm.

As I approached its usual berth, I was pleased to see the *Euphrates* there. I noted that Eddie had given the boat a fresh lick of paint and put new car tyres – painted in red, green and gold – all the way around the hull to protect the new paint job. But my delight at seeing that Eddie was around quickly turned to suspicion, because as I approached I noticed two policemen standing on the towpath and a few more on the boat's foredeck.

My first instinct, seeing coppers swarming all over the *Euphrates*, was to walk past and keep going. It smelt like trouble, and besides, it occurred to me that Eddie might be embarrassed. Then there was the reporter's predicament. If Eddie was being busted, the police would no doubt tell the newspaper, and I'd be duty bound to write something in the *Evening Press And Star*, especially as I'd have seen the raid taking place. Eddie was my mate, and I wasn't exactly keen to cover his misfortune.

Before I had the chance to turn heel, I saw him coming out from the cabin, led by two police officers, and he saw me, too. He looked mortified. But then I thought that he may also want someone there to be an advocate, to bear witness, and a reporter is as good as anyone to have about to make sure the police behave themselves. I took up my stride again and approached the *Euphrates*, ready to flash my reporter's credentials if need be.

'Can I help you?' asked one of the uniforms as I came to the boat.

He bore down on me and pulled some aggressive body language. It pissed me off.

'No,' I replied. 'I don't think so. I've come to visit my mate Eddie. What's going on here then?'

'None of your business,' the officer growled. 'Your friend is busy. Move along.'

I refused to do so. I was on a public towpath and there was no way I was going to simply walk off because some fresh-faced PC told me to hop it.

Eddie smiled at me and said: 'Don't worry, mate, a misunderstanding, that's all – they want me to go down to the station. I'll be back soon – come back in a couple of hours and let's have a pint and a catch-up.'

His confidence was such that I felt assured nothing could possibly be wrong, and shouted over the heads of the officers taking him away that I'd go for a walk and see him on my way back. He turned again and flashed me another smile as the officers clasped his arms and marched him off.

Later that day, I did return to the *Euphrates*, but it was all locked up and there was no sign of Eddie on board. I wondered whether his confidence was misplaced, but there was little I could do, so I scribbled a few lines on a page in my notebook asking him to call me, ripped it out and shoved it under the door.

*

I knew there would be little point in looking for Eddie and the *Euphrates* during the week in Camden Town, with his routine being to save his overnight stays on the temporary berths for Friday and Saturday, and I was so busy at work I didn't have time to pop down and see if he was about anyway. But I was pretty worried when I left work that Friday and went to find him, as he'd not answered my note.

The *Euphrates* wasn't pulled up in its normal spot, tied to one of the ancient iron rings set into the towpath by the market, and after speaking to some of the traders it was clear there had been no sign of him since he was arrested.

I feared the worst.

My next move was to see if any of the people in the houseboat moorings towards Primrose Hill had heard from him, so I strolled further along the towpath, out towards the Zoo and Cumberland Basin, leaving the market behind.

It was a pleasant enough evening, and I thought I would reach some of the barges pulled up past Regent's Park before dark. The people there were bound to know if the *Euphrates* had passed recently. To my relief, as I came under the bridge by the Broadwalk leading into the park, I saw the familiar red, green and gold craft tethered up on the far side of the canal.

As I approached, I saw the lights on inside and wisps of smoke coming from the chimney in the cabin.

I stepped on to the prow, called his name, and Eddie opened up.

We exchanged the usual pleasantries, he poured me a pint, and then I broached the subject as to what had happened the weekend before.

He gave a deep and reassuring laugh.

He told me he hadn't got to the bottom of it, but suspected one of Abdi's previous 'associates' might have got wind of where his new source of dope was coming from and not been overly happy about it.

'They didn't take too kindly to Abdi saying he wasn't selling puff for them any more,' said Eddie. 'They'd watched him, and seen Abdi coming on board to visit me. I don't suppose it was too hard for even those knuckleheads to realise I must be involved with the cheap ganja being flogged around the place, especially after they had seen The Micro coming and going with a few suspicious packets under his arm.'

Instead of coming to the *Euphrates*, heavy handed, Abdi's original suppliers had tipped off the police, and let the Old Bill do their dirty work.

'I asked Abdi about it, and he agreed it was the most likely scenario,' said Eddie. 'They'd been giving him and his mates grief. He said they'd have come by and done me over if they'd thought I was a gangster, if they'd thought that was what I'd have done if I was in their shoes. But they thought I was just some dumb old hippie, and it was much less hassle to let the police get me out of the picture.'

'So is that it? You got done?' I asked.

'Well...' he said, sinking down into the biggest leather armchair the bar had and grinning in a way that suggested otherwise. 'Well, they turned the place upside down and inside out. They were looking for my dope, of course. At first I thought it must have something to do with the liquor licence. Never really kept on top of all that sort of thing, but I soon realised it would be a council officer knocking, not about twenty rozzers and their sniffer dogs. It took them ages to search the old girl. You know what this place is like. Any number of places you could hide your stash. I actually rather enjoyed watching them getting angrier and angrier every time they found a new cubbyhole.'

'So what did they find? Did they nick you?' I asked, dreading the answer.

'Nope. They didn't find fuck all, and they let me go after letting me sit in the cells for the best part of a day.'

'Phew. That was lucky.'

'Luck, my friend, has nothing to do with it...'

He smiled a mischievous grin, and, leaning forward, he said in a conspiratorial whisper: 'I'm far too clever to get nicked by the bloody drug squad...'

While he had told me all about his growing-and-smuggling operation, I'd never really asked him about where he stashed his product. It seemed rude to do so. I imagined it would have been in a cupboard, or maybe under the floor. I'd never really thought about it until then, but I knew he had lots of nooks and crannies around that could hold a few hundredweight of greenery. However, I was also aware that the police don't raid somewhere unless they know they are likely to find something, and if they think there are drugs in a place, they will turn it upside down until they get what they are after.

'So how come they didn't get anything?' I asked. 'Why aren't you facing some kind of charge? Possession with intent to supply? Dealing?'

'It's like this,' he said, grinning. 'You remember I told you I put those car tyres around the edge of the *Euphrates* as I didn't want to scratch the paintwork when I went through the locks? Well... let's just say that's only partly true. Come and have a look.'

We climbed out of the prow door and on to the back deck. Eddie looked around, scanning the peaceful canal. There was no one in sight. The sun was beginning to sneak down past the cream-stucco homes of Regent's Park to the west, and the zoo's Snowdon Aviary was standing tall in the late summer air. He smiled at me. There was not a soul about. He leant over the side of the boat and took hold of a rope with a tyre on the end, pulled it slowly on board. At first glance, there seemed to be nothing different to it: it was an old Dunlop tyre, hoicked off a skip on a garage forecourt, with a worn-out tread and a green, slimy sheen where it had been submerged.

'Well?' I asked.

'Aha!' he said. 'Look at this.'

At the bottom of the tyre, on the inner rim, was a rubber flap. He stuck his hand inside and pulled. It was a false, waterproofed bottom, and inside was a sealed bag holding a fat stash of his finest weed.

'They never thought of looking here,' he said, grinning. 'And if they had, they wouldn't have noticed anyway. I've designed it so it looks just like the inside of any old tyre. The fact that it was under-water meant their bloody dogs couldn't smell it, either. I've got pounds of the bloody stuff left.'

'You genius,' I said, laughing.

'Stick on a record and skin up.'

POLICE IN DRUG MARKET CRACKDOWN

Drugs Squad officers conducted a series of high-profile raids over the weekend in an attempt to stem Camden Town's flourishing cannabis market.

Officers visited a series of addresses and used stop-and-search tactics in a bid to send a message to street dealers that they could no longer expect them to turn a blind eye to small-scale drug dealing that they claim is rife in Camden Town. The market area has, in recent years, gained what police sources called an 'unenviable reputation' for the availability of cannabis resin and stronger forms of marijuana, know by users as skunk weed.

They also raided a popular floating bar, the *Euphrates* Karaoke Barge, but came away empty handed. A source close to the investigation said police had acted on a tip-off, but were now satisfied the proprietor, Eddie Roll, had nothing to do with the street trade in marijuana that has become prolific in the neighbourhood.

MRS COLLINS AND
THE KING

I SHOULD, WITH hindsight, have realised how strange this raid was going to be.

Usually the police would tip reporters off as late as possible. This was their way of paying lip-service to confidentiality, to ensure you didn't ring up every one of your underworld contacts and say: 'Oi, someone, somewhere, tomorrow morning, before the sun is up, is going to get their door smashed in.'

You would get a call asking if you'd like to be at the police station first thing – meaning 4.30am – and they'd say they couldn't tell you much about what you were going to witness for 'operational reasons' but add that it would certainly be worth your while. Depending on the officer in charge, you might get a little titbit, a morsel to get the news-nose twitching – 'it's drugs' or 'it's counterfeit items' or 'prostitution and people trafficking' or 'stolen goods' – but with this one I was given no clue. A detective I knew called me much earlier than usual – around lunchtime – and said that if I met him the following day they'd take me on a house search that would give me an interesting story but refused to expand on what that meant. I was intrigued.

Then there was the start time. The copper added there was no need to come too early and that 7am was fine. He said it wasn't exactly a dawn raid and chuckled.

I wondered if this was a sign that those involved were mixed up with gambling scams. I'd heard of these all-night games, which were fronts for money laundering or round-table big-stake matches set up to mug high rollers with loaded hands of poker. They wouldn't finish much before seven, so maybe we were going to raid a game, catch the culprits as the final sting was administered.

I had to set my alarm anyway. It was early enough for me, and I wanted to give myself plenty of time to eat some breakfast.

I'd been on jobs like this before after hurrying out of bed, throwing clothes on, brushing teeth frantically, stumbling half asleep out of the house… and then cursed myself later as I spent a boring few hours while the police staked somewhere out or meticulously sorted through box after box after box of potentially stolen items in a cold warehouse. I would be given dark looks by detectives if I got in the way, and my belly grumbled as I cursed my hunger and the fact that I was, again, ill-prepared for an early start.

Before I left, I brewed some coffee and scrambled a couple of eggs, which I covered in pepper and wolfed down on a couple of slices of toast. I packed a bag with my notebook and a camera, threw in a load of pens and checked my phone was charged.

Dawn had broken as I left the house. It was a clear morning. I strode through empty streets, feeling a mix of nerves and curiosity at what might lie in store.

When I reached the police station, its front entrance was still locked up, so I called the detective who had asked me along. He didn't answer, so I left a message and texted him, too. Eventually he emerged from a side door and told me I was late and had missed the briefing. He led me in silence through a staff entrance, across a yard of tightly parked patrol cars and then into a windowless incident room where five uniformed officers and a couple of senior detectives were sipping instant coffee in foam cups. It was quiet and calm. There was not the usual air of macho adrenalin I'd witnessed before in the build-up to the execution of a warrant. As I'd missed the officers being told what they were due to encounter, I asked one of the sergeants what the raid was all about and he simply gave me a big grin and said: 'You wait and see.'

This strange atmosphere continued before we went into the target house. By the time I stood on a balcony of the post-war block in Holloway in the quiet of the morning, I had become increasingly confused as to who on earth the person on the warrant could possibly be. Everything about the operation seemed wrong.

I had noticed that the officers didn't have their usual sniffer dogs,

Kevlar vests and drawn truncheons. The lead officer simply looked at his unit, said 'Right, guys, here we go', went up to the door, tapped on the knocker and then bent down to peer through the letterbox. No battering rams, boots or shoulders were being used to enter the flat.

And then there was the music coming from within. I heard it as the officers paused briefly for the sign from the detective sergeant in charge that it was time to get started.

Sometimes, when I'd seen drug dealers raided, officers would steam into the middle of a party. There would be people lying around in various states of intoxication and the grumbling basslines of dubstep or some other sub-genre of dance music, providing the type of soundtrack cop-show writers would suggest in brackets in their script. Instead I could hear, gently coming from the other side of a set of net curtains, the sound of Elvis Presley singing 'The Girl Of My Best Friend'.

*

The first parking-meter in the world was installed in Oklahoma in 1935. The Model T had spent a good twenty years clogging up the thoroughfares that had once been the preserve of feet and hooves. It meant City Hall, Small Town America, was under pressure to do something to bring some order to Main Street.

It took London longer to come to the idea that road space had a price. Britain's first meter was installed in Westminster in 1958. The borough councillors said it was because of the increasing traffic and the rising cost of keeping the roads shipshape. Opponents said it was simply a good way to earn the council money. Whatever the reasons, it only took a couple of years for the meter to spread across the country, and by the mid-1960s there wasn't a local authority that hadn't set up a dedicated parking section in their roads and traffic department.

Peggy Collins spent the majority of her working life in the employ of the council. She started emptying parking-meters in the 1960s, when they used the old machines where you stick your cash in, click the lever around and watch the red-triangle sign tick-tock away. She moved on to the pay-and-display units when they were introduced in the 1990s, being given responsibility to go around the car-parks the council managed and collect the takings.

She was a valued member of staff. She never had a day off sick. She was always hardworking and courteous. However, she wasn't what you would describe as popular. She didn't socialise. She never joined her colleagues for a drink on Friday night, but they respected Peggy. They knew little of her home life. Some of her long-standing colleagues were aware that she was a widow, but the circumstances behind this personal tragedy had never been public knowledge in the department – and no one felt comfortable prying when she made clear, through her polite but guarded conversation, that her private life was just that.

Later, when I found out more about her background, I discovered the circumstances behind her husband's death and the effect the loss had on her.

Peggy was a Londoner who had joined the RAF as a civilian in the 1950s. She was offered a job that promised travel – she had dreams of bases in Germany, Egypt, the Far East – but instead was sent up north. She had been working behind the bar at the NCO mess at the RAF's Scottish Air Traffic Control Centre in Prestwick when she met her husband, a handsome fellow Londoner with neatly cropped, carefully Brylcreemed hair, called Peter Collins.

He had been called up to do his National Service and had chosen to join the RAF. They fell in love and married. Their time together was deliriously happy. Peter and Peggy were well-suited and very much besotted.

Peggy had been well-turned-out when she was a youngster. She told me how she loved catching a glimpse of herself and her boy in shop windows as they stepped out together. He looked gorgeous in the grey-blue of his RAF uniform, and she loved standing next to him with curls in her hair and a box-hat sitting high on the back of her head.

It was easy to relate this image of Peggy as a young woman with the lady I would get to know. She cared about her appearance. She liked a touch of rouge on the cheeks and having her hair done, and wore sugar-bag blue blouses to highlight her eyes. Her home smelt of talcum powder, her dressing-table held various lotions and potions and she by habit dabbed a touch of musk behind the ears before leaving for work each morning.

But Peggy and Peter's relationship was to be short-lived.

In 1959, Mr Collins died in an accident during a training flight. Peggy did not tell me the details, and it felt too intrusive to ask directly. Instead, a search through RAF records revealed that the plane he was crewing had a problem with its undercarriage and crash-landed. It burst into flames, and three people died.

The young widow continued to work at RAF Prestwick for a time after the crash. She never remarried and received a small pension from the Ministry of Defence.

If you had to select waymarkers on the road of someone's life, for Peggy you could say her decision to join the RAF catering corps was one that had ramifications. Another was reciprocating the smile given to her by the handsome young serviceman in the mess bar. Another was an event in 1960, which, by fortune, saw Elvis Presley touch down at the Prestwick airbase while en route to Germany. He had been drafted into the US Army and, while his transatlantic plane was being refuelled, he did a meet-and-greet for screaming fans. He was taken to the officers' mess for a drink, and it was here he met an attractive barmaid with sad eyes. He posed for a photograph with her, flirted a little, held her hand and gave her a lingering kiss on the cheek when it was time for him to go.

Before this, Peggy hadn't been an Elvis fan. She'd been bemused rather than impressed with his jerky-hipped dance moves. When her husband was alive, the pair of them liked big-band and swing music. Rock and roll had yet to hit the Scottish airbases, and since the accident she hadn't wanted to listen to the songs that brought back memories which still hurt far too much to cherish.

That evening, she saw a photograph of Elvis in the paper, and she stared at it for some time. When she was lying in bed, she recreated in her mind the touch of his hand and the smell of his hair cream.

That chance meeting changed her life. Peggy became a confirmed Elvis fanatic.

In the mid-1960s Peggy began to emerge from the grief-induced lethargy that had struck her down. After much lobbying from her parents, she packed up her life in Scotland and moved back to London. She got the job at the council, first as a parking warden, in a crisp uniform that was, in her eyes, pretty close to an RAF blue. By the end of the decade she had graduated from giving out tickets to emptying meters.

Peggy remained single. She moved back into her parents' council flat on the Holloway estate where she had grown up and lived on there after they died.

She retired aged sixty. The department bought her flowers and a cake. The mayor came in and said some kind words about how people like Peggy were the backbone of public services and the world was a better place for the likes of her. He said she'd be much missed, and they took her photograph with him for the council's staff newsletter.

It was only at the end of March the following year that a mild discrepancy emerged in a column of figures totted up by staff in the office of her former work. It was then investigated by a zealous audit clerk, and a mild discrepancy became a huge one. This set in motion a series of events that culminated in me standing in her neat little flat, watching the same sad eyes that had intrigued Elvis Presley. She sat shaking on a cheap settee while police officers, armed with the search warrant bearing her name, carefully picked their way through her cherished, treasured possessions.

It transpired that Peggy had got herself what seemed to be a sure-fire, foolproof scam that lasted for most of her working life and was only discovered after her retirement when the takings from the pay-and-display machines on her beat rocketed.

Peggy, still dreaming of the day she met The King, had become slowly more obsessed with Elvis. She began filling the box room in her flat with his singles and albums. This quickly escalated into fanzines, magazines, anything that had his image on it, anything connected to Presley. The vast number of products available to those inclined to look for them stunned Peggy, and became an all-encompassing, uncontrollable obsession. And her obsession got worse when he died.

No longer content with items merely relating to The King – and that equated to millions of quiff-bedecked trinkets, from Elvis dolls to copies of his films, picture mirrors, canvas portraits, badges, clocks, all manner of tacky rubbish that only a true disciple would want – she started dreaming of some serious Elvis collectibles, those unique items that were in some way linked to the man himself. And, to fund this addiction, she cranked up her fiddling.

The old parking-meters stood in uniform rows of sticks with bulbous heads, and there was no way to measure how many pounds and pence had been shoved in. She would empty the meters and put half the takings in the council's cash satchel, which she carried over her shoulder. This would then be carefully locked into a strongbox in the back of her van.

The other half would go into the shoulder satchel she carried everywhere. The old meters had a dial that clicked round each time a coin was deposited, which would have, if monitored properly, allowed someone to tot up how many hours of parking had been bought. But the council relied on the people emptying the machines to make a note in a small blue book, making it easy to doctor. Peggy also found that it was easy to manually wind the dial back, so, even if she had been suspected of pilfering, the evidence simply wasn't there.

Each day, she would choose a shop, a bank or a post office and change the coins into notes then go home at lunchtime and leave a wad of cash in a shoebox on top of her wardrobe. She'd do the same in the afternoon. It was simple and straightforward thievery.

The introduction of pay-and-display machines didn't stop her. She had to empty the change on her rounds and then replace the ticket rolls inside, and there were still no immediate checks and balances. She could take the cash, fill in the large blue takings ledger she used for the accounts department, and no one was able to see if Peggy's figures made sense. As a council officer would explain under cross-examination in court, no one suspected her for a minute. She was one of the longest-serving members of staff and, as he put it to the mild amusement of those listening, and to her shame as she stood in the box: 'She really didn't strike one as the sort of person who would go in for stealing 20ps…'

Peggy had started by keeping her 'valuables', as she called her Elvis memorabilia, in the box room at her flat, except for a mirror with his face etched across it that she had on the landing and a print of The King, dating from the early 1960s, which was by the dressing-table in her bedroom.

The box room had a wardrobe, and when the police officers opened it that morning, they found the Presley clothing she had bought stored neatly inside.

It ranged from outfits that included some of the more striking designs from the Vegas years to a handful of items he had worn as he slummed about the kitsch rooms of Graceland: two pairs of jeans, three pairs of nylon flares, a collection of shirts and T-shirts and two pairs of shoes.

Peggy knew Elvis's body shape from the clothes she had bought, and had an image of every muscle, every contour and every crease of his skin imprinted on her mind.

His shoes showed he had big, wide feet. Until the years of the deep-fried peanut butter and banana sandwiches caught up with him, Elvis had a narrow waist. He had broad shoulders and, judging by the width of the two hats she had bought from a sale in Cincinnati, a rather large head. She particularly liked the fact that the hatbands still bore the stains of his favoured hair cream. She believed, as she pressed her nose to it, that she could smell its lingering scent.

In shoeboxes under her bed officers found hundreds of ticket stubs to Elvis concerts. Presley bubble-gum cards, a set of twenty-five and in mint condition, were kept in a stamp-collector's album. A set of cufflinks – a present from Liberace, according to the dealer she had haggled with – were stored in tissue paper and placed carefully in a cigar box. At an auction in Memphis, she had found what was described as Elvis's 'personal juice glass', featuring 'a gold-and-white harlequin design', given by his sometime girlfriend Linda Thompson to Jimmy Velvet, the president of the Elvis Museum in Tennessee. Peggy had written this information on a piece of card and carefully slipped it inside the glass. She had a flight log for his private jet, signed by Elwood David, his personal pilot. She owned a car registration document, signed by Colonel

Tom Parker on the singer's behalf, for a two-seater, soft-top 1963 Mercedes.

There were statements for royalties paid for the songs 'Lawdy Miss Clawdy', 'Long Tall Sally' and 'Rip It Up' from Gladys Music and Chappell & Co., and – perhaps one of her favourite items and certainly the most valuable – was a Bible that Elvis had owned since 1957 and which was full of his own notes and annotations with sections underlined.

Peggy wasn't religious, and the Bible as a tome of belief meant nothing at all to her, but she loved to look through the thin paper pages and wonder what was going on in Elvis's mind as he high-lighted a passage.

I watched officers chuckling among themselves as they began carrying such items out to a waiting van, placed in see-through plastic evidence bags. Accompanying a police raid often made me feel unpleasantly voyeuristic as I stood in the background and officers did their macho crime-busting thing in the homes of gang-sters and drug dealers. The embarrassment of catching a big man clad only in his underpants in a wholly uncomfortable situation was offset a little by the fact that the person at the business end of the truncheon was fully aware that their criminal behaviour ran the risk of a battering ram being taken to their door frame.

But this was excruciating, and I made an excuse to leave. Peggy's humiliation manifested itself in choking sobs as she watched her home being pulled apart. I felt responsible, as I stood there with my notebook open, for adding to her distress.

On the doorstep I took down her address and decided to follow her case as it went through the criminal-justice system and, once it was all over, pay her a visit. If she didn't fancy telling me the story of an Elvis-obsessed meter maid, I thought I could at least apologise for the intrusion.

*

Three months later I sat in the gallery at the magistrates' court and heard how some diligent investigation by accounts staff, spurred on by a sudden leap in takings as soon as Peggy retired, had brought her actions to light. There was CCTV footage of her emptying machines, examples of the figures logged and further footage showing many more paying motorists than had been registered. It was pretty mind-numbing detective work but conclusive – and Peggy had automatically admitted her crimes, dating back to the 1960s, as soon as she was in the back of the police van.

I watched as sentence was passed. There was an element of pity in the tone of the beak, but the seriousness of the offences, the large amount of cash involved and the time period over which the crimes had been committed meant 'a custodial sentence is the only option'.

Peggy was given eighteen months.

*

A year later I found myself back on the doorstep of her first-floor flat. Having climbed the stairs I paused before ringing the bell. I had decided to write to her while I waited nearly a year for her to get out of the open prison where she had done her time. I wanted to ask her politely for an interview, not doorstep her again, especially considering what had happened the last time I'd shown up at her home unannounced. Perhaps I should ask her advice on buying Elvis memorabilia or just write something about The King. I thought it would be better to do that rather than wait for her to come out and knock on her door. I imagined she'd want to keep a low profile and would take some careful persuasion.

I sketched out a letter, explaining who I was, focusing not on her crime but what she had bought with the proceeds. I told her I was a fan, which was not such a lie (I mean, everyone likes a bit of Elvis sometimes, don't they?), and had been very impressed with what she'd bought. I told her I wanted to hear where it had come from and how she had made her choices.

Perhaps I got the tone right, perhaps it was the dullness of the days inside or perhaps Peggy simply liked the idea of having a pen pal take an interest; anyway, I received an equally polite reply, and she said she hoped to be home soon and would be happy to meet when she was.

*

Peggy sat on her sofa and offered me a French Fancy. The pink-and-yellow icing matched her make-up. She was nervous. I imagined what the first few days of freedom had been like – a mixture of exhilaration, I guessed, and shame. She must have wondered what her friends and neighbours thought and how much they had gossiped. Perhaps her return home saw her freeze when the doorbell or phone rang. Perhaps she scurried along the communal balcony to her front door, eyes down, a scarf pulled over her head, desperate to remain incognito. Perhaps she hadn't gone to get the daily paper in her normal corner shop. Perhaps things were pretty unbearable since her release. And perhaps my appearance was only adding to it.

She was playing with her fingers, interlocking them, twiddling her wedding ring round and round, doing 'here's the church, here's the steeple, open the doors and you'll see all the people...'

I tried to look straight at her and smile, tried to make sure she felt relaxed, but she was so embarrassed I gave up. I couldn't help but think the experience of watching policemen carry away box after box of her treasured tat had broken her... the raid... the arrest... the questioning... the solicitor taking notes... court appearances... sentencing... being driven off in a police van to serve out her time... the realisation that it had all come home to roost.

The days and nights in the open prison had aged her. I wondered whether she was trying to shake off the prison pallor of her skin by taking an extra layer of care over her appearance. Gracefulness now teetered on the edge of garishness, subtlety replaced by slapdash.

She seemed so discombobulated, so out of it, I scrapped the list of questions I had mentally prepared and decided gentle conversation was the best way forward. If she wanted to speak about her spree, so be it, but looking at the grief wrapped round her I couldn't bring myself to become an interrogator. I hoped it would be to my advantage that I hadn't barged in. This hadn't been an aggressive, foot-in-the-door job. She was allowing me to sit in her flat and ask her questions. Then it occurred to me that I was, in her eyes, another part of a process she was resigned to going through, another step in the ordeal of being found guilty. Speaking to a reporter was a natural part of paying penance. So we drank tea and ate cake and chatted about Elvis.

Slowly, Peggy warmed up.

Her wariness towards me was diluted, I felt, because she told me she read *The Press And Star* each week.

'Didn't realise how much I missed it till they locked me up,' she said, and I saw a smile, the first since I had been invited to take a seat.

She told me we had published an obituary of a friend of hers who lived on the estate. Her neighbour had run the gardening club and won an award during the Camden In Bloom competition. I smiled when she told me this. I had written the tribute and suitably cele-brated a life – and we remembered her friend together. This, followed by further small talk, began to make her feel at ease, and I could sense she wasn't finding the idea of telling me her story quite so frightening.

She said she had thought about the effects her behaviour was going to one day have on her each time she put more notes in the shoebox on top of her wardrobe. She was aware that eventually, maybe, the police would knock on her door, and the press would no doubt follow.

All the while, I could hear the gentle strains of Elvis songs in the background. I wondered if the music was coming from a large radiogram in the corner of the room. I glanced at it and saw its tuning panel was lit with a slightly orange light and had a series of stations marked along the dial – Radio Luxembourg, Budapest, AFN, Lyons, Brussels, BBC3, Hilversum, London, BBC1, Athlone and Marseille...

As the song came to its end, a voice said: 'That was "Blue Moon Of Kentucky", the 1947 hit written by Bill Monroe, which Elvis recorded in 1954... You're tuned into the number-one Elvis radio station in the world, The EP Graceland Express, playing The King, twenty-four hours a day, seven days a week...'

It wasn't the radiogram after all. The music was coming from a small digital radio on a shelf above the gas fire, and it allowed Peggy's days and nights to be played out to a soundtrack of Elvis songs.

As we sipped tea in chipped china teacups – 'They took my Graceland mug, my Have An Elvish Christmas mug, my Sun Studio mug... they took the lot,' she said bitterly – she began to warm to her favourite topic.

Peggy admitted that it wasn't simply the collecting of an item which, like her in 1960, had been near Presley, that she loved. It was the thrill of going to the auctions. She liked to meet others who were as infatuated as she was. Her appetite started long before the internet offered the chance to buy online, so she would traipse the country searching out sales and try to make it to an Elvis convention in the US once every couple of years.

'The Americans? Well, *they* know how important he is,' she said, stressing 'they' as if the USA was full of mad Presley-heads, while the population of the British Isles was stupid for not sharing their infatuation. 'You meet some very interesting people, real King fanatics there,' she continued. 'They are very determined, you know. People who know everything. People who want to own everything...'

She was part of a community that saw nothing odd about the obsession they had with the singer.

It struck me then that my assumption that loneliness was a key factor in her criminal motivation was flawed. She had friends and acquaintances around the world, all linked by the snake-hipped, blue-eyed singer who could reduce a girl to a shaking wreck with the curl of his lip.

The trips to Las Vegas and Atlantic City, to Chicago and Memphis, to check out a big Elvis event were wonderful holidays, she said. They were made all the better by the polite gentlemen who would tip their hats, remember her name from previous visits, ask how she was and introduce her as 'the UK's number one Elvis fan'.

She spoke with both awe and anger about others on the Elvis circuit. Some were sleazy, some were charming. It was clear there were some proper characters at these Elvis sales, people who competed with each other to hoover up the ridiculous items you could buy if you were that way inclined.

There was the intimate stuff, from clothing to combs to toothpicks to nail-files. There were the rare items, tinged with historical importance – dub plates of unreleased singles, dodgy radio-show tapes, cine footage of shows recorded from behind pillars, the back of house or the stalls of gigs in small towns, footage that if Colonel Parker had known about it would have involved the Sun Records lawyers. But there was also the tat – mass-produced rubbish that showed how the record companies were cashing in on the teenage pop market. This often included items he'd signed, but, according to Peggy, he had scrawled on so many items over the years that his autograph, even today, added little value.

Peggy came to recognise the different types of collectors and what they wanted. There were those with real cash who were savvy investors. There were those who wanted to be in that bracket, but didn't have the resources, and would look resentful when outbid. There were the Elvis fans, the daydreaming wives who decided that splashing their nest-egg on something that was once The King's was justifiable because it would gain in value and provide a lovely item they could cherish, an object to dust or polish and which they could leave in view on a sideboard.

I felt Peggy would have been in the second camp but for the fact that she had become something of an expert due to the time and energy she had spent finding out about this strange world of Elvis collectibles and kitsch memorabilia. She knew what people should be paying – although this would frequently get turned upside down by the appearance of a maverick bidder with their heart set on a rare single for a purely sentimental reason. It was almost always an anniversary present for a husband or wife, purchased tenderly because the song was playing when they first kissed.

*

While I waited for Peggy to be released from prison, I wondered what the authorities would do with a job lot of Elvis gear. I called a contact at the Ministry of Justice who works on the disposal of the proceeds of crime. They said they'd look into it and a week later rang back. It was going to be auctioned, and the cash would be given to the council to cover the money stolen.

It took them a few months to sort out, but I kept an eye on the auctioneers the ministry used. Around six months after Peggy had gone down, I was sent a copy of an auction-house brochure, and there was her collection.

The foreword was written by the chairman of Elvishly Yours, the British branch of the Elvis Fan Club, and there was another essay by an expert in pop culture from the V&A. Peggy's obsession was described as 'the most complete collection of Elvis items ever placed for sale outside of the American continent', and it was added that the range meant there were things for both the serious collector and the part-time fan.

There was no mention of Peggy. The brochure said the items were 'from a private collection that had recently come to light'. It added that many of the pieces had not been seen on the market for decades, were in mint condition and had guaranteed authenticity.

I thought I would go along and perhaps bid for something. The Elvis bubble-gum cards were almost within my price range, and I thought I'd keep them safe for Peggy until she got out.

I got to the auction house before the sale started so I could have a mooch through her stuff. It was astonishing to see Peggy's Elvis obsession laid out. I'd only seen it in shoeboxes and cupboards as the police sifted through it all and then as a list of confiscated items on a memo put together by the Ministry of Justice. The auctioneers had mannequins sporting his clothes and display cases full of trinkets and curios.

I watched the auctioneer work through Peggy's hoard. There was a good atmosphere in the room when the salesman stood at his lectern, banged his gavel and announced: 'Lot 1'. The bidders were keen. The bubble-gum cards, slated as going for £40, sold for £200. I saw husbands and wives deep in hushed conversations as to how much an Elvis mirror was worth to them, and I saw telephone bidders, presumably from the USA, compete to land various items of clothing at extraordinary, five-figure sums. And so it went on. Every guide price was smashed, and it became clear that Peggy's Elvis clobber, which had cost at best £50,000 over the years, was going to bring in at least ten times that amount.

I finally managed to buy a set of badges, produced to celebrate the opening nights of his films *King Creole, Blue Hawaii, Flaming Star* and *GI Blues*. They cost me £65, and I felt a bit guilty as I bought them, as I'd outbid a Teddy-Boy-quiffed pensioner who looked like he had never stopped being seventeen.

It was also pretty sad. Peggy seemed like a good person. I couldn't believe she had spent a lifetime thieving loose change. I mused how the loss of her husband meant she did away with any sense of fairness or justice.

Perhaps it put a kink in her moral barometer.

As the final hammer fell, I saw a pair of parking-department council officials who were Peggy's former colleagues standing at the back of the hall. They wore wry smiles as they left.

I caught up with them outside.

'We've made a fortune,' they said, with undisclosed glee.

'Seems letting Peg invest her booty in Elvis was a wise financial move.'

I totted it up. She'd stolen around £50,000 over the years, according to the court, although it was obvious to all that the figure could have been much higher. The auction had raised nearly £1 million. It would go into the Town Hall's general budget, the officers told me. I made a few calls to councillors I knew the next day to see what they made of it all. The chair of the finance committee said they were planning to use the windfall to offset cuts to meals on wheels in the coming year.

I wrote this down, thinking it would make a good top line.

Sitting in Peggy's front room, noting the shell shock of a few months in prison, the realisation that her life of crime was public knowledge and the fact that she had returned to a flat that was now emptied of her King collection, I passed her the badges. She turned them over in her hands and laughed when I said how much I had paid, telling me they had cost her £3 at a car-boot sale.

ELVIS-OBSESSED PENSIONER IN FIFTY-GRAND PARKING FIDDLE

A trusted parking officer at the Town Hall, who ran a scam for more than three decades before she was discovered, has inadvertently made her former employers a £1m windfall, *The Press And Star* has learnt.

Peggy Collins, 62, was arrested when an audit of parking machines revealed that she had been skimming thousands of pounds from the takings.

Mrs Collins's scam came to light after she retired from her job at the Town Hall two years ago. Wood Green Magistrates' Court heard that she had spent the proceeds of her criminal activity on funding her obsession with collecting Elvis Presley memorabilia. She was sentenced to eighteen months in prison.

It has since emerged that her collection – which included clothing, a signed Bible and other Elvis-related objects – has been sold at auction by the Ministry of Justice.

A Town Hall spokesman said that the council is reviewing its accounting procedures and tightening up the system for collecting parking fees.

TEA AND SYMPATHY

THE PROPRIETOR OF the Sunrise-2-Sunset Café was called Emilija. She came from Latvia and employed other Latvian women she had met in London to work the kitchen and tables.

She was kind and caring and not afraid of hard graft. She opened the doors at 7am for the first waves of workmen and did not stop till way into the afternoon, give or take the odd fag break. She would snatch three or four puffs before stubbing out her rollie, balancing it on the rim of an overflowing ashtray, and heading back inside to deal with another order for a set breakfast.

She teamed a quick efficiency with a smile and made people feel welcome.

Perhaps it was this natural friendliness, fostered by her memories of once being a stranger in a strange land, that attracted Michael through the doors of the Sunrise-2-Sunset Café. He was a notable figure in the cafés, pubs and hostels of NW1. If he wasn't loitering on a bench or a doorstep, watching horse races in the bookies or nursing a pint at The Osprey, he could be found whiling away the hours at Emilija's, drinking cups of tea, and always without a penny in his pocket. But she would never shoo him away, and at regular intervals offer a refill. She would smile and ask if he fancied trying the day's special, which she would never accept payment for, knowing that he didn't have the funds anyway. As the day's special was always onions, liver, mash and gravy, a particular favourite of Michael's, and as he was perpetually broke and perpetually hungry, he never turned down her generosity.

Other cafés in the neighbourhood saw Michael as being bad for business. He was always in a terrible state, and if you got too close he didn't smell pleasant. He was prone to hogging the day's papers and muttering to himself about the stories he would spend hours carefully reading through cloudy, rheumy eyes. But Emilija didn't mind him slouching in the corner seat and greeted him warmly every time he appeared with a hungry look about him.

He considered her a friend, and she considered him a good Catholic fallen on hard times. She believed their shared God had somehow guided him through the doors of her café in Camden Town and put her in a position by a hotplate and a stove in order to help the weaker members of His flock, weaker members such as Michael, who needed a Holy-Mary-Mother-Of-God-type figure like Emilija to be there when times were hard.

Michael's hair was white and thin. He had a nut-brown scalp, scarcely covered by the remaining tufts on his pate. On his left temple he had a huge liver spot, the size of a two-pence piece, and a constellation of moles on the other side of his face. His mottled cheeks were stretched over bone until they reached his mouth, at which point they sagged, giving him dog jowls that wobbled as he slurped his tea.

Michael had a face that would have made a painter from the Camden Town Group hold a thumb up and gaze quizzically. His chin was sometimes bearded, sometimes not; the hair would grow not through laziness but through lack of money. He always liked to use a new razor when he shaved, something that on his meagre income was not a regular possibility.

When he was a boy, the priest from his home village of Creggan-baun, in County Mayo, had said something that had stuck with him more than any other sermon on the Good Samaritan or St Christopher, which were the Father's favourite lessons. The priest chose the Good Samaritan, as he hoped a story of simple, selfless deeds would make his flock less trying and the parish more pleasant. And St Christopher was a favourite, as he saw every young man and woman leave for new pastures as soon as they could and hoped the story of the patron saint of travellers would stand them in good stead as they spread around the world.

The priest would raise chuckles when he told the congregation that 'Jesus Shaves' and would bemoan the numbers of bearded labourers he had among the believers that perched uncomfortably on his pews. He made a point of telling the altar boys, as they donned their smocks, that he wished his flock would appear on a Sunday with clean chins.

'Jesus, contrary to what many a Protestant or similar Dissenter who has turned their back on the Holy Roman Empire would have you believe, never sported a beard,' he would decry. 'How could he have achieved so much and been Our Saviour without being neat and tidy?'

Quite where the old padre had gleaned this information from had never been made clear, but the idea stayed with Michael. He took a razor when he could afford it and enjoyed running his hands over his smooth chin when the job was complete.

It was the only neat thing about him. His clothes were old and worn. Suit jackets from charity shops provided a sartorial theme. The lining of their pockets had holes in them, and he would have to fish for anything he placed in there. But, rather than being an annoyance, it meant he would occasionally harvest a lost cigarette butt or a coin. They were welcome finds that would brighten up his day.

His feet were shod with shoes that had broken uppers, cracked heels and split soles. They had been fished from recycling units in a supermarket car-park or begged from the cast-offs thrown out by the same charity shops who kept him in blazers. He wore greasy trousers. They had worn thighs and grubby ends that dragged along the floor as he shuffled through the dirty north-London streets going about his daily business.

Arthritis in the fingers made it hard for him to roll his own cigarettes, meaning his efforts were loose and shaggy. He'd tuck the ends in and suck furiously on tar-browned tips to draw the smoke, to get some purchase, puckering his lips and pulling in his cheeks dramatically. He would hold the smoke in for an extravagated length of time, hoping to get each drag's worth before exhaling equally dramatically, as if he were blowing up a balloon.

When the smoking ban started, Michael steadfastly ignored it, or forgot it applied to him, and Emilija would have to quietly shepherd him outside. He would clasp his cigarette with grim determination, puffing away as he went, his cheeks filling up like a trumpeter's, annoyed that a society that had ostracised him in so many ways still expected him to play by rules he found inconvenient.

*

Emilija was not the only Samaritan who looked after Michael.

Father Dominic at Our Lady's would slice him doorstep sandwiches. He spread the pickle and mustard on thick and put slabs of waxy cheddar between them, hoping they'd stave off the hunger for a few more hours. He would let Michael doze in a chair by the gas fire in the clergy house while he attended to parish matters.

The newsagent who ran the street kiosk by the station would give him a handful of cigarettes or tobacco, and, being a fellow Irish exile, would sometimes hand over a copy of the *Connaught Free Press* or the *Western People*. He hoped the news from home would keep alive the slender link Michael still had with the land of his fathers, a place he'd not seen since leaving to work in London during the post-war building boom.

There were others. The cleaner from Lesotho who worked at his hostel would check up on him and call him 'my dear'. She made him tea and put aside donated clothes she thought would fit him. There was the hairy and eccentric poet, originally from Cornwall, who asked Michael how he was in a slow West Country burr. The poet lived in a large, rambling house off the high street and had given Michael an occasional sofa in the depths of winter when he'd not the cash for a hostel. There was the Somalian taxi driver who ran the cab firm at the Lock and would stand him the money for chips or a pint or a flutter.

Michael had an uncanny knack of attracting a series of good deeds from a number of people who had been seduced by his frail appearance, scruffy attire and soft Irish accent.

*

Michael's lilt was noticeable, but it didn't stand out from the other elderly Irishmen who had made Camden Town home, and the archetypal Irish charm and chat wasn't his style. The closest he came to a line of patter was his regularly espoused defence of James Joyce's views of the Catholic Church: 'Have you ever read *Dubliners* or tried to read *Ulysses*? Joyce was a very mixed-up young man, you know...' And he delivered it in a brogue so strong that I suspected it wasn't a device used to chisel funds out of people, as it took a real effort to clock what he was going on about. It was inspired by a genuine intellectual curiosity, not a street-drinker's attempts to curry favour.

He had lived the classic lifestyle of an itinerant labourer, moving from one bedsit to another or spending weeks in temporary hostels. He didn't mind; he was used to it, and despite the fact he'd not crossed the Irish Sea for more than fifty years, he still considered everything to be temporary until he returned to his parents' small farmstead outside Cregganbaun.

It was either falling behind with his rent that forced the issue or his inability to keep a tidy home. One or the other would mean it was time to pack his ragged belongings into a battered suitcase and search out new digs. He was extraordinarily messy. He seemed unable to throw out rubbish, and could reduce a fresh-scented room to a grim-smelling pit within a fortnight.

He was a relentless and indiscriminate collector of refuse, with neither aim nor purpose. He struggled, for example, to throw away plastic milk cartons, leaving them in every corner. It wasn't solely laziness or the lack of domesticity carved by not having a place to call his own but partly due to his upbringing. He had ingrained within him a sense that everything had an intrinsic worth, everything had been created by the sweat and spark of human ingenuity – or through God's grace, as his mother would tell him – and he felt it was disrespectful to the Great Inventor and the raw materials provided by Mother Earth to throw things out. Those milk cartons could be used as cloches to protect the early spring vegetables from slugs, or to collect water, or scoop oats for feed; his imagination created a multitude of uses for all kinds of rubbish.

His parents had reused absolutely everything, and he could conjure up in his mind the response his mother would have given, if she'd lived today, about the packaging and waste surrounding him.

She even felt a milk bottle, which would be washed and used again, an extravagance. It was normal for her to ladle out the morning's milk direct from the bucket it had been squirted into by her cow. It meant Michael couldn't help but let junk pile up. Eventually the landlord would enter his room, see the mess and chuck him out. It was always a race between falling behind on the rent or filling up his bedsit – whichever came first led to eviction.

His daily routine, I learnt, was mainly spent trying to keep warm. Even in the summer months he dressed with layer upon layer of scraggy cloth under his jackets, and I'd often find him tucked away in a pavement-side nook or cranny, hoping for some respite from whatever weather was out there. He had a pathological fear of being chilly, ingrained through years of rough living. Instead of being hardened to it, he fought it constantly and feared it more than anything else. It was a remorseless and never-ending war of attrition between Michael and the elements.

Through our conversations I gleaned information about how he spent his days and filled in gaps by speaking to Emilija, Father Dominic, Seamus the newsagent and the others who had taken it upon themselves to be his guardian angels.

Around the time I really got to know Michael, he had moved from a Kilburn dosshouse to a bedsit off Chalk Farm Road. He appeared, for once, to be settled and spoke to me of how friendly the place was. He had a habit of finding plenty to criticise when it came to his living arrangements, so I was pleased to hear him react positively to his latest move. Yet he still yearned for the mythical 'good old days' when the Irish were by far the biggest ethnic group in Camden Town and had created a solid community that worked, ate, drank, fought, worshipped, procreated and died together in a two-square-mile area.

'Back in the day, we'd go into one of the old houses, the derries, round Somers Town,' he told me over a cup of tea at Emilija's. 'There were streets and streets of empty homes, and we'd climb in, and no one would disturb us. It was a dosser's heaven, it really was. There'd be a fire in the grate, a billycan on the boil, people to talk to, drink to be shared.'

I asked him whether he kept up with his old friends, how people had fared, imagining them sitting together around tables over lunches of beef, spuds, carrots and gravy at the Irish Centre or meeting on Sundays as Father Dominic delivered another sermon on the dangers of temptation and of being led astray from the one true path by boozing it up.

He looked at me incredulously, as if I had asked a completely ridiculous question.

'Not at all. They're all dead, and if they're not dead through the drink, they've been taken away to be "looked after" by the authorities,' he said.

I wondered aloud if that meant a stretch in prison.

'No, no, no, not prison.' He shook his head at my ignorance, and grinned a toothy grin. 'I mean your sheltered accommodation, hostels managed by the housing associations, that type of thing. And they've changed, too. We used to turn up and pay 30p for a kip for the night and they'd throw in breakfast. You could leave your bundle there during the day and come back again later if you felt like it. Now they get you to sign a tenant's form, have a check-up, ask how many points you've got, if you've been sent there by a housing person from down the Town Hall.

'Granted, it has got rid of the lice and the bed bugs and the scabies on the whole. We used to spend our days scratching away – scratch, scratch, scratch. Used to be teeming with lice, but it's so regimented now, regimented and cleaner. I may not be squishing bugs in my trousers any more, but it's not for me, you know.' He shook his head as he pondered the individual freedoms lost to the local authority's reorganisation of adult social-care practices. 'It used to be that you'd choose a place each day where you'd end up each night,' he said. By lunchtime you'd know where your mates were kipping, so you'd make your way there. Not any more: when I'm in-between sits, I spend half my time looking for a kip. And there's virtually no squats left, not like back in the day. Every street had one. No longer.'

*

Unless he had made one of his fairly regular pilgrimages to the northern fringes of his stomping ground and woke up in Kilburn or Cricklewood, Michael's mornings would start with a cup of sweet and milky tea, either bought or blagged, from the Rumbeltums van that pulled up on the industrial estate around the back of Kentish Town. He was a long-term customer. If the old man who ran it was working, he'd get a tea and an egg or bacon sandwich for free. If one of his staff was on duty, he would be charged – 'Not mine to give away,' they'd say – but he didn't mind too much. The number of freebies he'd had off Rumbletums over the years was so large he felt he had to occasionally give something back to ensure they could stay in business, as he put it, and he could still touch them for a brew.

Then it would be a walk along the canal into Camden Lock to meet with others, to sit on a bench and hear the day's news, watch as some of the heavier drinkers opened their cans of super-strength lager, passed around bottles of cider and fed their aches.

Michael had told me how he used to drink. He passed much of his middle years staving off the loneliness of dreary boarding-houses by spending his evenings in pubs, nursing pints of Guinness, soothing the pains caused by early starts, cramped spaces in the backs of the vans and the brutal hours hacking into the London clay with pick-axes and shovels. But, unlike many of his contemporaries, his drinking was a pastime, not the be-all and end-all. He knew he was lucky to have a constitution that did not really agree with booze. He drank, but not to any real extent, unlike some of his peers, and he found that as he got older he couldn't hold his drink like he used to. He looked with distaste at those around him, swigging it back every morning, stinking of booze and piss, any last semblance of dignity stripped away by their thirst for alcohol.

After having his fill of the towpath gossip, he would head to a haven provided by one of the borough libraries for a few hours with a newspaper or a book. He read the same things over and over. He loved Irish history and Irish literature, enthralled by the stories and words of his countrymen. This would last into the afternoon: it was no accident that he'd spin out the reading as long as possible, as he found his chances of getting a free lunch increased as the day wore on. Café owners did not take kindly to a valuable seat being taken up by someone who had no funds for food and whose smell and appearance put people off their dinners. Even Emilija didn't have the time to play host properly if she was cooking up and fetching and carrying plates of steaming hot all-day breakfasts. And after lunch there would be a certain amount of grub going to waste – the ready-blanched chips, the beans in a pan and not in a can, the par-boiled spuds and part-fried sausages which the café owners would scoop into the bin if Michael wasn't there.

He would go to the Sunrise-2-Sunset Café three or four times a week, or the Greek place on College Street, which had three generations of the same family working the kitchen, counter and tables and was known for its huge portions. He'd stay as long as he could and then take a stroll to the benches at the old burial ground in St Martin's for a cigarette and a muse on whatever it was he had read in the papers that day. He would watch the pigeons, watch the dogs being exercised, watch the parents and toddlers play on the mud-patch grass.

*

Michael had occasionally earned a few quid in the afternoons helping the scrap-metal men load their van with rubbish off skips – he'd sit in the cab as they drove around the neighbourhood, looking for the tell-tale signs of scaffolding outside the old, four-storey homes being converted back from flats into family houses, as that would mean there might be a bath, piping, guttering or something else they could swipe. He didn't do that often any more – he was no longer strong enough to be much help – but in the past the fivers he was paid were helpful, as was the warm cab to sit in, the heater blowing soothing air on his feet.

Then, as evening approached, he would return to his bedsit, hostel or squat. If it was his bedsit – as it was in the final days I knew him – he'd have a walk through the vegetable market in Inverness Street and see what was left over. He'd be given a few potatoes by the traders, cut out the eyes and blackened bits and boil them up on a hob in the communal kitchen before smearing on marge and eating them on a bed of cabbage.

Sometimes he'd have a chip supper from the First Choice Take Away on Kentish Town Road, carrying his meal well-wrapped back to his room, where he would squish handfuls of chips between slices of bread. Like the cold, he had a longstanding fear of hunger. It was the other dominating factor of his daily life. He devoted so much time to scavenging grub, and was so skilful at it, that he usually managed to fall asleep each night with the pangs staved off for another day – often thanks to the small acts of kindness he encountered.

*

Michael had many strange habits, and they included traditional superstitions he'd inherited from his mother. He would always cross himself when he passed a church, mutter a prayer when he saw a hearse and walk three steps along with the funeral procession to stave off bad luck. He knew that if his left palm itched he would lose money, while if his right palm itched he'd come into some. If he heard ringing in his ears – and he did regularly after years of working a jackhammer – then it was a sign of souls in purgatory calling out for him to light them a candle and say a prayer.

And there were other superstitious quirks he stuck to whose origins were less obvious. He had a habit of carrying around strips of brown paper he had torn from bags he collected from grocery stores. As I learnt from Emilija, he would carefully take out a length from an inside pocket and smooth it flat on the table in front of him. He would then take a stub of a pencil or one of the small pens he was constantly filching from bookmakers, and in delicate, printed, thin handwriting carefully write her out an IOU for the price of the meal she had given him. He'd leave it under the sugar pot or prop it up among the sauce bottles. He would write the amount and beneath add 'inc tip' before signing his name. He would hand over an IOU to the newspaper kiosk, where Seamus had a habit of sticking them in a drawer under the counter and forgetting all about them. They would not always promise cash. He would leave an IOU on the sideboard in the poet's home, stating that he, Michael Corcoran, was available for an afternoon's work in the garden or some other offer of a few hours' labour. The poet didn't throw them out either. He thought they were rather enchanting and had a vague idea he would one day make them into a collage for the wall of the downstairs loo.

The only person he didn't leave an IOU with was Father Dominic. Perhaps he thought the acts of generosity were part of the job and he would be amply rewarded in heaven – or was being rewarded well enough on earth already.

*

I'd not seen Michael for some time when I heard about his final, eccentric behaviour, and his absence hadn't worried me. While he was often based in Camden Town, I knew of his sojourns in Kilburn and Cricklewood, which would last a month or two before he reappeared as if he'd never been away. But I had become concerned as I'd heard from three different people what he had done.

The first was Emilija. She had served me eggs, chips and beans, smoothed down her apron, ran her hands through her hair and said: 'I'm a bit worried about Mick.'

'Why?' I asked. 'What's the matter?' I had assumed he was on what he called a 'High Road Beano', namely hanging out on the benches that dotted the main thoroughfare of Kilburn. 'He's all right, isn't he?'

'I don't know. I'm worried about him,' she repeated. 'Take a look at this.'

She pulled a cheque from the pocket on the front of her apron. It was folded in half and drawn from an account marked 'Bank of Ireland'. It had her first name written on it in spidery handwriting, followed by the sum of £3,000, and a signature scribbled along the bottom.

'He left it tucked under a mug a couple of weeks ago,' she said. 'He didn't say anything. Just got up and went, and I've not seen him since.'

*

A conversation Michael and I had came rushing back to me, and I began to put two and two together.

A few months previously an advert in *The Evening Press And Star*'s classified section had caught my eye. It was by 'Aird Bourke: Notaries To The Public, Solicitors' from County Mayo. It asked for information regarding the whereabouts of an Aiden Michael Corcoran, and I subsequently discovered that the last will and testament of Aine Corcoran had been placed in their files.

She was the last of the Corcorans of Cregganbaun. While her brothers had fled Ireland in the 1940s, gone to work in America and London, she had stayed faithfully behind. She'd worked the land with her parents, and, as they declined, taken on more and more. She had a strong constitution, formed by the years of toil, but once both her mother and father had passed away, she became less inclined to look after the house and the surrounding land. She spent her final years alone. Her home began to leak, the chimney no longer drew the smoke properly, the roof sagged, tiles slipped, windowpanes broke and were replaced with newspapers and rags, doors were draughty and hung lopsidedly, gutters and downpipes were blocked and overflowed. The place was slipping quietly into ruin.

Aine would appear once a week in the town. She hooked up her pony and drove her trap down the rutted tracks. She always went to the post office, cashed her social-security cheque, bought provisions from the general store (including a half-bottle of cheap whiskey) and passed a few pleasantries with whoever was in the village going about their business.

It was when she didn't appear on her Thursday trip into Cregganbaun that people thought there may be something wrong, so regular was she, and so a small group led by the postmaster made their way up the hill, through the five-bar gate and into the house of the Corcorans. She was found lying next to the water pump. The doctor who arrived told the others who had gathered and were looking sadly down at the corpse that it was a surprise she'd lasted as long as she did, all alone up there, as she had a body wracked with a variety of maladies and illnesses, and the exertion required to draw water from the ground had probably done for her.

While she'd had no contact with her little brother, who was fifteen years younger, she never forgot him. When he was first born she had played the role of a second mother. She knew he lived in England, knew he lived in London, and had heard he was somewhere in Camden Town, so when her parents died and she inherited the farmstead, she made a new will, leaving him everything.

And this was where I came in, flicking through the latest edition of the paper the morning it came out. Sitting in the café, nursing a cup of tea while I waited for a fried-egg roll, I opened the paper on the classified pages and noticed the advert from County Mayo. It was pretty obvious this was an inheritance, although it wasn't made clear, probably to deter scam merchants and time-wasters.

After breakfast the front desk called and said there was a man waiting to see me. It was Michael.

'I want to ask you a question,' he said.

I was used to him 'asking me questions', which usually meant tapping me up to run an errand for him or provide the price of his favourite lunchtime meal of onion, liver and mash, which would instead be spent at the bookies.

'I think there is an advert in your rag that is about me. I'm a little worried, you know. I don't know what to do, but someone is after me, and I'd like to know why. Will you make a call for me? Can you do that?'

I did his bidding and, as was usual in our relationship, didn't see him again for another month or so.

*

'Let me tell you something,' he would say, so often prefixing a long, rambling lecture with these words. 'Let me tell you something...' and then his eyes would have that glazed, faraway look as he steeled himself, worked out how to open his story and then glanced at you to check you were listening. I waited for another lecture on why Joyce was really a good Catholic, and that he loved Holy Week and just didn't believe that those around him quite understood the glory of God.

'My ancestors, the first Corcorans to walk our land – though that name of course only came to us in the Middle Ages – were responsible for the peat. This was long before the Magnatai tribes of this ancient land had built the tombs, and three thousand years before St Patrick got rid of the snakes... the Corcorans had come to the country and settled and set about removing all of the trees so they could graze their animals... they'd brought with them their goats and sheep – did you know, before then, and we're talking the neolithic period (he rolled neolithic out as if he were especially pleased to be using such an intricate word), the Irish only had wild pigs to eat? It's why we make the best sausages in the world, you know. Three thousand years of practice. You want a good sausage, go to an Irish butcher. They know what a sausage should taste like.'

He cupped the mug of tea I had made him and paused to gather his thoughts. I knew him well enough to keep quiet during such pauses. It only interrupted his flow and meant it would take even longer to get to the point of what he wanted.

'These settlers brought with them barley and they brought with them wheat, and they started chopping down the ancient forests in the uplands and making themselves houses out of the logs and fields from the places they'd cleared... but they were wasteful, they were... they loved the views, I reckon, from the top of the hills and didn't want to move, didn't want to switch their crops, let the land recover. Soon overgrazing and erosion made the land turn, made the earth acidic, made it stagnate, and it was no good any more. But the Lord moves in mysterious ways. It meant the uplands turned into peat bogs – so our famous peat was caused by our neolithic farming ancestors.

'It was this lot were also responsible for my own set of stones. There were four barrows on our land, four almighty great tombs, and two still had stone-walled chambers, and we'd play in them as kids.

'My ma and pa told us they were built by giants, and we believed them, of course, because we'd seen giants... seen them playing the hurling, seen them playing rugby, seen them working in the fields... it made sense to me when I was a wee thing that there were giants sloping across our lands in the olden days...'

He paused again, took a deep swig from his mug, and gathered further thoughts.

Michael went on to describe how he had retraced those steps he'd made back in the 1940s. He walked from Camden Town to Euston with a small, battered holdall, caught a train there to Holyhead, bought a ticket for the ferry to Dublin then taken another train and a bus out to his old home... and climbed the stairs up to the offices of Aird Bourke, above the takeaway. He'd been welcomed in by the notary, offered a seat and then in silence handed a folder that contained details of his legacy.

After reading the will, he visited his parents' and sister's graves and then went to the old farmstead and had a peek about.

'Terrible state, it was,' he said. 'Terrible. Horrible. Awful.'

This was coming from a man whose living standards were hardly salubrious, and the idea that he wasn't comfortable with how the old place had become sent an inadvertent shiver down my spine.

He said he couldn't face living there. 'Everyone I knew was either dead, or senile, or drunken, or had never been my friend in the first place; that sorry old town meant nothing but death and decay for me.'

So he went straight back to the solicitors and told them to sell it for him.

'The thing was, no one wants to buy a ramshackle hill farm in the middle of nowhere,' he said. 'Not today. Not in Ireland. If she'd gone and died ten years ago I may have got something from it, due to all those moguls buying up land and trying to build estates and playing the Billy Big Bollocks everywhere... but not since the banks went coo-foddle... not since then.'

He didn't seem too unhappy about this and, as he paused, I managed to squeeze a word in. 'So what did you do with it, Michael?' I asked.

For a brief moment I had a vision of a free holiday. For once I would get something out of him, I thought. A trip to the west of Ireland. A remote farmhouse to hang out in for a week. I'd do some walking, some fishing, drink Guinness, listen to an old ginger-whiskered fellow play the fiddle as I sat by a roaring fire in the saloon bar of a pub.

'I thought about it…' he said, tilting his head and frowning, as if the memory was a difficult one to confront. 'You know, nature has the same power as an intoxicating drink, allowing man to laugh and sing and forget for a while the sorrow of his earthly miseries…' I wasn't sure who he was quoting, but I know it was one of his memorised phrases. 'And it is lovely up there, you know, lovely. But what the fuck would I be wanting with half a pitch of scrub and grass and a collection of cracked stone?'

'So what will happen to it?' I asked again.

'Well, I got a phone call from the Taisce fellow,' said Michael.

'The Taisce?' I asked, and he chuckled at my ignorance.

'It's like your National Trust over here,' he said. 'The Taisce. It's our National Trust, if you like. They go round looking after those giant stately homes the Brits built for the lords and ladies that oppressed my forefathers. Funny how things turn out: the homes of those who robbed our lands now looked after by our nation, preserved… Anyway, I never thought An Taisce could be the key to my fortune.

'They'd had a look round my barrows, nosed about the ground, decided the land was of some serious historical importance and that it must be bought for the nation. They said because we'd not done much ploughing over the years it was a pristine archaeological site… I wanted to say, you try and plough land on a gradient like that, land that was only good for grazing not crops anyway… the way the fella had said it, making out the folks were too lazy…

'Now, it wasn't quite striking oil, to be honest, nor getting your hands on some of that famous Mayo gold they go on about… No, it wasn't quite like that. But I'd have taken anything at this point, and the fact was the government was offering a grant they'd bagged from the EU, and the Taisce had cash and they wanted it, and there was no way I'd turn it down, so I sold it to them. Imagine that. My old home, with all those ancient Irish fellows lying up in that field and being something special for the historians.

'Imagine that, eh? You could say it all ended well.'

He swilled the last of his tea about and poured it into that cracked and shallow mouth. He smacked his lips with satisfaction:

a tea drunk and a good story told. He smiled at me, stood up, adjusted his coat and said: 'Cheerio, be seeing you, keep well, God bless...'

That was the last I saw of him.

*

Looking back, I suppose it wouldn't take a doctor to realise the years had taken their toll on his slender, hollow frame.

He had a cough so phlegmy it created a snowball of disgusting mucus, starting at the bottom of his lungs and growing bigger, bigger and bigger as it rolled up his windpipe and then into the darker recesses of his rotten-toothed mouth. And when it got up there he didn't have the required strength to project it any distance... rather than let it dribble out of his mouth and down his chin, he would take a small piece of paper and spit into it... and it wasn't always something absorbent like a tissue paper. Often it would be one of his IOU strips, and this foul habit was yet another reason he was avoided by so many and another reason those who did not avoid him were treated with graciousness and appreciation.

Michael acknowledged this and spent his last days handing out alms to those who'd looked after him.

After speaking with Emilija, I went to the newspaper kiosk and waited for Seamus the newsagent to finish serving a customer.

'Have you seen Michael recently?' I asked.

'No, and I've been wondering about him,' Seamus replied.

'A few weeks ago he picked up some papers – the *Connemara Journal, The Irish Times,* the *Roscommon Herald,* the *Tullamore Tribune* – and told me he didn't have the cash to pay for them, but was good for it...' He began fishing down beneath the counter, searching for something, and I knew immediately what was going to happen. 'He said he'd bring me "something" later. I hadn't the heart to tell him to stop fucking around and put the papers back. There was a queue and the last thing I needed was for Michael to make a scene. He could make a scene, you know, never with me, granted, but I had seen him shout and swear at those PCSOs when they told him to get up off a doorstep or told one of his friends to tip their beer away... a real scene. The following morning I found an envelope wedged in between the door and frame, and it contained this.'

Seamus passed me a folded piece of paper, and before I'd even opened it, I knew what it would say.

I spent the rest of the morning visiting his old haunts, and each time it was the same story. Father Dominic fished out a cheque from his bureau drawer, clasped it carefully and said: 'I found it pushed under my door... I thought, poor old Michael, where's he got this from? Then it occurred to me it was probably one of Michael's games or just another sign of his dementia. He had got very forgetful recently, you know... He had always been full of tall stories, but I noticed he was not as with it as he used to be. I thought about cashing it but hadn't got around to it and didn't for a moment think it would be good for the sum.'

The story was the same at the hostel. The cleaner from Lesotho carefully unfolded a cheque she had placed in her purse.

'Crazy old man,' she said, with a smile and a few taps of a finger on the forehead.

There were others who had been given cheques, and nobody had thrown them away, but neither did they believe they were worth anything more than as a souvenir of an eccentric down-and-out who had made them feel better about themselves.

When I told them about the place in Cregganbaun their eyes lit up. I told them I suspected the cheques were good and each had the same look move across their faces... a moment of wondering if the cheque meant real money and then, if it did, what would they do with it?

I went off back to the office and began ringing around hospitals, wondering if any of them had him tucked up in a bed somewhere. I had no joy, so I called a Camden Town GP, and he took Michael's full name down and said he'd look into it. He rang back later that day and told me Michael had passed away three weeks previously.

'He was found on a bench, down by the canal, and apparently he was pretty far gone,' the doctor told me.

'At first it seemed there wasn't too much wrong with him, except for the fact that he was a little on the thin side and seemed exhausted. But his cough was a worry, so the hospital ran some tests, and he had late-stage lung cancer. Three days later he was dead. Among his possessions were instructions for his body to be taken back to somewhere in Ireland, to the place he came from, and the address of a solicitors that had the funds to pay for it...'

Returning to the Sunrise-2-Sunset Café, I told Emilija about Michael. We sat together and shared some memories, and then I explained that she was one of eight people holding a share of Michael's inheritance. After a short silence, Emilija came up with an idea.

'I could do something nice with this...' she began, and I expected to hear of the holiday she'd take or the improvements it would pay for at the café.

'If there are eight cheques, and each is for £3,000, that means it could be as much as £24,000 – imagine the number of sandwiches and teas Father Dominic could provide for all the other Michaels with this money.'

I was pretty overcome by her generosity and said we should move quickly. She left her waitress and cook in charge of the café, threw a coat over her apron, and we went to visit Father Dominic. By the end of the day, seven of the eight cheques had been collected together – the eighth was held on to grimly by its recipient, who shall remain nameless so as not to embarrass them – and the funds, once the cheques had been cashed, were put into a pot controlled by Father Dominic to run a lunch club in the vestry for Michael's street-drinking peers.

Looking back, I'm not sure if Michael would have approved – he wanted those who had always shown such kindness to benefit, not his contemporaries, people he so often avoided, so often was furious with, so often spoke harshly about.

But, even in death, his sponsors, remembering Michael, did a good thing.

THE SECRET FORTUNE OF
MICKY CORCORAN

Good Samaritans across Camden Town were left scratching their heads this week after discovering a down-and-out they would look out for was a secret heir to a fortune in Ireland.

Michael Corcoran, who died four weeks ago, was well-known in the NW1 area and lived in the Crossroads Hostel in Levering Road.

Before his death, the seventy-seven-year-old retired builder left a series of large cheques for people who over the years had looked out for him.

They included sums of more than £5,000 to Our Lady's Church, where he was a parishioner.

Father Dominic Flaherty told the *Press And Star*: 'I knew Michael for many years, and he never mentioned any inheritance. He was a good man who lived simply and would often rely on friends to provide a warm meal.

'After I last saw him, I found an envelope addressed to me pushed under my door. In it was a large cheque. Michael was somewhat eccentric, and I wasn't sure if this was some kind of mistake.'

Father Dominic discovered that others who knew Mr Corcoran had been given similar sums. They contacted the Bank Of Ireland and have since found that the cheques are drawn on an account that recently received a large deposit. It is believed the funds came from the sale of the family farm in County Mayo, where ancient burial grounds dating back more than three thousand years have been discovered. It has been bought by the Eire equivalent of the National Trust, the Taisce.

Father Dominic added: 'The majority of the money Michael gave away will now be used to set up a fund to provide services for others in need, in the parish where he was so well-known and loved.'

GRAND THEFT AUTOBUS

MECHANOPHILIA IS THE love of machinery.

It is a condition that relates to the physical effect Modernism has had on human beings, and its meaning has changed with technological progress. It originally described the sensations felt by the shiny-eyed generation of the early decades of the 20th century, who thought technology would create a better place and decided to pre-empt (or welcome) it through artistic movements such as Futurism, Cubism and Post-Impressionism. This trend was undermined by the mass mechanical slaughter of the Western Front, which prompted a backlash against the evils of the industrial age, articulated by people such as JB Priestley and Laurie Lee, who recalled a bucolic, cottage-garden, rose-trimmed doorway world of William Cobbett and prompted fresh interest in the Diggers, the Luddites and the Arts And Crafts movement.

Mechanophilia also has a second meaning.

This is the product of the dawning of that same post-Victorian, mass-industrial age. Psychologists use the term to describe a physical lust towards mechanical objects – a state it seems we all suffer from to varying degrees today, with smartphones and tablets and other gizmos everywhere, giving the psychologists plenty of new work around the addictive behaviour of tapping away on a small screen.

Mechanophilia comes in different shapes and sizes. As well as the enjoyment felt when holding a new gadget in your hand, it includes the thrill most of us get when revving an engine, pulling a lever or pressing a button. Such actions prompt our brain to release endorphins and flood us with a sense of well-being. Simply operating machinery makes us think, 'Clever me, I did that'.

This syndrome, which we all experience and are partial to, can manifest itself in mild forms. If you have ever experienced satisfaction when using an electric drill, you've had a touch of it. The wood succumbs to your command, a shave of it curls out of the hole you've made, you pull the bit out and blow away the dust, yet can't help yourself squeezing the trigger again and giving the bit a rev or two, even though the hole you needed to make has been created.

Then there are more extreme examples, caused by the hardwiring in the brain of the person affected, flooding the mind with extra feel-good chemicals. Mechanophilia can be intense and make people behave in unconventional ways. For example, it is the uncontrollable motivation behind those tales you read in the papers relating to someone who has uncontrollable sexual urges towards cars and lorries. I've seen newspaper editors' eyes light up when a deviant gets caught in the midst of doing something quite unfathomable in a garage, car-park or lay-by.

So, mechanophilia has many degrees of severity, and the story of Bobby Dove, whose court case I covered, is an example of how it can manifest itself in some strange forms.

*

I met Bobby Dove on the steps of the magistrates' court. Normally, if a defendant has been tried and found guilty, you have to approach them with a sense of humble trepidation. You need to introduce yourself with care, make sure you don't become the conduit for a grand sense of injustice and potentially the subject of verbal abuse or a physical assault.

But with Bobby it was very easy.

To start with, there had been no one else in the court except Bobby, three magistrates, a prosecutor, his defence solicitor and me. It meant that when he looked around with wide, moist eyes, seemingly stunned by the series of events that had led to this day in court, he'd seen I was there. I smiled at him. He smiled back. I gave him a nod of the head and he'd given me a thumbs-up. Bobby grinned an embarrassed grin and did a little shoulder shrug as if to say: 'Well, shit happens, huh?' I'd seen his charge sheet and was curious. I thought his case might make a left-hand page filler for

The EPS, a humorous tale of minor criminality that people would enjoy, a 'nowt-as-queer-as-folk' yarn.

He had already pleaded guilty by then, already heard his crimes described as being 'fortunate not to end with a much more unpleasant and possibly deadly outcome' by the Queen's Counsel who was prosecuting the case with an air of importance that suggested Bobby's slight frame hid a truly dangerous criminal.

The defence solicitor had read out a long series of reasons why Bobby Dove deserved sympathy, a well-crafted, if somewhat clichéd, back story of mitigating factors about his tough home life and troubles at school. As I wondered if such blabber would influence the beaks, he added something that knocked me dead – and the magistrates, too, judging by the look of incredulous horror on their faces: 'He also wants you to consider two hundred and eighty-nine further counts,' said the solicitor quietly as he made his closing remarks.

At first I thought, well, that is rather damning, and decided that the story would sit further up the paper and on a more prominent right-hand page. This was hardly an isolated lapse in an otherwise blemish-free adolescence. But then it occurred to me that his admission was another sign that the court should realise that poor Bobby simply couldn't help himself. He had an extreme case of mechanophilia.

After he was released and told he would be sentenced at a later date, I approached and introduced myself, and Bobby simply said: 'What do you want to know?'

Now we were on the street he hesitated to make eye contact. It was as if the courtroom had forced him to simply smile at everyone as part of a ruse concocted to get him as little punishment as possible. However, as I began chatting to Bobby, trying to earn his confidence, I discovered his distracted body language had nothing to do with me. We were near a bus stop, and he kept peering over my shoulder, and in such an obvious fashion I had to turn my head to see what he was looking at. He just couldn't help but stare as double deckers pulled up, opened their doors, let passengers off and on and then pulled out into the traffic. It was only when there wasn't a bus going past – and we were on the Holloway Road, so this was for but a brief moment – that he spoke to me directly.

'Do you think they'll lock me up?' he asked.

And what could I say? 'Yes, you are going down for sure. I've never heard of such a huge number of previous offences to be taken into account, and I'm surprised you were given bail before you are sentenced...' But I just couldn't bring myself to say anything that would upset his gentle, innocent demeanour.

'I don't think they will, Bobby, or they probably wouldn't have let you go today. But if you get caught doing it again...' I heard myself telling him, as he looked at me with wide, scared eyes, gazing as if I had any sway over his future.

I asked him if he wanted to go somewhere more comfortable to have a natter, and he said he could do with a pint, so I suggested The Wig And Gown around the corner. As we set off, he began speaking rapidly. I had half a mind to ask him to save it for when we were seated and I had a notepad in front of me, but it seemed he had sorted out his story in a chronological and rational way, had decided what he wanted to share, so I didn't interrupt and break his flow. I pictured the quotes I'd pull out of this conversation, made bold, highlighted on the page as column breaks. It would make a great page lead: *Bobby Dove, The Serial Bus Thief*.

*

We stood at the bar, and while our pints were being poured Bobby Dove's confession continued.

'The first bus I stole... well...' he paused and broke into a big smile. It made him look even younger and more innocent. 'The first bus I stole was made by Corgi. It was pocket-sized, a 468 London Transport Routemaster, on the 19 timetable, and I pinched it from a crate full of battered old cars, trucks, tractors, trailers, snowploughs and emergency vehicles that was in a corner of my classroom.'

I chuckled, thinking he was joking, but a glance at his expression told me he was deadly serious.

He looked pretty harmless, a geeky kid, but the more we spoke, the more I sensed there was something not quite straight about him. He had an air that made me think he had been an outsider at school but probably wasn't bullied like the other dweebs in his class.

Bobby Dove had been left well alone. Friendship was an oddity, not the norm. There was something undeniably lonely about him, and something strange, something different, something so off the scale he wouldn't have been a target for the name-callers, the lunch-money thieves, the toilet-block administers of head dunks, dead arms and wedgies. His character seeped out of him, highlighted by every tic that the other kids would pick up on. They would subconsciously know that if they did push a button, the wrong button, crank him up a bit, call him a name, say something nasty about his mum, he would turn, turn rapidly and violently and no longer be harmless. I imagined few had seen him totally lose it when something inside that head, topped off by a mop of unruly hair, went pop. Perhaps the commotion it caused had become a minor legend among his peers, as it had resulted in a smashed window in the head teacher's office. Such iconoclastic behaviour made them call him 'mental', and while it meant he didn't have any close friends, it also meant he didn't gather gangs of enemies, too, unlike other unpopular children. He was simply one to be left alone, avoided and allowed to play with toy cars in a classroom corner in peace.

We'd supped half our drinks before I could comfortably interrupt his flow, and so when I got the chance, I thought I'd cut to the chase.

'And when did you start stealing real buses?' I asked.

He didn't answer, but drank some more of his pint.

'They've got very smooth floors, the garages,' he continued, with a hint of wistfulness that made me think he was not sorry at all to have become Britain's biggest bus-jacker, as I knew our sub-editors would relish calling him, just sorry his run had come to an end under the circumstances they did.

I waited again, for a moment. Sometimes these types of interviews panned out where you would ask a question but not get an answer. Then you would pause and wait some more, and this would prompt the person to tell you something more insightful. It wouldn't be what you were expecting, but I found I was given the proper juicy stuff if I let my subject just say what was on their mind.

I had been to the garage Bobby Dove mentioned. When the new Routemasters were introduced by the then Mayor of London, I'd gone to write a piece and grab a photograph for the paper as the first one went out on its maiden journey. He was right. I remembered it clearly... the garages did have unnaturally smooth floors, really quite slippy. The concrete had been buffed by giant wheels rolling tons of steel across them for the past sixty years, day after day, week by week, month by month, year in and year out.

The scene of Bobby's crimes had two depots, back to back from one another. One exit and entrance faced north, the other south. One was used solely for the daytime bus routes, the other for the 'N' routes that operated over twenty-four-hour shifts.

Bobby had a manic glint in his eyes as he told me about the day garage. It was a cherished memory, and he described everything in great detail. He told me of the huge doors that slid back on themselves so three double deckers could go in and out at the same time.

'Can you imagine,' he said, with a hilarious, wide-eyed sense of awe at such a design, like it was the cleverest thing in the world.

He described how at one end there were offices behind jerry-built partitions, where pine-effect doors with frosted-glass panels led you into a corridor. It held the drivers' and mechanics' clocking-in machines and a rack for time cards. A supervisor's area was to the right, with glass windows running the length of the office, so the depot's senior management could keep a watchful eye on the garage floor. Further down, to the left, was the mess room. It held sagging old armchairs, dirty coffee tables with peeling laminated tops, battered metal-grey lockers and combination padlocks, while some of the lockers had bent doors that had been forced open. The floor was covered in worn carpet tiles, the area by the sink and tea urn heavily stained with the drips from teabags, sticky from spilt sugar and worn down by the feet of the drivers.

There were loos and showers in an annexe off the mess room, and old graffiti on the cubicle walls. Some of it was scrawled in pen: 'Jamie fucked my cat', 'MJ you tosser', 'Your Mum' and 'Andy Armpit is a Gay Lord'. There were less offensive tributes scratched haphazardly into the doors as well as the walls – crossed hammers and 'Irons', 'AFC', 'THFC', 'CFC'... a popularity graph of London's football clubs.

Another section of the garage housed an area for the mechanics. It had a row of overflowing bins, which were full of rags, empty oil bottles, spark-plug boxes. One corner had piles of scrap ready to be dumped – carbon-scarred exhausts and all manner of gear cogs, camshafts, hubcaps and batteries.

Workbenches stood along a wall, with clamps and vices mounted at intervals and tools stored above them. There were grubby posters advertising motor oil, and pictures of semi-naked women with out-of-date hairstyles pouting towards the camera. Spots of grease and oil on the floor showed where buses had been worked on. Stairs led down into a dark pit set in the floor so mechanics could get beneath the buses and have a look at the undercarriages. There was a stack of old tyres and wheel rims, and jacks and air hoses and pressure gauges, and everywhere the smell of engines and grease, petrol and dusty upholstery, cigarettes and exhaust.

'It was easy enough to get in,' said Bobby. 'I hadn't really planned to. I didn't set out thinking, I know, tonight I'm going to nick a bus,' he confided. 'I used to go and sit in the street, sit on the bench outside the gates. I'd write down the times the buses left in the morning and the makes and models and numbers, for my notes, you see, I liked to know what time they'd be off out and see if they were sticking to their timetables...'

At this point things began to become a little clearer. It dawned on me that just as you get trainspotters, you also had bus-spotters – and Bobby was a bus-spotter extraordinaire. He had that same condition that makes someone stand on the edge of a railway platform waiting excitedly to spot the 11.14 from Uxbridge chug into King's Cross, and, rather than just write down numbers in a notebook, he'd not been able to control his urge to get as close as he could to the buses.

'I'd always wanted to go inside the garage and look around, but I didn't have the guts just to walk straight up and ask the foremen if I could have a tour,' he said.

Bobby paused and took another long swig from his pint, then rolled the lager around in the glass, as if contemplating whether he should save what remained to sup while he told me the rest of his story or whether he could knock it back and touch me for a second drink. I noticed this and wanted to get to the meaty bits. Another pint wouldn't break the bank and could oil his vocals and give me more material.

'Drink up,' I said. 'Let's have another one.'

He didn't need encouraging. His Adam's apple went up and down rhythmically as he finished off the lager and placed the empty glass down with a satisfied clunk. He let out a deep burp without any semblance of self-consciousness.

As I bought the next round, I drew up in my mind a list of what I needed to know. I wanted to discover how he stole a bus, where he went when he was behind the wheel and hear of some of the adventures he'd had... But, most of all, I wanted to learn a bit about why he did it, why he became a regular joyrider, what led him to run such risks and what made him unable to control his urges.

'So how did you get hold of a bus?' I asked, when I returned with the drinks. 'It can't have been easy. I mean, you don't just walk into a depot and drive off... or do you?'

Once again, he ignored my question. He took another swig and let out another contented belch. 'I dunno why I decided that night to go and have a look round the place. The bit I climbed into wasn't an all-night garage, not like the Tottenham Swan depot, for example, where the buses go in and out twenty-four hours a day. It shuts up pretty early, with no night-bus service coming from the place.

'That all happens round the corner, and because they are next to each other, they don't bother with nighttime security in the daytime bit. They just close the doors and go home when the last bus comes in. It means it is quiet from about midnight. I was out that night, yeah, and thought I'd go past the buses on my way to watching some snooker at the snooker club, man. It's always open late and there are some pretty good players there, y'know. My mum's boyfriend was round. They didn't notice I'd left the house.

'So, I was out, and I walked past the garage... It was all locked up and dark, and I just thought, why not? Why not have a little look, go around the back and have a butcher's? That first time I climbed through a window at the side. The garage is next to railway lines, and all I had to do was get over the fence – it was so easy, so easy, man... You walk along the tracks and then clamber over another wall into this patch squashed between the railway and the garage. It was full of brambles and rubbish and broken bricks and all sorts of crap...'

Bobby described how he spotted a toilet window propped open and shoved himself through it, and there he was, in the garage, and that was that. 'I clambered in to have a little mooch about,' he said. 'I didn't think of nicking a bus that night, I really didn't, I swear. I thought I'd have an explore and wander around, maybe get in the cab and have a wiggle of the steering wheel, fuck about a bit, have a bit of a laugh. But when I got in and no alarms went off, and I saw all these keys hanging up, I knew I had to have a drive in one of them. I swear I didn't plan it in advance. It was just one thing led to another. That little window led right into the driver's mess room, and on the wall was a box full of keys – the keys for every bus in the garage. I couldn't resist it. I had a cup of tea and ate some biscuits they'd left out and thought about it. But, come on, what would you do? You can hardly blame me. It was too good to be true.'

What would I do? he had asked. What would I and possibly every other person on the planet do...? I hadn't the heart to tell him. He was totally delusional.

Bobby paused. It was the first time he'd stopped for breath for a while. I'd been writing as quickly as I could, my scrawling shorthand getting bigger and bigger on the page as he spoke faster and faster and faster, as he became more excited reliving his exploits. The sudden break took me a little by surprise and allowed me to catch up with what he had just said. But I also feared that it might be the last I heard.

As I said, I find with interviews that when the person I'm speaking to stops, they are expecting you to ask another question. But if you pause, too, they start up again – and give you the answer to the question they think you were going to ask. Unsurprisingly, it is often much more revealing than anything you could have tried to squeeze out of them. I would let Bobby lead the way. I took a glug of beer and flipped back over my notes.

'So what bus did you take?' I asked.

'The first bus I got into was the Number 24. An Alexander ALX4000, on a Volvo chassis, a B7TL, registration number YG76YUX.' He peered across the table at my notebook to see if I had written this detail down accurately, and looked disappointed that I hadn't bothered.

'The cab was open, so I sat in the seat, adjusted it a little... the driver must have been a right shortarse, I could hardly get my legs under the steering wheel, the seat was so far forward, man... it was a lovely little cabin, so well-designed, you know... a seat on a pneumatic cushion... big steering wheel, set at a nice angle, with good handgrips... gear stick to the right, automatic, of course... door-operator lever on the left. Great dashboard, so neat and clean and easy to understand. Speed counter, rev counter, fuel. Radio to the left, on top of the dash, with a stretch lead attached to a mouthpiece, hanging on a little clip. Up above, the crank handle to set the destination board... the cashbox on the right, the ticket machine – this one had an Oyster reader retrofitted...

'Scandinavian designed, built in Coventry. Lovely bit of design, lovely, man.

'I wondered what to do. I had to fire up the engine, stick the key in the ignition, rev it a little. I didn't have to take it for a drive... I didn't have to actually leave the depot, I thought. Just turn the engine on and rev it up, hear it go... but then, well, why not just spin it round the courtyard, try a three-point turn? And then I saw on the console in front of me a grey plastic box with a button on it. I knew that it must open the gates out the front, and that was that, man.'

He told me he drove around for a while on that first night, kept the *Not In Service* sign up on the front, and after about half an hour of careful pottering through silent back streets he returned to the garage. When he left, he pocketed the electric fob that opened the main gates and garage doors but replaced the ignition key on the hook he'd taken it from.

'I knew it was a bad idea,' he said, smiling, like it was the best idea he had ever had but also realised that somehow, inexplicably, others might not agree. 'No, I promise, I honestly did. But I also knew I couldn't just hang the keys up. I had to keep them.'

He returned the following night, let himself in, and this time went into the mess room, found an open locker and changed into a driver's uniform. He admired himself in the mirror. Took a selfie on his mobile. I later found it uploaded on Facebook with the caption 'First day in new job'. It had been 'liked' by two people.

'When I first turned the key in the ignition the engine made my bones bloody rattle,' he said. 'They have 4,460cc engines with 174 brake horsepower. Saw a *Top Gear* where someone had reconditioned one and stuck it in the back of a Mini. Needed massive spoilers and fins to stop it flipping itself over. Rear-wheel drive. Awesome.'

I asked Bobby how he managed to drive a twenty-foot double decker with no training or experience, and with no mishaps at all.

'I just took it slowly,' he said, looking at me as if I were stupid. 'And after I'd done it a few times, and then a few more, well, you couldn't say I was inexperienced.'

I could hardly argue with that, and asked him where he went.

'Oh, here and there,' he said. 'I decided it would be better not to spend too long on the less-crowded bus routes where I might be spotted, so I went to see the sights. I thought I'd blend in. I went down Trafalgar Square and along the Embankment and saw the Houses Of Parliament, went down across Westminster Bridge and then back up over Waterloo Bridge, along The Strand and home via High Holborn, Euston and Camden Town.'

'Did you do this every night?' I asked him, and again he looked at me as if I was stupid.

'Of course. That was my route,' he said simply, and I didn't really know how to answer that.

Bobby had got himself a route: he'd driven it every time he'd gone into the depot after hours and borrowed a bus. The way he saw it, this was just something he did – no big deal.

While he had told me his story in a marvellously rambling way, I wanted to flesh it out and run some checks on what he'd said. I suspected I'd heard a version, that while true in his eyes it didn't say all there was to say about this strange episode. I decided to speak to drivers at the depot and see what they knew about this story. He hadn't told me how he'd been nicked, for starters. I needed to see the police notes on his arrest and the case made against him. I imagined that a criminal psychologist's report, briefly referred to in court, could also give me another angle from which to consider Bobby Dove's bus rides.

I could get these documents in two ways – befriend the solicitor representing him, or go to a police source. I tried the solicitor, but there were factors that made this tricky. The firm was overworked doing criminal legal-aid cases handed to them when people were arrested and held in custody. Bobby was one such case. He'd been given the duty solicitor when he was caught. Previous experience told me they would have more pressing things to do than meet me, and would have no real motivation to help – the case had been concluded, bar the sentencing. It would not only require a fair amount of work, but there was the unwritten rule that solicitors should err on the side of caution when speaking to reporters. There was always the fear that if something appeared in the paper before sentencing it could influence the punishment.

Getting hold of the police file on Bobby, on the other hand, was solely down to the discretion of the officers I knew. Interview transcripts and the arresting officer's notes would have been typed up and logged on a central computer.

I merely had to ask a source politely, chat them up, make out I was being thorough and responsible in my news-gathering, making sure I wasn't just buying the story of a convicted criminal...

'It's a minor matter,' I'd say, 'but I want to make sure I get it absolutely, crystal-clear right. Here are the details – I just want to check if what I've been told stands up.'

Ask the right officer on the right day and my experience told me they would be happy to help.

I arranged to meet a police contact, bought him a coffee and pastry in the City Snacks café near Holborn Police Station and told him what I was after. He remembered Bobby Dove The Bus Thief – 'How could any of us forget? Fucking hilarious' – and he'd see what he could do.

While I waited for the officer to call me back, I went to find some bus drivers who'd be happy to chat. I got on a bus at the first stop outside the depot. I was the only person on board, so I stood by the driver and told him who I was and what I wanted.

He laughed. 'Yeah, we all heard about it. Bloody funny. We can't wait to get out of these sodding buses at the end of the shift. Can't think why anyone in their right mind would want to drive one in their spare time. Total loon.' He said he couldn't speak while driving but told me his name was Brian and that he was happy to meet back at the depot at the end of his shift. 'I finish at 3.30. Come and ask for me. Don't worry about the foreman,' he said. 'We'll sit in the mess room, and I'll tell him to fuck off, it's union business.'

I went back later, and he was waiting for me at the gates.

Over a cup of tea, Brian filled me in. 'With hindsight, it seems obvious. We'd all wondered for months if something strange was going on. One of us lost a uniform. Buses were left parked up in a different spot to where we swore we'd left them the night before. Logbooks were missing. Fuel gauges seemed to have been read incorrectly when we handed our keys in.

'Once, a nasty scratch down the offside appeared on one of the buses. The sort you get if you take a corner too tightly. If something like this happens, you are meant to fill in the incident book. It's not a big deal, you might get a bit of a ticking off, but you just log it, and if you don't, well, the foreman notes it and asks you why. My colleague swore he'd not done it, but it looked like he was lying.

'It bugged him, and he wondered if it had happened without him noticing, but it was a big old mark, and it isn't really possible to cause that type of damage without knowing. It led to a bit of an argument and a bad vibe that lingered for a week or two. The driver eventually accepted that it was his fault, and that pissed us all right off.

'For a while none of us put two and two together. After a few months of these random odd happenings – we started joking about there being a ghost in the garage – our suspicions became more concrete. We didn't do anything about it, though. I mean, no real harm was done – and then a bus was found, run out of diesel down the road, and it was obvious something was actually up.'

'Is that how he was nicked, then?'

'Well, sort of.'

It transpired that Bobby had taken a bus out on his usual route with the *Not In Service* sign displayed as he drove past late-shifters and West End revellers waiting at stops, and then gone back to park up. But he'd run into some difficulty.

Bobby was always diligent with his driving – checking his mirrors, indicating, textbook stuff – but that night he'd overestimated the amount of diesel in the tank. About a mile off the depot the bus started to splutter and cough. He'd run out of fuel. He turned the engine off, closed the doors behind him and walked home.

Seeing as the bus had been signed in last thing at night, its driver wasn't blamed. The police were called in, and it became clear that all the unexplained happenings over the past few months were perhaps explainable after all.

*

The police officer came back to me three days later. We met again in the City Snacks café for a coffee, and he passed me a folder.

'Here is all we've got,' he said. 'Interview transcripts, arresting officer's report, investigation review. You owe me a drink.'

I thumbed through the sheaf of papers when I got back to the newsroom.

The documents were written in that formal, mangled language known among reporters as 'plod speak'. The charge sheet explained how officers were called to the garage after a bus was found a mile away from where it had been left the night before. It was a mystery. No damage had been done, but it had been reported missing by its driver, and once the control room had turned on its tracker they'd gone to find it and realised it had been left where it was because it was out of fuel.

The report went on to say that the police interviewed the foreman working the night before, who not only swore blind he watched the bus park up but fetched the signing-off sheet he and the driver had filled in before going home. The officers believed him, and asked if they could access the CCTV archives for the past twenty-four hours to see if it held the answer. The report went on to show that the CCTV was managed by a security company, and it was going to take a day or two to get what was needed.

As the officers were about to call it a day, the driver joked that it was probably the ghost that had moved in who was responsible, and that throwaway line led to Bobby Dove getting his collar felt. The odd happenings of the past year were related to the increasingly bemused PCs, and another call was put into the security firm, this time asking for all the CCTV footage they had as a matter of urgency.

Once it was supplied, a joyrider's late-night runs were there for all to see, but the CCTV evidence was inconclusive. In the grainy shots they had, Bobby's face was hidden from view. He was wearing a bus driver's cap, and the angle of the camera was such that no real distinguishing marks could be seen. Officers went through the footage, logged up night after night after night of breaking, entering, taking and driving, but nothing linked Bobby to the crime scene. They swabbed down steering wheels for DNA and dusted for fingerprints. He had no previous, so there was no record they could cross-check against. They then searched CCTV footage from the surrounding streets in the hope of getting a better glimpse, and although a couple of images did emerge, they merely confirmed the profile of the thief that the detectives had expected. They were searching for a young adult male, and that was basically all they had to go on. The detective overseeing this strange case decided they'd do better not to scare off the bus thief, keep the investigation secret, make no changes to the depot's security and try and catch the perpetrator in the act.

Bobby, however, had had a bit of a scare when he ran out of diesel. He knew questions would be asked and so decided to lay low for a while. This event was, I found out later, also coupled with two unconnected events in his home life. His mum's boyfriend had moved into a new flat nearby and she was spending nearly every night there, giving him some peace and quiet at home. And the latest version of *Grand Theft Auto* was released around the same time. This included plenty of opportunities for hijacking a large variety of public-transport vehicles and driving them at breakneck speeds in front of admiring, scantily clad women. It meant his bedroom was a more attractive place than it had been, and he decided to shelve the bus-stealing gig until a later date.

But Bobby wasn't in the clear.

A few months later, the bus company running the garage was being taken over by a rival firm. The franchise was nearing its end. As new terms and conditions for the drivers were being hammered out by the union, the issue of uniforms was brought up.

In one meeting, a shop steward said he understood that the company taking over would want them decked out in new colours and livery, but he wasn't standing for cheap, scratchy, ill-fitting trousers and short-sleeved shirts. He wanted his fellow drivers to be able to walk to work with dignity: 'Not feel like some schoolboy in a cheapskate uniform,' as he put it. 'The members must be able to sit at the wheel in comfort.'

No half measures, he warned the management, jabbing his finger across the table, no Primark cast-offs. Something dignified, and three sets issued per driver, too.

The management had already got themselves a more attractive package on the table – longer shifts and less overtime – so this was a concession they were happy to make.

'Give us some suggestions,' they said, 'and we're happy to consider them.'

Later that night, the shop steward went online and searched for bus-driver uniforms. As he looked through the images, he found the home page for a bus enthusiasts' club, and finding the concept distracting, absentmindedly clicked on it and scrolled through the photographs of old Routemasters and related bus paraphernalia that the members had taken. He clicked a link on the website that took him to a series of pictures of bus conductors in grey caps and smart uniforms, of drivers in shirts with epaulettes. And there, sitting among this motley collection, was a picture of Bobby. The search engine had pulled up a selfie he had posted on Facebook and forgotten about, the line 'Me in my bus driver's uniform' offering itself up for perusal.

The steward wasn't one to snitch, but the episode had caused bad blood between his colleagues and the management. They suspected the joyriding episode was one of the drivers playing silly buggers, couldn't understand how someone could break in so often and take a bus out – and only get caught when one ran out of juice. They'd called a meeting and threatened everyone, en masse, said it had to stop immediately or serious disciplinary action would be taken... So when he looked closely at the picture and recognised the mess room, he felt duty bound to tell his superiors that a bloke called Bobby Dove had posted a picture of himself in a stolen uniform and may hold the key to the mystery.

The police found Bobby the following day, and he confessed everything.

*

I saw Bobby again at his sentencing. He had been scrubbed till his face shone a fleshy pink and was wearing a carefully ironed shirt and an ill-fitting suit. He had his mum and another person with him, who I guessed must be the boyfriend he'd mentioned. He was given a suspended prison sentence and a heap of community-service work. I approached him afterwards, and he seemed relieved. I'd watched him kiss his mum goodbye on the steps of the court, so I offered him a pint and he accepted. We went back to the pub where we'd first talked, and I bought two lagers.

'Okay?'

'Yeah, okay. Mum'll be pleased I'm not going to prison.'

'Yeah. It'll be done before you know it, the community service.'

'Got to wear a tag, too. Not allowed out at night, and not allowed to go near the bus depot either.'

'You got a driving ban as well.'

'Yeah. Not got a licence anyway.'

'I did wonder why you didn't wait and apply for a job as a bus driver, Bobby. You're nearly the right age now, after all.'

He stared at me. 'I hadn't thought of that,' he said, glancing away and falling quiet for moment. He looked at me again, with sad eyes. 'Don't suppose they'd let me now...' his voice trailed off.

I drained my pint. It was getting on, and I had to file a piece about his sentence for the next edition. I got my coat off the back of the chair I was sitting on and shook his hand.

'No harm in trying, Bob. They may not notice your record. And if they do, they may not care.'

'Perhaps,' he said. 'I suppose I could say that I've got previous experience.'

I left him alone, silently sipping his pint, with a faraway look, no doubt dreaming of getting back behind the wheel of a bus again soon.

The Evening Press And Star, page 4

'LUCKY YOU DIDN'T KILL SOMEONE' – COMMUNITY SERVICE FOR SERIAL BUS THIEF

The joyrider dubbed 'Britain's Most Prolific Bus Thief', who was behind the worst ever public-transport crime spree, has been banned from using buses for five years after pleading guilty to nearly three hundred counts of stealing vehicles over a twelve-month period.

Bobby Dove was also handed a two-year suspended prison sentence and ordered to do four hundred hours of community service. He was told by Justice Whittingham at Highbury Corner Magistrates' Court that he was 'extremely lucky' not to be going to prison.

'This was not a victimless crime,' Justice Whittingham said. 'You could easily have killed someone with your reckless behaviour.'

Magistrates heard that Dove had broken into the Archway Bus Garage in Kleanthe Road and driven double-decker buses through the streets of London in the dead of night, often five times a week. He was caught after he was forced to abandon a bus that had run out of fuel.

Police later found a picture on a social network site of Dove posing in a driver's uniform and boasting of his 'new job'. Sentencing, Justice Whittingham added that he was shocked at the lax security regime run by North London Buses and suggested they review their procedures. The court heard from Dove's legal team that he had long held a fascination with buses and that he was seeking professional help.

KERMIT THE HERMIT

I REMEMBER A night spent as a teenager trekking up Hampstead Heath, walking along paths, heading through wet undergrowth and entering a dew-soaked meadow on a clear midsummer's night.

One of my peers had been told there was a party going on somewhere, and so my youthful self and friends had set out to find it. I followed the others, blindly – one of the group knew where we were going, and it was enough to be outdoors at 1am with friends sharing a sense of building excitement. The destination of our late-night walk hardly mattered. The journey was the thing, swigging from bottles of fortified wine and cans of cheap lager.

We had reached a fence that signalled the end of the Heath and the start of a private garden. It was rotten, ramshackle and easy to climb over.

'This is the place,' someone said, and we could hear muffled beeps and basslines coming from up a hill, behind trees and bushes.

We followed another path and then, out of nowhere, a man dressed in a tatty cap and a green trench coat stepped in front of us and said: 'You want to go that way. Follow it round and take the fork on the right. Enjoy yourselves.'

We'd been surprised by his appearance. He had come silently out of the shadows. We'd stopped, expecting trouble. This was, after all, an adult, and he had caught us trespassing. But, instead of ticking us off, he showed us the way. After a few more twists and turns along overgrown paths, we came out on to a large lawn, and there, ahead of us, was the semi-derelict Heathwood House. It was a rambling old mansion, poorly boarded up and badly shuttered, left to the mercy of the elements – and where someone that night had decided to place a sound system inside its large hall and throw a rave.

I recalled that youthful adventure many years later, and realised the man who came out from behind a bush to give us directions was Kermit The Hermit. Two decades on, I would get to know him and write the story of how Kermit, a tramp who had made a makeshift home in the grounds of a prime piece of north-London real estate, went toe-to-toe with a billionaire property developer.

The story went like this.

*

In the 1800s, when London was growing quickly and angrily, its noxious industries in the east pushed housing north and west.

The suburbs had yet to develop, as the tube was still merely an engineer's daydream, but farmland, heath and common around the northern edges of London – Hampstead, Highgate, Finchley, Hornsey – were greedily eyed up by speculators. It was land that could provide a standard of living your well-heeled country squire would recognise but was still close to the beating fiscal heart of Queen Victoria's Empire, providing a best-of-both-worlds scenario for the *nouveau riche* businessman of the period.

One such plot lay on the old Hampstead Lane, a snaking road that traverses the brow of the Highgate and Hampstead hills. This was a well-grooved thoroughfare, its importance as a route marked by a tollgate. It was flanked each side with pasture used by sheep drovers, while evergreen Scots pines had been planted along its route to act as year-round waymarkers for the shepherds and cattle-men to see from afar. The drovers, who would bring their flocks into London for slaughter via the Lane, would find sustenance at the famous Spaniards Inn, a popular hostelry that legend stated was the haunt of highwaymen who preyed on travellers laden with riches heading in and out of London.

Along this route there was a farmhouse and dairy. It was a holding mentioned as far back as the Domesday Book. But, when Lord Mansfield had Robert Adam build Kenwood House next door in 1764, much of the attached farmland had been lost to Capability Brown's sculptured gardens. Once the grand, stuccoed house was completed, the farm was no longer a viable economic entity in its own right. It lacked the necessary pasture and had gradually become a smallholding for generations of land workers who earned their daily bread selling their labour to the big estate next door, using their own patch for raising supplementary vegetables and livestock.

By the mid-1850s, with land prices rocketing as the Georgian house-building boom rippled into the Victorian era, the site was put up for auction and eventually bought by a northern industrialist called Joseph Wilkinson. He was searching for a seat that was a short journey from Westminster, where an electorate of his peers in a rotten borough had sent him to further the interests of the cotton-mill owners of Lancashire.

He set about pouring his wealth into the creation of a home he believed would last generations. It would be a place the Wilkinson family would live in for as long as a quarter of the globe was coloured pink, as long as there was an empire on which the sun did not set. It would be an edifice that would honour his business acumen long after he had returned to the earth.

Wilkinson's architect had one eye on the commissioner's ego, which meant fancy frills and dainty touches, and another eye on his fee, which meant more of the same. It was a beautiful example of the period, but, by the time my friends and I came across it, the building had slipped into disrepair.

When I first nosed around the halls and corridors, as a sound system blasted out acid-house music, peering into rooms smelling of rising damp and dry rot, and watching my step on creaking stair-cases, it had been empty for a few years.

Called Heathwood, it had twisted terracotta chimney pots in a neo-Elizabethan style and fish-scale slates across the sixteen different roofs that covered its extensive wings, bays and towers. It had copper-lined gable ends, decorative guttering and a weather vane, long turned an oxidised green. The red brick that was predominant was offset with sandstone lintels around doors and windows. The mortar was crumbling and the stonework chipped.

Fine detailing above the front entrance included images of Ancient Greek physicists Archimedes, Empedocles and Theophrastus in a nod to the fact that Wilkinson had made his fortune manufacturing chemical dyes for the cloth trade.

In its original state, Heathwood boasted a glasshouse accessed through a central hall. This had long been demolished, although the foundations remained and marked where it had once stood. Rusted iron bars poked upwards from its cracked, Cornish-granite base. These had once stretched high above the palms and fronds below, creating a skeleton to hold large panes of glass in place. Now water seeped in through nooks and crannies. Every winter its dilapidation increased until it was dangerous enough to warrant the owners' attention. They found it easier to bring the whole thing crashing to the ground rather than repair it.

The hall, unlike much of the building, was in fairly good condition. It had been lined with mahogany, and the varnished hardwood had stood time well.

The panelling, running from floor to ceiling, gave it a serious feel. In a room used for entertaining – and where my friends and I had found ourselves at that rave – it felt oddly like it meant business. It gave the impression of being a gigantic boardroom. One side had arched windows facing south, with double doors accessing a terrace tucked beneath a colonnade that created a first-floor balcony for a cluster of upstairs bedrooms.

Elsewhere, a maze of musty corridors took you deep into the building. The domestic machinery needed to keep such a big place going was found on the northern wing. The kitchens and 'below-stairs' elements, including a vast laundry, were utilitarian in design. There was no plaster detailing or fancy architraves here. Instead, the rooms were marked by simple fireplaces and plain doors. The northern wing's fourth floor housed servants' quarters, with its own staircase to allow staff to get about without ever crossing the path of the Wilkinson family.

On the first and second floors were large bedrooms with separate dressing-rooms and, in what was seen as a modern must-have at the time, bathrooms with taps that ran hot water directly into big baths. These were heated by an immense coal-fired boiler in the basement, which took a huge amount of sweat and toil to keep it fired up and running. It was a grand lodge, built in the fashion of the day. It had plenty of charm and was in a wonderful spot.

*

Heathwood's landscaped surrounds included a rose garden, a box-hedge maze and long lawns bordered by ornamental rhodo-dendrons. There was an avenue of birch and lime, and the western and southern perimeters were marked by horse chestnuts. A series of connected, formal Italianate ponds, each with a cherub spouting water into its basins, ran from the terrace to the foot of the property.

When finished, it was still essentially on the outer fringes of the city that it overlooked from its perch on the hills of Hampstead. Even as London gradually crept northwards, eating up the fields and turning tracks into roads, it felt cut off from the sprawl. The garden headed down on to Hampstead Heath, which by then was protected by the 1871 Act of Parliament and secured as open common land. It meant its residents could stand on the terrace and gaze south into London over a green expanse that stretched for many acres.

*

During the First World War the Wilkinson family's only son and heir had slowly drowned in his own blood in a muddy rut in a field near Ypres. Grief-stricken, the now-childless parents handed it over to the Ministry of Defence and headed back to their Lancashire home. They would both be dead before the war was out.

The government used it for convalescing soldiers. For a time, the psychologist Dr Rivers, who treated Siegfried Sassoon, held clinics there. After the Armistice it never returned to private ownership. Between the wars it was used as a grace-and-favour home for the Master of the Rolls, and from 1940, it became an RAF officers' training centre. In 1948 the NHS took it on, and it became a home for older people too fragile to live alone after a stay in hospital.

The glorious interior gradually took on an institutional feel. Patterned ceramic tiles with lily motifs were covered with linoleum.

The larger rooms were used as wards, while others had partitions added, carving them into offices, consulting rooms, stores. Eventually, after fifty years of wheelchairs, walking frames and slippers buffing corridor floors and making tracks in the gravel paths of the garden, the NHS considered the house surplus to requirements, too costly to keep, no longer fit for purpose, and it was put up for sale.

Heathwood lay empty for a few years. No buyer could be found, and a recession further delayed its disposal. It was around this time that I went to the party there.

Eventually, when new money found a haven in London property, it was sold on. But it still lay empty while its new owners drew up plans to build flats in part of the gardens and then deal with the crumbling old home. It was squatted for a while, first by homeless people looking for shelter, who kept their heads down in the hope their occupation would last, to others who saw that it made a great venue for all-night raves, which hastened a visit from the bailiffs.

All this time, while the NHS used it and then when it had moved on, a solitary man lived quietly at the bottom of the garden. He slept in a tumbledown potting shed. He minded his own business and was rarely seen by nursing staff and patients, nor by squatters, surveyors, architects, estate agents and the representatives of potential buyers as he shuffled along paths between overgrown rhododendron bushes and ornamental ponds now clogged with weeds.

He was known as Kermit The Hermit.

*

I had been trawling through council planning-application reports in search of a story lead. It's a hefty document published each week, containing details of homeowners wanting to add a new extension or change their windows and housing developers planning new estates and blocks.

I noticed the old house had been sold on again and that the buyers planned to knock it down and replace it with a neo-classical mansion with all those must-haves for the modern oligarch – an enlarged basement with swimming pool, cinema, cigar room and wine cellar, a car lift, servants' wing, library, entertainment suite, and bedrooms with bathrooms and dressing-rooms. The architect's images lent credence to the adage that the more money you have, the less taste you possess. It was truly something, a marble-clad lair that dominated everything nearby. I decided the pictures alone would make a little story for *The Press And Star*.

I wondered what would come of Kermit The Hermit once the work started. He would surely be an unwanted folly in what would become the back garden for a non-dom family who'd rarely walk the manicured pathways.

Tired of reading through the planning records at my desk, I decided to go for a walk up to Heathwood to see Kermit. It was an excuse to get out for a bit, away from the phone and the chatter and the tapping of keyboards, and speak to him directly. I knew his reaction would give me a fresh top line.

I would visit Kermit armed with my packed lunch – a bag of cheese-and-pickle sandwiches – and use them as bait to get him talking. I knew from previous encounters that he could be spiky if disturbed, but he liked a sandwich. I'd sit on one of his dilapidated garden seats, share my food and quiz him. So I scooped up a handful of chewed biros, shoved a dog-eared notebook and a camera into my bag and headed off to see what Kermit would make of the new owners of the land he had lived on for thirty or so years.

*

I had met Kermit properly a few years before, when I covered a story involving stolen vegetables and vandalised allotments. A group of disgruntled growers who tended plots near Heathwood had sent me a letter chronicling a series of thefts from their beds.

'Perhaps if you write about it, the person responsible will be scared off,' one plot-holder had said.

I covered their annual vegetable show and enjoyed their hospitality at their summer barbecue, and I wanted to see if I could help them out. The secretary of the Park Allotments told me crops had been uprooted in the middle of the night, and some of the less forgiving gardeners believed it may have been the work of 'the old tramp who lives up by Heathwood'.

I knew they were referring to Kermit. His home was a short walk away, and he was regularly seen leaning over railings, chatting to some of the allotment holders, talking vegetables, the weather and the like.

They were a mixed bunch on those allotments. You couldn't tell who did what during the week as they dug the communal soil in tatty Sunday afternoon gardening outfits. This being north London, there was a good mix of the type of people who could give you story tips. There were some successful solicitors and high-flying lawyers, a film director who had made a cult Brit-flick in the sixties, a TV scriptwriter responsible for a famous sitcom whose cast still earned good money doing a Christmas special. There were a couple of actors, a well-known sculptor, three novelists, an academic of Irish literature and a physics professor who had worked with Peter Higgs of Higgs boson fame. Other allotments were tended by teachers, doctors, a fireman, three bus drivers, a lifeguard and a number of people in various trades.

Those who were less kind in their ways said it must be him, that tramp, snagging their produce, passing judgement with no evidence to go on but their own prejudices that the eccentric old fellow looked like the culprit.

This petty thievery had gone on sporadically for some time when one late-summer's evening I was invited to a barbecue to celebrate the year's corn harvest. We had the charred cobs with sausages and halloumi cheese in pitta bread. As we glugged down beer and got progressively drunk, the conversation turned to the vegetable thefts. Then, watching the sun slip behind the western hills, my plot-holder friend Bill and I decided that instead of heading home we'd kick back in the easy chairs in his shed, sup a few more drinks and keep an eye out the window and see if a nocturnal visitor came.

Sure enough, a little after midnight, we saw a figure clamber over a gate. Bent low, the intruder snuck along the small earthen paths, looking left and right, clutching a bag and pausing here and there as he searched for a plot to raid.

I could make out his silhouette under the clear night sky, and it definitely wasn't Kermit The Hermit. Kermit was a short, tubby man with a straggly beard and hair all over the place. He always wore a seaman's cap. His portly shape was accentuated by the threadbare green raincoat he wore everywhere, no matter how pleasant the day. This interloper was much taller, much leaner and well-dressed.

Fuelled by beer, we decided to confront him. We slipped out from our chairs, quietly opened the shed door and, crouching low behind a row of gooseberry bushes and sweet-pea frames, we stalked the trespasser.

He paused at a bed of good-looking leeks, thick-set and growing in neat rows. I handed my camera over to Bill and told him to start snapping as soon as I was close enough to approach the vegetable heister.

'Gotcha!' I roared as I stood up tall from behind a row of runner beans held high by bamboo canes. As the flash of the camera popped, he turned to me, let out a high-pitched curse, dropped his bag and raced off.

I gave chase, half wondering if doing so was such a good idea, as he was bigger than me, and the thought of rugby-tackling him into a compost heap held little attraction. I also reminded myself I was a reporter after a story, not a well-meaning vegetable vigilante hoping to enact a citizen's arrest. My conundrum of what I'd actually do should I get close enough to grab him was solved by the fact that it was dark, I was tiddly and he was spurred on by fear. He was much quicker than I was, and soon heading towards the iron-spiked railings that ran along the allotments' borders, and in an athletic movement far beyond my ability to mimic, he swung himself over and was heading down the road before I could do much more than shout out that we'd caught him on camera and now he was for it.

I watched him disappear and then walked back to where we had disturbed him and found a hessian bag with a Waitrose logo abandoned by the path. There was nothing inside to nail the man, no evidence we could use to track him down bar the snatched image we'd grabbed. Instead, we giggled at a supermarket receipt at the bottom of the bag. It showed a bill of over £100 for a couple of good bottles of French wine, a packet of Duchy Originals cheese biscuits, a goose *pâté*, a whole wheel of Stilton and, much to our childish delight, two packets of a high-fibre powder you mixed with water to relieve constipation. Such a shopping list made the nocturnal thefts of prize vegetables even more bizarre. This man could clearly afford to eat well, and while I was wary of making accusations in print as to his identity, it gave me a hilarious top line for the story I was planning.

When we met back with the Allotment Management Committee and explained what we had seen, it transpired that the suspect had been a regular complainer to the allotment holders, writing angry letters saying their plots looked 'like a bloody shanty town', and he did not appreciate the imaginative use of scrap wood to build sheds. He called the site an eyesore and said it ruined his enjoyment of his nearby house and impinged on the Holiest Of Holies, the prospective price he'd get for his home should he ever wish to sell up. Such claims fell on barren ground with the growers, who mumbled they'd been there far longer than he had, that the plots looked wonderful and he could get stuffed. I hoped our work would not only scare him off but would make a cracking page-three lead on the feud between a disgruntled Nimby and the gentle vegetable growers of the Park Allotment Association.

More importantly, it allowed me to dispel the nastier allegations by some of the less-thoughtful allotmenteers that old Kermit The Hermit was a wrong 'un.

*

Because Kermit had been accused by some of the growers, when we revealed that he'd had nothing to do with it I was given a box of vegetables by the embarrassed Allotment Management Committee member who had made the accusations and asked if I would hand it over as a conscience-salving peace offering. Since Kermit didn't know his innocent habit of leaning over the fence and passing the time of day with some of those digging the earth had led to such suspicions, he was pleasantly surprised when I clambered through the thick copse that surrounded his home, clutching a box of bounty.

We settled down, and, over a tea brewed up in a smoke-blackened billycan, I heard his story.

Kermit was originally from Northumberland but had left that wet, green, hilly county in the 1960s. He'd signed on with a merchant line in Newcastle, with the vague idea that by working his passage he could eventually settle in Australia or America or somewhere that spoke English but wasn't as damp as the North East.

I got to know him over a period of years. I'd take him the odd gift – a pair of walking boots, a hamper from the newspaper's Christmas fund, a scarf I no longer wanted – and he accepted them without comment and did not make me feel like I was being condescending.

He never told me his real name but did say he'd been christened Kermit by gardeners due to the tatty green coat he wore all year round and, of course, because it rhymed nicely with Hermit.

Kermit lived in pretty dire surroundings but seemed healthy enough. His makeshift home was full of bold and friendly rats and ringed by rubbish. He had a collection of rotten deckchairs stolen from the gardens of Kenwood House that were arranged around a fire pit. A piece of mossy tarpaulin was stretched out from the crown of the potting shed's roof and was tied off to sycamores that formed a natural stockade around his space. It was a token attempt to create a fairly dry outdoor area.

His sleeping quarters were in the cave-like interior of the crumbling outbuilding. I dared not venture into the darkened recesses, but from the wide entrance – bricks had been dislodged and never replaced – I could see a camp bed along one side with piles and piles of blankets laid out on top. There was a rickety chest of drawers along the opposite wall and a stool with a paraffin lamp perched on top. There were plastic bread-crates stacked up containing all manner of oddments. Another area acted as a kitchen store with blackened pots and tin mugs and plates.

It didn't look nice. It didn't seem comfortable. But Kermit The Hermit had survived there long enough, was in as good a condition as any man of his advanced years could expect, and he called it home. It had been home long enough, too. Kermit had, thirty-odd years previously, jumped ship at Tilbury and, looking for somewhere hidden and quiet to rest up for a few days, had clambered into the grounds through a gap in a rotten fence, found the abandoned potting shed and laid his head down.

Kermit's absolute rejection of material comforts beyond keeping his feet relatively dry and the rest of his body relatively warm, eating three times a day and sometimes washing in the showers at the Men's Pond, was a lifestyle that was hard to fathom.

I found it occasionally repulsive but, for the most part, admirable. Here was someone who, in the centre of London, had managed to find a place to live for the best part of four decades, and to do so completely off-grid. He used minimal resources such as heat and water and had avoided having a National Insurance number for most of his adult life, only coming on to the state's radar when he got older and a well-meaning doctor, who sometimes gave Kermit the once-over, helped him wangle a small old-age pension. He did not, I assumed, hoard for the future but lived in the very present.

It seemed at first that his existence was a rejection, a response, to a modern world whose comforts did not suit him and which he felt were unnecessary. It looked like a challenge those reality-TV show producers cook up where they dump people on an island and tell them to fend for themselves for a few weeks.

Kermit's life looked tough. I don't want to romanticise this. He'd chosen to live in semi-derelict surroundings, yet his liberty was hard-earned, and he was conditioned to it. His situation reminded me of another Northumberland man I'd once read about. He was called Jack The Blaster, and one day over an ash-tasting cup of strong tea I told Kermit his story. In the 18th century, Jack carved a grotto in cliffs at Marsden Bay in South Shields after falling out with an absentee landowner who demanded he pay rent on his paltry smallholding. Above his hearth, an admirer had scoured the legend: 'Ye landlords vile, whose man's peace mar, come levy rents here if you can, your stewards and lawyers I defy, and live with all the rights of man...'

Kermit liked this, so next time I was walking nearby I popped in with some chalk and scrawled it on a wall of his living quarters.

While Kermit was a man of few words, I did chisel some biographical facts out of him and began to put together a reasonable series of assumptions as to why he lived where he did and in such a manner.

Kermit had taken his P&O merchant ship to the southern hemisphere, working the route as a deckhand. He told me of visiting the tropics for the first time, how a boy from a soggy valley near Lindisfarne reacted, heading through the Suez Canal, going over the Equator, port-hopping down the coast of East Africa, the immense space of the Indian Ocean. Although many years ago, he had a clear memory of those days and spoke with an understandable wistfulness about his youth.

I asked him how it ended, what brought him back ashore, why he had left the maritime service and ended up here. Why had he quit the globetrotting voyages, seeing new places and feeling settled by the regulation of the crew shifts and the cash that he earned?

'It went wrong for me on a return trip from Australia,' he said. 'We'd been in the port of Belawan, on the northeast coast of Sumatra in Indonesia. Been there for the best part of a fortnight, unloading freight and then filling the holds again. Our ship was huge – a freighter, an MPV taking timber west. I had an accident, and it made me scarper when we got back to London. I was never going on board of one of those things ever again.'

I asked him what had happened, and he told me that when cargo had been taken on board, one of his jobs to was to check the ratchet straps holding crates in place were properly tied off. Any movement could put the ship at risk on the high seas, and it was a role he took seriously. He'd climbed down a steel ladder to the very bottom of the largest hold and run through the checks he had to do. But while he was ticking off the straps in the lower hold on his inventory one of his fellow crew, aware the ship was running late to catch the next tide, had secured the upper doors. He was locked inside.

'I nearly died,' he said. 'I was trapped for a week. I found some water I could drink from a fire bucket, but there was no food and the temperature was furious. The deadlock on the hold door, which you were meant to be able to open from the inside, was rusted shut. Couldn't move the damn thing at all. I banged and banged on the doors, but no one could hear me. When they'd done their roll call, they assumed I'd jumped ship and stayed in Indonesia. It wasn't unheard of for crew to do that.

'I only got out when I found a mallet we used to drive stakes into the logs we'd loaded up and smashed it continuously against an air vent. Someone heard me and told the engineers. They thought a bearing in the prop drive was out of sync and came to investigate. By the time they found me, I'd lost about three stone.

'I've had claustrophobia ever since, and when we got back to the Port of London, as soon as the wood was unloaded and I'd got my back pay and my shore pass, I walked down the gangplank and vowed I'd never go on one of those freighters ever again.'

Craving land – 'real land', as he put it – he'd left the East London streets with his pay in his pocket and headed out to Hampstead Heath. He was desperate for something resembling the green of Northumberland, hoping it would help stave off the nightmares he'd had since his accidental incarceration.

'I climbed through the garden fence to this place,' he said. 'I found this hut, curled up in a corner, wrapped myself in my seaman's jacket and fell asleep. I've been here ever since.'

I asked him why he hadn't been thrown off. He explained the groundsman who occasionally saw him didn't care what he did. Eventually, when the nursing staff discovered their unofficial tenant, they reacted with kindness.

'They'd bring me lunch, check up on me, hand me clothes, blankets, all sorts. Angels, they were. No one asked me to leave, so I didn't.'

He told me a friendly doctor, one of the allotment holders, gave him the odd check-up and looked out for him. This doctor allowed Kermit to use his house as an address so he could claim a state pension when he reached sixty-five and brought him food and clothing. He survived, able to satisfy his basic needs of warmth and shelter, and was helped along by the kindness by others.

*

The Lazzeer Property Development Company was registered in the British Virgin Islands. It was formed by a private equity firm based in Cyprus, a vehicle for investing the fortune of a man called Alexandr Bromotov.

Bromotov had, in the late 1980s, found himself well placed to benefit from the collapse of the USSR. He was a high-ranking civil servant and close to the fire sale of state assets put into place by the Russian government as they raced to privatise as many nationally owned industries as possible.

Bromotov attracted Swiss-based investment into the firm he registered the day the Boris Yeltsin government took power. He bought swathes of industrial plant and accompanying contracts for raw materials. Within five years his firm had assets worth over £5 billion.

He then turned his attentions to using the profits to invest overseas in what he considered to be more stable states than the new Russia.

Via a financial-products company managed from a small office in Limassol, Cyprus, he established LPDC in the British Virgin Islands, using it to buy land in the UK. He saw this as a safe invest-ment and, following his banker's instructions, was happy to see his wealth secured in such a way.

He personally had little interest in the minutiae of the myriad deals he signed off. He trusted his lawyers to do so. One day a brochure crossed his desk showing a 'unique, once-in-a-lifetime opportunity' to buy a 'rambling, beautiful Victorian mansion in need of comprehensive updating... offering its new owners a premium site in one of London's most sought-after enclaves'.

Bromotov, a committed Anglophile, saw the picture of the front door of Heathwood with its Grecian figures. He loved them. On the strength of this detail, fuelled by a fantasy of being a landed English aristocrat – he had once watched the *Brideshead Revisited* film on a transatlantic flight – he instructed his lawyers that he would very much like to be the new owner of this decrepit mansion.

*

Perhaps, if it had been left solely to Bromotov and his architect, the plan to build apartments in the gardens of Heathwood would not have materialised. Maybe they would have merely set themselves the task of converting and restoring Heathwood to former glories with modern twists.

While a businessman seeking decent returns on his investments, his equity profits were in the metals industry and on a scale so vast that property development of this type was simply too small to register. He also saw the purchase as a private matter. This was the chance to buy and build a London house, mirroring the way Joseph Wilkinson had been drawn from the north to the capital to show off his wealth.

No doubt his lawyer and personal-equity investor saw the land around the home and knew their annual bonuses would benefit from a balance sheet that showed the cost of Heathwood and that rebuilding the pile had been offset by creating apartments in the gardens. They suggested it in such a way that Bromotov probably nodded sagely when he read their report through, and with no further ado scrawled a signature giving the project the go-ahead. In doing so, he was unwittingly turning Kermit's home into a building site.

*

Kermit didn't know about the plans until I visited him. He'd missed the nurses once the place was sold, but life went on. The regular meals they'd brought down the garden paths had been offset by the kindness of other neighbours who knew the canteen calories he'd once relied on had disappeared and so upped their attention.

The film director, who lived nearby and loved the eccentric nature of Kermit's lifestyle, took it on himself to ensure the void was filled. The closure of the NHS institute actually resulted in nicer dishes being offered up by those who saw a need and were happy to step in.

Kermit, living for the day and not seemingly having the wit to ponder or be bothered by an unknowable future, did not worry that Heathwood was in a state of limbo. It also allowed Kermit to feel more comfortable about relieving himself behind bushes and trees. He could now go about his daily movements without the fear someone would take offence to him dropping his trousers and crapping in a shallow hole scraped into the undergrowth.

I didn't like the part of my job that sometimes made me the bearer of bad news, but Kermit was stoical and said he knew the place couldn't stay empty forever. He wondered wistfully, and somewhat fantastically, if he would be affected by the noise of the building work. He hoped whoever bought the apartments wouldn't have dogs roaming the gardens, which he'd have to fend off, or rowdy barbecues, as he didn't want his peace disturbed too much.

'Kermit, they will ask you to move,' I said, feeling like a doom merchant. 'What if they evict you? These types don't muck about. The place has been sold, and it doesn't mention in the brochure that it comes with a man living in the potting shed. Where will you go? What will you do?'

I was surprised by his calm reaction.

'Don't you worry about me,' he replied, smiling a toothy smile and leaning forward, putting his hands on his knees. 'I will not be going anywhere,' he added conspiratorially.

I didn't know if this was Kermit indulging in some wishful thinking or whether he hadn't fully understood the gravity of the situation.

'Kermit, I do understand this is your home, but the new owners… well, they won't be turning a blind eye to you, not like the nurses did. No, they'll be sending in their builders soon, once they have got permission – and they will get it, mate – then you'll be moved off, moved away. You do realise that, don't you?'

Kermit smiled again, and then spoke to me gently, as if I were a child: 'My dear fellow, don't you think I have long known this day would come and that I'd have to be well prepared for it?'

With that, he gave a little chuckle, tapped the side of his nose a couple of times, and rose from his chair signalling my visit was over.

As he headed into the depths of the potting shed, he turned his head and said: 'You don't worry about me. I don't want any fuss and bother.'

*

After the planning application for the new Heathwood had been lodged, the owners had to wait six weeks for any interested parties to come forward with observations. A couple of civic groups made their views known, saying the new outbuildings were acceptable if the house itself was fully restored, while conservation bodies focused on the main building's slow decay and questioned whether the new apartments could pay for it to be put right. There was no mention of Kermit The Hermit, and I wondered if it was the paper's duty to make a fuss about his precarious position.

I wanted to write his story, get a headline asking what the future held for him, create a David-and-Goliath-type tale and whip up some sympathy. Perhaps it could lead to a compromise, I thought. Perhaps something could be done. Perhaps he could be given a flat somewhere; perhaps the council would have to rehouse him.

To do so, I'd need Kermit's permission, so one slow afternoon I trekked up to see him again and explained what I feared was about to happen and how I hoped the *Press And Star* may be able to help.

I was to be disappointed. After gently outlining my plan of action, he steadfastly refused to accept the gravity of his situation.

'I won't be paraded about in your paper,' he said. 'I'm not in need of publicity. I don't want no one knowing about me up here. I keep myself to myself and don't do any harm to nobody.

'They aren't moving me anywhere, and I don't need your help,' he said, spitting into the fire pit. 'Trust me.'

I tried to explain that in a matter of weeks the new owners were likely to get their permission, and then a man would come walking down the garden path armed with a sheaf of legal notices, and they'd hand them over to him, and that would be that. He would be served notice on his little woodland enclave, and he'd have to gather up what meagre possessions he could shove into one of the rickety, rusted trolleys dotted among the trees and get off the land, never to return.

'No, I won't,' he replied simply. 'No. They won't be getting me out.'

I just didn't think he understood the seriousness of the situation, but couldn't see what else I could do. I left with a heavy heart, sad to see another old-school eccentric defeated by the unstoppable power of wealth.

I waited with trepidation for the Town Hall's planning-committee meeting which would judge the application. I knew once the plans were discussed in public, I could write about Kermit without breaking his confidence. Hopefully, somehow, after he'd been turfed off, the relevant social service would step in and look after him.

*

The meetings were held on Tuesday nights in the Town Hall's main chamber. Pine benches with green leather cushions gave the place a civic air and a sense of authority. A group of councillors, which con-sidered the merits of each proposal, sat on one side. The committee's chair was on a desk at the front, flanked by the borough solicitor and the head of the planning department. Opposite them sat planning officers, who would talk the councillors through the individual appli-cations. In the public seats would be the developer's representatives, architects, planning agents, and then there would be others who had an active interest in the schemes being considered, such as neigh-bours, ward councillors and residents' associations.

I settled into the press bench. Heathwood was third on the agenda. It didn't take long to reach it. I noted in the meeting's papers there were representations from a civic group and another from an individual whose name I didn't recognise.

After the plans had been presented, the chair invited the civic group to speak first. They rattled through the history of the house, explaining why it had enough architectural merit to be saved, but their argument was based on aesthetics rather than recognised legal reasons. I couldn't see how the committee would use it as an excuse to block the apartments in the garden being built.

The chair then called the next objector and, to my surprise,

Kermit appeared in the chamber dressed in a natty tweed suit, flanked by the lawyer I knew from the allotments.

He laid on the table in front of the planning committee a large leather briefcase. He flicked two bronze catches, lifted the lid and said in a calm, clear voice: 'You must dismiss this application as it stands, because the applicants are wrong in surmising that the entirety of the land they purchased is theirs to build on.

'I, as will now be proved to you, am the legal occupier of an acre of the gardens of Heathwood House. I have claimed squatter's rights and registered such rights with the Sheriff of the Property Division of the High Court.'

There were audible gasps from the representatives of Mr Bromotov, and the council's planning clerks looked quizzically at one another. The councillors on the committee turned to the chair for guidance, but she merely waved him on.

The old rascal, I thought. Bloody hell.

'My name is Terence Trevelyan, and I have with me my legal representative, Mr George Ballard, QC, of Chambers, Lincoln's Inn. He will prove I have been in occupation of a section of the land this application refers to and therefore this project cannot legally go ahead without my say so,' said Kermit.

Ballard, who was a retired Wig and whose main focus in life was no longer saving criminals from the clink nor ensuring society was kept safe from brigands but growing various types of tomatoes under glass, went to the briefcase and began to pull out A3 sheets of paper. Each had a photograph on it.

'I will now provide the committee with some background,' he said and smiled at me. 'My client first took up residence in a dwelling in the grounds of Heathwood in 1971. As you are no doubt aware, if it can be shown beyond reasonable doubt that a person has been in continual occupation of a dwelling for more than twelve years, they are given leave to claim squatters' rights, which my client, as mentioned, has done.

'I have here a series of photographs, taken on the first day of January each year, from 1972, with my client standing, as you will note, at the entrance of his place of habitation. This is accepted evidence of the longevity of his occupation and has been logged by the Sheriff of the Property Division as such. Furthermore, I have with me twenty sworn affidavits signed by numerous others who will vouch for my client's continual residence at his abode, which, for the sake of ease, I shall from here on refer to as Number One, The Potting Shed...'

He began to read a list of eminent names – all allotment holders – who had signed statements in Kermit's favour.

I watched Mr Bromotov's agents hurriedly consulting each other.

After some furious whispering, which prompted the committee chairman to call for 'some respectful hush in the chamber', one flush-faced man in a suit scurried quickly from the public benches, mobile phone in hand, no doubt frantic at the thought of the reaction his boss was about to offer.

I grinned at Kermit, aware I had a golden story to tell. He stood passively by, calmly listening to the case being made in his favour. Once the project was unanimously dismissed by the committee, he turned quietly, thanked George Ballard and left the chamber to head back to his tumbledown home.

I rushed back to the newsroom to file the story. Kermit tickled me no end, and when the story broke it went all over the place. It received nationwide attention, ripped by national reporters directly from the pages of the *Press And Star*. Kermit had a good laugh about that. The journalists who seized on it and tried to pass it off to their news editors as their own repeated some of the more fruity lines which were frankly an exaggeration on my part. I had described Kermit's patch as being in gardens 'directly influenced by the Palace of Versailles' and 'featuring ornamental watercourses mimicking those of the ancient city of Babylon' – whatever that meant. Such grandiose claims gave Kermit much satisfaction when he next invited me in to sit by the fire pit in a home he could now genuinely call his own.

The Press And Star, page 1 splash

HERMIT HOME RULE: OLIGARCH MEGA-MANSION SCUPPERED

A billionaire oligarch's plans for a controversial housing development were left in tatters yesterday (Tuesday) when the tycoon discovered he had no legal right to commence building work – as the land earmarked for homes was already owned by a hermit.

Terry Trevelyan – known by friends as Kermit The Hermit – has been granted the legal right to stay on land he has lived on for more than three decades after a judge granted him squatters' rights.

Developers LPDC, an investment vehicle owned by Russian metals magnate Alexandr Bromotov, had hoped to win permission to build twenty-six flats – worth around £3m each – in the grounds of the Victorian mansion Heathwood House. This boasts gardens modelled on the Palace of Versailles and includes watercourses inspired by the ancient hanging gardens of Babylon, which Mr Trevelyan has long used to bathe in.

At a Town Hall meeting last night to decide the fate of the site, Mr Trevelyan gave evidence and produced a series of photographs taken over the last three decades showing him clutching a dated newspaper in the same spot on the land he was claiming as his own.

The hermit's solicitors have provided further evidence in the form of sworn affidavits from numerous neighbours including doctors, lawyers, nursing staff and the cult Brit-flick film director Johnny Cousins, stating that Mr Trevelyan has lived there for more than twelve years and therefore could not be legally removed.

The plot near Hampstead, which consists of around 120 square metres of woodland and a small brick shack, has been Mr Trevelyan's home since the early 1970s.

He has remained tight-lipped about his case, but *The Press And Star* has learnt he called in the services of respected retired QC George Ballard, and after presenting evidence of the length of his tenure, the esteemed lawyer took up his case.

It is unlikely the land, which could be worth more than £2m if planning permission was granted for housing, could be sold by Mr Trevelyan for anything near that sum, as it enjoys the same protection under planning law as the Green Belt.

Mr Trevelyan told *The Press And Star*: 'I know my rights. No one can just walk in and flash their money around and take what's rightfully someone else's.'

Quizzed as to what he would do with the land now it was legally his, he said life would 'carry on as normal'. He added: 'I'd not want to sell it anyway. It has been my home for many years, and shall remain so.'

A spokesman for the owner of Heathwood House declined to comment specifically on the case, but stated: 'After taking legal advice, our client has accepted the ruling and will now redraw their plans to take this into account.'

THE DUKE BOX HAZARDS

I HAD COME to see my mate's band play – but it was really an excuse to get drunk. It had been a long week at the paper, and we'd covered some fairly grim stories. I fancied forgetting much of it with the aid of some lager.

The Duke Box Hazards were a rock-and-roll outfit staffed by people I knew, and I had seen the band countless times before. They were a kicking little combo, so I thought I was ready for what was coming – but that night led to a series of events that, when I embarked on my drinking session, I could not possibly have foreseen.

*

'A one, two, three, four – here we go... opening chord... and then whump, straight into it.

'It's magic, the way the brain works, isn't it? I can sense it inside, what's going to come next, because I've played this tune hundreds of times, over and over again. But it still makes me marvel at the way my fingers move – apparently without me telling them to. They just do it. Like walking. You know what comes next, it's obvious, and it just happens.

'And then the chord change – as we go into the middle eight, the fingers on the end of my hand know exactly where they need to go, the different position on the fretboard, and when, precisely, to make that move, and how it changes from what I was doing a moment ago... my ears pick up the changes and, as I look down at the neck of the guitar, for that one split second I marry the shape and position of my left hand to the noise my ears are picking up.

'It's lovely.

'But.

'Suddenly, commotion. I catch it out of the corner of my eye. There's a problem. I can't hear Sam singing any more. All I can hear is... expletives... strong ones, fucking fucks... and breaking glass... "Fuck off, fuck off, fuck off," shouted over the PA.

'And that's not how this song goes, I remember thinking. I remember that very clearly.'

I was sitting by Greg's hospital bed, and he continued: 'You do shorthand, right?'

I replied: 'Yes, course.'

And he said: 'Well, I've got a bit of a confession to make. I've got something on my mind and I want to tell someone. I have to get this off my chest, and I want you to write it down for me, okay? You could even stick it in your paper if you want. There's a story here.'

Greg was an old friend. We'd gone to school together. He was a bicycle courier by day and The Duke Box Hazards' lead guitarist at night. It felt a little like a last will and testament he was after sharing, and he was clearly high as anything off the morphine they'd given him, and frankly I thought his gallows mood was misplaced. The doctors had said he would make a full recovery, it would just take time. But then again, I hadn't had almost the entire right side of my body basically studded back together with metal pins, half my skull taken out and replaced by an acrylic paste, and I wasn't facing an uncomfortable 'procedure' to remove a tube draining fluid out of my spine... so when he said 'Take this all down, please, will you, mate? I need to tell someone this,' I could hardly refuse.

I got out a biro and my notebook, and here is what he told me, pretty much verbatim.

'My first thought that night when it all kicked off was, what is he doing, who has he antagonised this time? Okay, not fair really, jumping to conclusions, but Sam is known for doing what he wants, whenever the fancy takes him... that's what makes him a good front man, that arrogance. But also it is what makes him a daft fucker that gets me, all of us, into trouble... although he doesn't see it like that, doesn't see a hundred people aching to rip his head off as strictly trouble, just another day being Sam.

'But I can see someone. A big, brawny, drunken bloke who has no cares and is fearless in his bulk, and he is lurching forward at the front of the stage, and there's no bouncer in the shadows to offer us protection. Why would there be? I mean, you know The Green Onion. It's a crappy back room in a crappy pub.

'But there again, we may piss someone off enough, or perhaps – and I am being frank here, not really trying to downplay our talents, just be truthful about them for once – perhaps someone will think we are just so terrible, our music so objectionable, that they feel like throwing a bottle or two at us and laughing as we duck.

'Crunch. Glass underfoot. It happens so quickly, and the mood of the place now changes from indifference to antagonism.

'Wallop.

'This bottle came flying at us, and it hit my amp, which pissed me off, because an amp will not heal itself. At least if it had clonked me one it would leave a scar and that would be that. It took a nasty chip off the amp as it shattered, and then the beer spilt across the cones, and I thought for a moment I was going to kark it right there. Zap – death on the stage as the electrics get soaked. A good way to go – if it's Wembley in front of three trillion fans. Not so good when it's the back room of the fucking shabbiest pub among the many in Camden Town.

'It's an odd-shaped space, that stage, with acres of leg room where you don't want it – behind an antiquated PA system which no one uses – and none where you do. You want some room so you can have a boogie and a little hip wriggle while your fingers run up and down the fretboard.

'So the band always gets squished and funnelled into this little space at the front of the stained, rotting platform, and we feel unable to move for fear of knocking our instruments into each other. It wasn't gratifying, and the thrill we'd first felt when we were booked to play there had long since worn off. But it was a gig, and that was what The Duke Box Hazards were all about. It had to be. Live music. No choice, because no one was ever going to give us a record deal.

'Rich, well-hidden at the back, was still bashing out the rhythm of the song the rest of us had abandoned long ago. He was mesmerised by fear, caught in a drum loop that he couldn't escape from, although he was the person in least danger.

'When the crowd turned he wouldn't get the first shower of crap, and he had much more to hide behind if a stray missile got through the human shields me and Sam provided.

'And Rich made it worse, because the drums on their own sound like some kind of totemic war dance bang-a-clang-clang-clang, clang-bang-a-lang-lang, and I reckon it incited the crowd even more.

'Sam was shouting and swearing, and the fat bloke at the front was shouting back and swearing, and neither of them could hear each other or know exactly what they were complaining about.'

I remembered it clearly now. Sam's enemy tried to clamber on to the small stage and sort the argument out. Drunk, fat, big puffed-out red cheeks, he was comically struggling to hoist his frame up and not getting very far.

'Sam had an advantage,' Greg continued. 'His foot was about in line with the bloke's chest, and, as the man decided it was too much effort to join the band on stage and instead he'd bring Sam down on to the dance floor, his big, grappling arms reaching out to grab Sam by the ankles and drag his impertinent little arse into the crowd for a thorough kicking, Sam lashed out, booting him in the chin and then, swinging the microphone like a mace above his head, smacked the attacker across the forehead. Using the microphone lead, lashing it about, he forced the crowd to back off.'

I recalled Jimmy Jennings, an Irish bloke with a Peter String-fellow haircut whose pub it was, arriving with help, and the band was safe – for the time being.

'Not again,' said Jimmy to the stunned wreck on the floor. 'I told you before, Seamus. Leave my musicians alone. You want a punch-up? Do it after they've finished. I want my money's worth.'

'Thanks, Jimmy,' Greg had said.

'So we were out of danger, but only while we entertained this squalid pit. Sam's antagonist was so drunk he seemed to forget why he was on the floor. Alcoholic weariness spread across his face, and he was now more concerned with getting to his feet. For a moment there was an angel on his shoulder – probably with the voice of his long-departed mother – saying "Now, now, Seamus, why d'ya get yerself in this mess, boy?" and he looked like he wanted to curl up and sleep and was praying under his breath, apologising to the voice of his dear old ma.

'So we're safe, although none of us wanted to continue, and, like Seamus, I just wanted to go home. I wiped the beer off my guitar and I was pleased – it still worked.

'Jimmy said something like "That's that then. What you waiting for? Get on with it"… I glanced back at Rich – click, click, click, click – he counted four on his drumsticks, and we launched into that song I wrote called "Acute Girl Trauma". Sam liked that one when he'd had a ding-dong because it allowed him to shout a lot, so we indulged him, and it went down quite well – better than any of the shitty numbers we had forced on the binge-drinking crowd at Jimmy Jennings's place so far.'

I remembered the events Greg was describing. The Green Onion may have seen better days, but I suspect it was never a classy joint, always a shithole. There was an unmistakable stench of violence in the air. It wasn't just the rougher elements of the clientele who didn't appreciate The Duke Box Hazards' efforts to entertain. No. It came deep from within the crumbling late-Victorian edifice to alcohol, with its frosted windows, chipped paintwork and rogue buddleia bush sprouting from the window ledge on the first floor. The oppressive air seemed to emanate from the faded gilt cornicing that ringed the room. It stank. The Onion had its own atmosphere created by the lingering fug of stale fags, long since stubbed out but still there… beer served through never-cleaned pipes… fake designer aftershaves… spilt beer and peanuts and alcopops. But worst of all was the underlying damp, noxious odour of human origin: predominantly sweat mingling with the pong from the gents, a smell that seeped out from under the cracked and battered door to the toilets.

*

Greg looked knackered lying there, stunned by the pain. Despite the drugs they had given him, you could tell he was uncomfortable.

There was crusty snot and blood forming a congealed ring around his nostrils, and I wanted to get a cloth and clean it up... but there was this tube disappearing up his nose, and I didn't dare in case I wiggled it free. And, to be honest, I didn't really want to touch him. His chest looked weak. It wasn't the chest that puffed out like Keith Richards's when he was on stage. It was more like a chicken breast hanging in a butcher's. Devoid of life. Pimpled. Shallow. Horrible. His skin had a sallowness, as if the accident had drained the pigment from him.

I'd scribbled down what he had said, humouring him, wondering what the relevance of it all was, hoping he'd reached the end. Sitting on a plastic chair next to a hospital bed had begun to give me the freaks. He'd been so handsome. Looking at him, all smashed up, with caked blood and dried snot and the tube up the schnozzle and a drip in his arm... well, it made me feel vulnerable. It made my skin itch. It made me think there but for the grace of God go I. And while I wanted to be a friend, write down what he told me, I also wanted to get out in the fresh air and escape the hospital for a while. I could sense Greg knew this, and he said: 'Listen, I really appreciate this. My insides are so battered, my spleen half gone, my kidneys bruised... I feel like complete shit. Please bear with me. I need to tell you about my accident. I need to tell you why it happened.'

*

While I took down Greg's musings, I thought about the flyer advertising that night. It was printed on green, orange and white paper, A5 size, done by the photocopy shop on Holloway Road. It had not been cut well. The top left-hand corner was wonky and sliced off part of a sentence reading 'Jimmy Jennings, Promoter, Presents...' And then there was their name: 'The Duke Box Hazards, live at The Smeg Club, presented by The Green Onion pub.'

Theirs was not the only name on the bill. Jimmy would never say no to a band that wanted a gig. He had a scattergun booking policy, convinced that among the grit he would eventually book a diamond, and it would be his club that they would cite in interviews years later as the place where it all kicked off for them.

By the entrance to the darkened hall at the back, on a green, yellow and white poster, in the same font as the flyer, the other names on the bill were advertised.

With The Hazards, there was D'Archangel. They were a bunch of gothic rockers playing music which they described as post-industrial – perhaps, I ruminated with Greg, because it sounded like the sort of noise that we imagined haunts former steelworks. It was typical fare for the Onion.

That evening's entertainment included The Honolulu Fridays, a three-piece girl vocal group who accompanied themselves on ukuleles. There was Hounslow, a four-piece wearing black shirts and white bow ties who played music as depressing as the place. There was The Gingernuts, who turned out to be a bizarre covers band, mixing The Kinks and The Beatles with Abba and something I could not recognise but sounded a bit like an extended Human League B-side. Their lead singer had ginger hair. I suppose that's where they got the name from.

Others filling the 7pm-to-4am bill included a teen metal-band called Vomit. They were followed by Brows That Meet, which I suppose was indie, for want of a better description. There was the popular ska-fusion-rock outfit The Chineapple Punks, who were 'headlining' the evening. ('Not actually too bad,' said Greg, breaking a strict piece of Hazards etiquette. 'Lead singer quite a nice-looking girl with a voice and a half to boot.')

For their final song they did a pumped-up jump-around version of America's 'Horse With No Name'.

'Well we've been through the motherfucking desert on a motherfucking horse with no motherfucking name, it felt good to be out of the motherfucking rain grrrrrr...'

It went down a storm. The crowd loved it. They sung the bah-baaah-baaah-bah-bah-baaah-bah chorus bit at top speed while having a pogo.

Free entry, Fosters £1.50, bar till 4am.

It was partly the booze-mottled punters whose Friday nights had long lost any flavour and who were attracted to the Smeg Club that caused the colossal fight between The Duke Box Hazards and almost everyone else in that dingy room. The Sam and Seamus set-to was merely a warm-up. It would be wrong to blame the pair of them entirely. They just helped a dam of bad vibes the Green Onion had created to break and wash across Greg and his band.

Here's how it started. The Seamus incident had set the scene early on. There were a few in the crowd who stood out in the haze and warm fog of fag smoke and beer belches. One sloshed-up regular, decked out in high red heels and a red dress to match her complexion, kept requesting songs. Most were either Tom Jones numbers or, when she got really excited, Debbie Harry classics. She was having some kind of high-strength-lager-induced I-am-Blondie trip in luminous make-up and an unkempt mop of bleached hair.

She had taken the lead from Seamus and kept trying to attract Sam's attention, and when he ignored her she took umbrage and made a pretty game attempt to wrestle the mike off him. Sam was feeling pissed, aggressive and annoyed that his vocal artistry was being ignored (by some 'pickled old trout', as he unkindly put it). She looked a lot harder than all of them and was aching to chin someone if they asked her to get the fuck off the stage in a way that she took offence to. The Hazards were feeling edgy. The crowd sensed it and seemed ready for a lynching.

The band ran through their usual repertoire and avoided between-song banter, lessening the opportunity for catcalls and hollering.

Their opening number – 'Grandmother Mayhem', a fast rock-and-roll number in the key of E – was met with heads nodding politely, but I noticed there was a rush on the bar. Always a bad sign. Their second song – a country-inspired ditty, snappily titled 'I've Been Whaling Over You, But Now The Blubbering's Gotta Stop', failed to ignite the crowds as it had done once or twice in the past, namely Greg's cousin's wedding and my thirtieth birthday party.

A few more mates turned up for the end of it, and they cheered and whooped self-consciously before heading to the bar themselves, which made me feel doubly depressed. I felt sorry for The Hazards up there. Even their friends weren't pretending to love them like we all had when they first started.

They moved swiftly on, hardly looking at each other, standing still, trying to ignore the heckling that grew as they worked through the first part of their set, which ended with the attack by Seamus the lashed-up brawler. Jimmy sorted it for them, although by the frowns on his fat, pasty face it seemed he thought it was their fault.

Hoping that was the evening's trouble out of the way, the band began again. A few songs down the line Debbie Harry's wannabe *doppelgänger* started shouting, and Greg tried to humour her. She was not into their next tune, an ironic masterpiece Greg told me he had thought of while on a courier run to some trendy internet firm just south of the river.

It was called 'Waterloo Sunrise' and about someone waking up with a minging hangover on The Embankment and wondering how he got there and then realising that he had been living rough by the Thames for the past eight years.

I thought it was brilliant, although Greg would be the first to admit the chorus, which required a change of key, needed tweaking, and the rhyming of 'cardboard box' with 'holes in my socks' was not quite Ray Davies. I liked it, but Debs did not and slurred to Sam: 'Lemme 'ave a go. You lot are fucking shite.' He replied: 'This ain't karaoke, love'. Someone else heard him, and in a pitted, deep voice, scarred and mangy from many Rothmans Number Ones, snarled: 'It fookin' well should be, sonny, more fun than you daft fookers,' at which point Sam, who had the advantage over the heckler that he was miked up, told him to go fuck himself.

But the crowd thought he was addressing them in general, and a ripple of discontent flowed towards the band. I stepped back, ready to duck outside. I hoped Greg would find cover behind the antiquated PA. The 1970s stack of bass cones and valve amps would provide a form of safety if bottles or pint glasses were thrown.

'Not again, Sam, leave it out, mate,' growled Greg. 'I've had enough for one night.'

Rich clicked his sticks four times, and I was hoping another tune would gloss over the latest confrontation, but Sam was in a mood and did not come in when he was meant to. They had to play the first eight bars again.

Debs Harry, her bravery fuelled by downing another double peach schnapps and lemonade, came to the front and started to dance, her drunkenness moving the soles of her feet without her brain really knowing what was happening, as if she were doing it by instinct, like a lab rat on ecstasy.

She kept it up for a couple of minutes before it leaked through her ears into her sodden head that they were not playing 'The Tide Is High' and then the abuse started again.

'Okay, you take the fucking microphone then, you daft tart,' shouted Sam as she wobbled up on to the stage, tangling herself in leads and wires and threatening to unplug everything.

She did not realise he was unhappy. Far from it. She grinned, leerily, at all and sundry from her elevated spot on the stage, waving at friends who were hooting encouragement. She draped a fat, pork sausage of an arm around his shoulders, her eyes going in different directions and her mouth drooling towards the microphone, her saliva causing him to recoil with disgust. For one awful yet brilliant moment she seemed poised to snog him.

Sam stalked away, picked up a pint and took some aggressively big gulps before tossing the glass to the floor and sending shards into the crowd.

'All yours then, sunbeam. Give us a song. Your audience is waiting,' he snarled.

Now she came to a little. Suddenly there she was, on stage, pissed out of her nut. Mike in hand. With an audience and her band. And fame beckoned. But... erm... I ain't never sung in a band before, nowhere except while scratching away at my armpits in the shower. And then I normally sing... what was it?... 'Simply The Best'... or... how does it go?... 'Black Magic Woman'... is that it? The semi-sobering realisation of where she now found herself struck home. She blinked rapidly, steadied herself, and the rest of The Hazards looked at each other, wondering if she was going to suddenly realise what was required and bottle out as gracefully as she could.

But this was too good an opportunity to let slip. She'd clearly always thought to herself, whenever she watched X-Factor on the telly, that I could bloody do that, nothing to it... and now she had the chance to prove it.

A shoulder strap on her Friday-night finery slipped down her arm, exposing more pinky-blotched flesh. I remember Greg trying to defuse the situation: 'Sorry, love, but we're in the middle of...' he said. The crowd had gone quiet. They sensed a coup had taken place.

'Blondie,' she shouted at him. 'You know Blondie? Let's do Blondie!'

She was not listening and Sam, sitting on a speaker to one side of the stage, was now enjoying himself. This audience participation was making the rest of The Duke Box Hazards squirm. Greg rolled his eyes.

He recalled this from his bed, and I remembered, too. I tried to make light of it, say no one cared and it was pretty funny, but Greg wasn't in the mood to make light of the incident that had pre-cipitated his spell in hospital.

'Will you fucking sort this out?' he had shouted at Sam. 'Get her off right fucking now. Get her off. Go on...'

Sam stuck a finger up at Greg and swore. 'You lot are such a fucking bunch of dozy wankers. I can't be arsed with this any more.'

I was watching with increasing interest and a growing sense of anxiety.

'I wanna do Blondie.'

I had gathered her name was Rosie by listening to the cat calls from her mates. She whinnied at them and turned her attention to Greg. He was cut in half by a withering look. Now he was frightened. He imagined the bruisers in the hall, waiting for their very own Rosie to entertain them.

Greg scowled again.

'Which one?' he ventured, sensing she would not be best pleased if they were to throw her off, and seeing that she had the crowd behind her. She was one of them, and they loved her. There she was, showing those youngsters in their flowery shirts and long hair that she could do it. Someone shouted from the back: 'G'wan, Rosie, give it some, ducky.'

Rich clicked his sticks, shouted '"The Tide Is High" in C,' and off they went, playing a very passable, skanking version of the hit... except Rosie remembered but a smattering of the lyrics and repeated the only words she could recall over and over again. I got into the spirit of things and tried to dance to it while Greg coaxed her cracked and horrible voice through the next verse, even though she refused to listen and kept reverting back to the opening lines.

Greg looked pained recalling the memory, but I suppose I was grateful, what with the bang to the head he received, that he could so clearly remember that night.

'She warbled into the crowd, and you know what? You know what was the saddest thing of all, the saddest thing among many other sad things that occurred to me that night? They loved her. They absolutely loved her to bits. She was shit, and so were we. We looked like morons, and in the cold light of day, her performance was moronic, too. But they loved her for it.'

The evening came to an abrupt and violent end as the song finished. The crowd bayed for another, and Rosie took a series of what she considered to be dainty steps back and forth, bowing and curtseying as she went. Greg said thanks to her, told the crowd to big her up one more time and tried to shuffle her away... but as he took her gently by the elbow she stumbled and crashed off the stage. It wasn't a big drop – three feet perhaps – but it was enough for her to cut her head and bash her nose and, when she came up, she came up fighting.

I only saw this from the back, but suddenly the stage was no longer the band's. It was invaded by the crowd, and I could see a mangle of fists and feet flying, and then I saw Greg's prized guitar raised above heads and crashing down to the floor, splintering into a sorry mess of wood, strings, fretboard, tuning heads, pick-ups and electrics, accompanied by a terrifying, yowling wall of feedback.

I knew the story of The Hazards, having watched them stumble from one false dawn of rock greatness and music immortality to another. I wondered why Greg wanted me to chronicle a story of a band that had failed, of a bar-room brawl, but even while lying in a hospital bed, tubed up, he had an eloquence that made it easy to take notes, and so without pushing him I continued to listen, hoping that the kernel of a story would emerge that I could use. I could see the feature – *'The Perils Of Pub Rock', by Greg Heyberg, lead guitarist of Camden's legendary Duke Box Hazards.*

But there was more to it than that.

*

Greg was a bicycle courier. He worked for Been There, Delivered That, the West End's premier delivery company, according to the side of their vans. He'd once dreamt of making a living as a musician, but the combination of talent and luck eluded him and the other Duke Boxes, so he played his guitar at the weekends for 'fun'.

'It's fucking horrible, my job,' he said.

'The constant threat of being made into marmalade by buses, lorries, 4x4s. You know how many cyclists get killed each year in London, right? It's bloody carnage out there. Then there is the rain. Wet Tarmac. Puddles in gutters. Litter. Raincoats and umbrellas and heads bowed, no one looking where they are going.

'And the shit I had to drop off to got right on my tits. They always looked down their bloody noses at you, when you went to do a pick up and drop off, and I was always aware that they valued the package I handed over more highly than they valued me. Never a please or thank you. I hated the crap I had to put up with.

'I made a point of moaning about it to anyone who would listen, because I didn't want to be a delivery boy. Who does? There's that put-down: "Whaddya think I am, some kinda delivery boy?" "Erm. Yes, actually. You are." That's the problem. And the people I worked with thought it was pretty fucking cool, so I had no one to commiserate with. Bunch of mugs, really. Mostly a load of Aussies and Kiwis, looking for quick cash while they bummed about in Europe, and this seemed easy to them, though they spent as long checking their map apps as they did cycling.

'And then there are the others, the homegrown "dudes", all should have been at university really, but too much into their drugs/booze/independent-film-making to get their heads down, and so they end up with me at Been There, Delivered That. And they all drove me mad after a bit. They were into what I call 'biker chic', and that made me mad as hell because it gave the job a flashiness it did not deserve.

'They swapped tales of fights with lorry drivers, verbals with cabbies, slanging matches with posh muppets in four-by-fours. They were always going on about new brake and gear systems, fixies, of high-performance rock oil and how to strip your bike so it weighed as much as a twopenny piece, new breathe-easy lightweight shorts that stopped you getting nappy rash, and of sunglasses, of gloves, of short cuts and of weekend scrambling sessions in the woods on the Heath or one-hundred-and-twenty-mile round trips to the coast... and of one million pieces of paraphernalia... bullshit talk that was part and parcel of the fashionable world of bicycle couriers.

'I remember sitting in the mess room at the HQ off the Euston Road, nursing a cup of tea, waiting for my next job, listening to all this macho crap. It really pissed me off.

'I'd only done one delivery that day, and we get paid by the job. I had cycled from South Kensington, up past Kensington Gardens, around Hyde Park Corner, up to Marble Arch, along Oxford Street – where some Japanese tourist stepped out in front of me by Selfridges – 'You stupid fucking fucker,' I shouted at her, disappointed that she failed to understand the vitriol I was gobbing as I shot past – and then at Oxford Circus I hung a left, up past the Beeb to Regent's Park, then on to some trendy music PR company in Primrose Hill.

'I got off my bike, having done the journey in about twenty minutes flat – not fucking bad – and handed over the envelope I'd whipped over there in double-quick time. The bloke at the desk signed for it and then put it in a wire tray for the big chops upstairs. I went back and waited, and a job came in, and off I went, and that was that. That was the one I got smacked up on. I don't remember the accident, but I do remember the mood I was in. Had a right strop on.'

It was hard work, sitting in the hospital, with the smell of disinfectant and everything that reminded you of how frail humans are, hearing Greg having a bitch. But at least I could get up and leave at the end of the visiting hours. Poor old Greg couldn't, so I persevered.

'You remember I needed a new guitar, after it got wrecked at the Green Onion that night?' he asked me.

'Yeah,' I said.

How could I forget?

'Well, we went down Denmark Street and had a look through the shops, something we had done many times before, and I had seen a Strat that became like the object of my desire. I'd fallen in love with it, and I lingered, at first too shy to approach the dream, like some spotty teenager who sees a girl he wants desperately but can't pluck up the courage to say anything to her because he believes the little pimple on his chin is a fucking volcano and will disgust her and disgrace him.

'It hung there in the window, a thousand-pound's-worth of American crafted guitar with a Rosewood sun-splash design and ebony scratchplate, and my must-have need for the thing was confirmed when I finally went inside after much umming and ahing, pretending I had some cash, and tried it out. Shouldn't have done. It was too, too nice. Way out of my price range. Way too nice for me. Still, I was hooked. I had to have it.

'A thousand pounds? You know me – my money situation was strictly hand to mouth. But then we had a lucky break.

'About a week later, we met an acquaintance, Holy Tone, in the Metro Café on the Camden Road. He was having a breakfast – eggs, sausages, bacon, fried bread, beans, canned tomatoes, bubble, black pudding, chips and brown sauce, washed down with two cups of tea and a pint of milk. He is a big bloke. He was holding court, talking about something or other, and I don't know who said what to who first, I was too busy reading the back pages, but I left that fry-up with a determined plan.'

Holy Tone – real name Tony Donoghue – was a legend in certain circles in our neighbourhood. He had, while in his twenties, earned a fearsome reputation as a no-nonsense midfield general in the Roy Keane mould for The Bell's Sunday-league team. He'd be the reason for ambulances to trundle across the pitches at Hackney Marshes at weekends, when his two-footed lunges at anyone showing any level of skill for an opposing side decided to try and sell Holy Tone a dummy. He was also known for being a reliable fence – always knew a man who knew a man – and would offer a wide range of knocked-off, knocked-down bits and pieces for sale, particularly kitchen appliances and white goods, which he would get hold of as a preferred contractor for various social-housing associations. New kitchens would be fitted and the white goods in there written off, no matter what condition they were in, and then flogged to favour his bank balances.

Other money-making projects were above board but just as inventive. Holy Tone had once earned five-thousand pounds in cash with the help of Greg and his friends over a weekend when he'd come across a lock-up in the underground car-park of an estate in Queen's Crescent. The council wanted them cleared for renovation, and its tenant had died with no family. Holy Tone found a large quantity of wig-making equipment inside – felt, brims, card, scissors, netting and a workbench. The lock-up also including bales of fake hair. Holy Tone had retired to the pub with the contents playing on his mind, and while supping away at his weekend beer, noticed that Wimbledon was on the telly.

It was the year Andre Agassi won the tournament, and he was lighting up the early rounds with his dash and verve. The world was going through an Agassi love-in. Holy Tone, ever inventive, immediately went to a Commercial Road rag-trade wholesaler and bought a job lot of cheap caps. He made a Nike stencil, sprayed five hundred Nike ticks on them, and then glued a shock of hair to the back.

Greg and his mates went to Wimbledon with Holy Tone's Agassi Mullet hats and did a roaring trade with those queuing up to watch the tennis. Since then, Greg had associated Holy Tone with get-rich-quick schemes of varying degrees of legality, and it so transpired that Holy Tone had struck a similar, mutually beneficial deal with Greg and the other Hazards over that breakfast.

'Tony works for O'Doul's, one of the biggest road contractors in London,' said Greg, shuffling up in bed.

He spoke in hushes, as if what he was about to tell me wasn't for public consumption.

'You know they have the depot round the back of Kentish Town Road, yeah? Tony has been a foreman there for years and years. But trouble was afoot. He told a tale of woe. "Little t'eeving boogers" as he put it, were following his gang around and pinching all their traffic cones and whatnots as soon as their backs were turned.

'This gang of highly organised criminals – the thought they could have been students on their way home after a night out at the Camden Palace escaped him – were costing his boss a fortune. Furthermore, other rascals were pinching the road signs they put up and selling them on to scrap-metal merchants.'

Greg told me how this had got him thinking, and after Holy Tone had finished his breakfast Greg took him to the pub for a pint with a deal in mind. This spate of thefts gave him an idea. He offered his services for a limited period as a righter of wrongs to Holy Tone, who said he'd pay good cash for road cones, the strips of red and white plastic that cordon off holes, in fact, anything at all that Greg could find round broken-up Tarmac and holes in the road from rival contractors.

'He told me he'd pay even better for road signs, because he had the contract with the Town Hall and Transport For London for them, and they'd have to replace what was taken. His logic was the more road signs I helped myself to, the more he would have to replace, thus making a tidy, profitable circle for all concerned.'

Holy Tone was good enough to acknowledge that the hoisting of a 'One Way' sign took more effort than the lifting of cones and would pay on a sliding scale. It would be easy.

So The Hazards, who are no slouches when there was a few bob to be made, got to work.

'Our nocturnal jaunts to building sites and roadworks around

Camden Town became a regular occurrence,' said Greg. 'In fact, while in the midst of our crime spree, the first thing we'd say to each other when we met up to jam was "seen any roadworks round your way then?" And if there was a positive answer we'd jump in a car and do a little lifting under the cover of darkness.'

It quickly became clear, as they waited around the corner of O'Tooles yard in Kentish Town, that this was all highly profitable. Tony was good for his word and would buy anything. Rates were low for your run-of-the-mill workman's stuff – cones in good nick had a going rate of about five pounds – but they were lying on the street and you could lift them without a second thought. Greg was not going to sniff at a score here and there. Road signs, as Tony had promised, were more profitable. After one particular job that netted eight Give Way signs, four One Ways, five 40mph limit numbers from various junctions on the A406 and a host of other orders and warnings from the streets of north London cut down from posts with a set of pliers, he made a tidy one hundred and fifty pounds. The guitar was soon his.

But Greg, as is his wont, got greedy. He had cleared over a thousand pounds and bought the guitar, proudly taking it out of its triangular cardboard box on the 134 bus after leaving Tin Pan Alley, and giving an unplugged show on the upper deck. But he had become addicted to the thrill of pinching signs and had begun to stockpile them in his back garden. No one ever went there, except cats who chose to shit undisturbed in the tall grass and scruffy bushes, and Greg's dad did not notice that his yard had turned into something akin to a junction on the Euston Road.

'And I think this side-line was what did for me,' Greg said, when I pushed him to explain how pinching signs to get a guitar had landed him in hospital.

'You see, I was going down Gower Street, and there is a turning to the left, Great Russell Street, that has a bike lane in it. I had a drop-off at UCL. Now, traffic isn't allowed to go down there. There was a No Left Turn sign... but we'd stolen it.'

Okay, I thought.

'I don't remember anything about the smash, but my mum told

me that was where I got hit. A lorry took a right where they shouldn't have done and took me out. And I'm afraid to say that it was probably my fault. I was given a twenty-pound fine for that one.'

The Evening Press And Star, page 7

THEFT SPREE:
GANG TARGETS STREET SIGNS

A spate of thefts that has seen scores of street signs disappear could be the work of an organised gang, *The Press And Star* has learnt.

Bills filed by the Town Hall's road department this year show a 5,000-per-cent rise in cash spent on replacing signs that have disappeared, while figures released by Transport For London show a similar increase. A police spokesman had 'no idea' why anyone would seek to steal signs, but the *Press And Star* has discovered that more than three hundred marking one-way streets, no right turns, weight and height restrictions, speed limits and other road orders have had to be replaced at what a Town Hall source called 'an alarming rate'. They added it was suspected a gang could be selling the signs on for their scrap-metal value.

However, a council spokesman said no evidence had emerged that they were being stolen nor that foul play was suspected. But it was added that the council had spent more than ten thousand pounds this year urgently replacing signs.

The spokesman said: 'We take this very seriously. Removing street signs can cause serious accidents. We will be working with the police to ensure the culprits are caught and brought to justice.'

DOCTOR ZIPP'S
AMAZING OCTO-COM

THE CORONER SHUFFLED and sat a little more upright in his chair. He gazed around the court and pushed his glasses back up to the bridge of his nose. They had gently slipped forward as he read over his notes. He took an audible breath, as if he were trying to give his final remarks the gravitas required. He cleared his throat.

'I conclude the cause of death was drowning,' he began. 'The water temperature was such that hypothermia may have been a contributing factor, but going on the evidence provided by the autopsy, I suggest prolonged immersion resulted in respiratory impairment caused by the lungs being full of water. I am minded to post a verdict of accidental death.'

I felt a shiver pass through me. As well as images of Dr Harry Zipp's cold and uncomfortable end, it was draughty in the courtroom, with its rotting window-frames, uncomfortable benches and grubby veneer panelling. It always seemed to me to be a suitably depressing place to put a full stop at the end of someone's life story.

'It's pneumonia weather out there,' a colleague had called as I left the newsroom – heading for an inquest I'd seen listed and which had caught my eye – and they were right.

It was one of those autumnal days where the light is weak and the sky murky. On my way to the Court House I'd turned my collar up in the vague hope of stopping the wind that was ripping its way down my neck and halting the drizzle that soaked me. It didn't work, and I was pretty miserable by the time I arrived.

I had said hello to the clerk at the door of the coroner's office and slid into the knee-tight press bench. The coroner was at his desk, shuffling through papers and occasionally peering over the top of his glasses at a computer. The clerk I'd greeted came in and handed over another file to add to a pile. A police officer sat quietly on a bench to the left of the coroner. He was concentrating hard as he went through his notebook. I saw his mouth moving slightly as he read through the evidence he had scribbled down.

I gazed about, waiting for the proceedings to start, and I had the same morbid thought I always got when I covered these proceedings. We were about to hear of events that led to the end of a life. It would often appear to be a set of circumstances colliding in a humdrum manner. Despite the many I had covered over the years, I still found myself feeling surprised that something so precious, so complicated as a human life, could be taken away in simple and innocuous ways.

As I tried to shake the morose sense engulfing me, I noticed the arrival of one more person in the near-empty courtroom, catching a glimpse as he sat down in the public gallery.

This man was, I guessed, in his sixties, and judging by his flushed cheeks, scraggly white beard and scruffy clothes, lived a hard life. I wondered which of his relations had passed away in circumstances yet to be ascertained, who on the coroner's list he was grieving for.

The coroner looked around, rose briefly and said to the clerk: 'Shall we begin?'

I opened my notebook, took the lid off my pen and began scribbling in shorthand.

*

The coroner opened the inquest by laying out some basic facts: 'Dr Horatio Zipp, aged seventy-six years, was found semi-immersed in water on a reef approximately eight hundred yards to the southwest of Vazon Bay on the island of Guernsey. I would like the court to note the inquest into Dr Zipp's death has been opened here today instead of in the Bailiwick due to the need for extra forensic examinations. An autopsy was carried out by pathologists in London to ascertain the reason his body was covered in lesions. It is noted that Dr Zipp was a senior lecturer at the University of London's Marine Biology Unit and lived in the district our court covers, so while it may not be usual for an inquest to take place so far from the scene of the deceased being discovered, there are practical reasons for this, and the States Of Guernsey coroner has given his permission for us to continue, with the results of this hearing being posted to him. I will move on to the findings of the pathologist's report in a moment, but before I do I would like to call PC Bougourd of the Bailiwick States Constabulary to the stand.'

The officer stood up, straightened his tie and waited for the coroner to continue. After being sworn in, he was asked for his statement.

'I believe you were the police officer who first saw the deceased's body?' the coroner said.

'I was.'

'Would you mind describing to the court what you saw?' the coroner asked, and the constable began.

'It was Saturday the 19th of August, and I was on an early.'

'An early?'

'That's a shift that starts first thing, 7am.' He looked down at his notebook and continued. 'I was at the station. We weren't on a patrol rota that day. The duty sergeant called us in from the mess room and told us to get down to the harbour. A body had been found on the Hanois reef by a fisherman, and my orders were to get on the lifeboat that would be waiting for me and go to the spot.'

The Hanois reef, as I discovered once I'd returned to the office and dug out an atlas, is a partly submerged slab of rock that runs on a north-to-south parallel along the western coast of the island. It is a place of wrecks and has a sinister reputation among sailors of the Channel archipelago. It is a stretch that is best avoided. The water between the reef and the coast is fast moving and treacherous. It moves between gullies in unpredictable ways. This is not a place that attracts pleasure craft. A few experienced fishermen lay lobster pots there, but it is a lonely, isolated.

'The duty sergeant wanted me to confirm the discovery of the deceased and secure the scene, as much as was possible considering the precarious nature of the resting place,' the officer continued. 'The duty sergeant told me to keep in touch via our radios, and he'd set about organising forensics. He added that he would put the call out through the harbour-master to check no one had been reported missing or that any boats had been in trouble in the area.'

The officer described how he had been taken out to the reef, and, when the boat was as close as the skipper felt was safe, he could see the body of a man. It was lying face down, approximately three feet above the tide line, and seemingly clinging to a jagged outcrop. The cadaver's legs were in the sea, and from the officer's first impression it seemed a strange place and position for a body to have been carried by the ocean. He went on to outline how they'd got a lifeboat crew that could handle the swell and the proximity of rocks, taken a forensic detective out to the reef and managed to reclaim the body.

The coroner said that an autopsy confirmed Dr Zipp had water in his lungs, and while this is never conclusive, as it can be a sign of respiratory or pulmonary failure, in this case, due to the other signs of lengthy immersion in water, the most likely conclusion was that Dr Zipp had drowned.

There followed a cursory investigation of his identity then a few questions asked over his movements in the days leading up to his death and his state of mind.

The court heard from a written statement by a colleague of Dr Zipp's that he was a marine biologist conducting a shellfish survey that involved shore-gathering and investigations along a coast with big tides and strong currents. He worked alone. These stated facts created a story of his demise.

'It was suggested by his injuries that he had been washed into the sea and fairly knocked about by the waves,' said the officer. 'As the pathologist's report outlines, the body also had abrasive, circular-shaped marks across its trunk and back.'

The coroner, who had been listening while also reading a written appraisal of the officer's evidence, asked him if he had anything else to add.

'My only other thoughts are these, sir,' he replied. 'Having seen cases of this type before, I would agree with the assertion that the death was caused by drowning, and, given the nature of Dr Zipp's work, it also seems likely he was knocked into the sea while collecting, or perhaps found himself caught out by the tide, and unable – or unwilling – to swim to safety due to the distance or the strength of the currents.

'However, neither of these facts explain why his body was found somewhere so far offshore. I have checked the tide table and know the currents well. There is no answer as to why a person would enter the sea on the beach Dr Zipp was last known to be working on and be washed to a reef so far away.

'Furthermore, the marks on his body are not consistent with an abrasive wound caused by a fall. I have not seen lesions of this type before and would like the court to note this.'

'As I am sure you are aware, the job of this court is not to answer such questions,' the coroner replied. 'It is merely to ascertain a cause of death, which in this case is drowning. I will, however, note there were a number of marks and lesions on the body of Dr Zipp, but I am confident they were not the cause of death and were, in all likelihood, inflicted on the corpse after Dr Zipp had died. How these lesions were caused is not our primary concern. Therefore I am minded to record accidental death as opposed to an open verdict.'

*

What a horrible way to go, I thought. Was Dr Zipp alive when he reached the reef? Was he left stranded on a rock, watching the tide slip closer? And how had he got there in the first place, if he was collecting on a seashore? Was he swept out to sea, thrown off balance by a wave… was there a moment where he felt his feet go… the safety of solid earth disappearing… the shock of the cold water… limbs aching as his waterlogged clothing became heavier and heavier… did he see the reef, and in one last, desperate attempt kick hard against the current to reach the exposed, jagged rock?

Dr Zipp was, as the court heard, an experienced marine biologist who had worked on many similar field trips. It struck me that while it was all well and good for the coroner to state his death was caused by drowning, it didn't really begin to answer why his life had come to a premature end in such a way.

I knew I had a story here for *The Evening Press And Star*.

I noticed the old man in the public gallery shake his head slowly as the verdict was reached, and in the silence of the courtroom I heard him sigh. He looked out of place. Under a heavy-duty wet-weather mac he wore a Guernsey jumper. He had a pair of tough canvas trousers stained with a fair few years of hard wear, and he wore a pair of stout boots. He looked like his natural home was on the deck of a trawler.

He left the gallery quickly when the coroner had finished. I decided to catch up with him, as I assumed he must have been a friend or relative of the deceased and could enlighten me as to the life and times of Dr Zipp.

I gathered my stuff up, nodded to the clerk and left, hoping to find him in the Court House reception, but he was nowhere to be seen. I went to the steps outside and looked up and down the street. He had gone, so I returned to the clerk's office.

I asked for a printed copy of the verdict. At the top of the page was Dr Zipp's address. It was a mansion block in one of the Blooms-bury squares. I decided a door knock on a few of his neighbours would be a good place to start. Someone must have known him and could tell me whether he lived alone or if there was a widow I could contact. If this wasn't fruitful, a visit to his department at the university would be my next port of call.

*

Harry Zipp had lived in a flat in a block off Tavistock Square. It was once a nice address, but the building had deteriorated through lack of care. There was a cracked window-pane in the front door and worn carpets in the communal hall that smelt of a mixture of cleaning detergent and unidentifiable odours from different kitchens. A lift announced its arrival with creaks and groans.

The block had been built in the thirties, and the cage had a con-certina gate you slid across. It went up the centre of a staircase that wound around it. I pressed the button for the fourth floor, and the lift rose slowly upwards, cranking and swaying. I got out into a dark corridor, and there, in front of me, was the old boy I'd seen at the inquest.

*

'Excuse me,' I said gently, and he slowly turned around. 'Excuse me... but are you a friend of Dr Zipp's?'

'Yes.'

'I'm sorry to hear of your loss... I'm from *The Press And Star*, and I wondered if you could spare me a moment?'

He nodded.

'He sounds like an interesting person,' I continued. 'I'd like to write an obituary...'

He looked hard, eyeing me up, and then his face softened. 'You're the reporter from the court, aren't you? You were at the inquest. I saw you there, didn't I? I tell you, Harry was a remarkable man with remarkable ideas...'

'Well, I was fascinated by what the coroner said.'

'Yes, really, he was an extremely interesting man. I'm Frank, and Harry was my partner. I can tell you all about him. And they said it was an accidental death, didn't they? Well, accidents happen for a reason, I reckon. They might have said how he died in that court,' he spoke slowly, choosing his words with care, 'but they didn't begin to ask why it happened. That's the story, young man. That is the story.'

*

Over the years I have been approached by countless people with tales so outlandishly fantastic that you stop writing after they have given you their name and said: 'No one believes me, but my cat is the Messiah.'

Occasionally, though, you will get an eccentric who genuinely has a yarn to tell, and if you give them five minutes you find yourself investigating something that produces an extraordinary tale. It happened to me when one of the fruit-and-veg men at the market came into the office and swore blind his granny had bought a Samuel van Hoogstraten at a car-boot sale. It turned out the Dutch master's painting had been stolen by the Nazis, 'liberated' by an Allied soldier and eventually made its way to a rugby-club car-park in Wanstead. It happened when the children of a neighbour of mine told me they had stumbled across an underground vault in the garden of a derelict house they had been playing in and been threatened by guards with certain death if they breathed a word of what they had found. I was to discover that the vault had been built as a wine cellar by John Nash and was still full of 18th-century bottles of plonk. It was days away from being secretly wrecked by an unscrupulous property developer. And it happened when I was tipped off about a seventy-five-year-old retired art teacher who went out in the dead of night armed with a folding ladder and a bag of spray paint... I was to discover he was behind some acclaimed street art that everyone had assumed was the work of a twenty-something Banksy disciple.

I sensed that it might, just might, be happening again with Frank.

*

'So tell me, when did you first meet Dr Zipp?'

'I have known him for years,' said Frank, fumbling with a set of keys. 'Come on in. Mind the mess. I wasn't expecting visitors.'

Opening the front door – it needed a shove as it dragged over a doormat – revealed a cramped and shabby home. In the cluttered entrance hall, a marlinspike was hanging from a wall with a print of Turner's *Van Tromp Returning After The Battle Off The Dogger Bank* tacked lopsidedly beneath it. A wooden hat-stand held weathered coats, a faded orange sou'wester, waterproofs and over-alls. The place smelt of musty books and damp clothing. There was a strange, pungent sense of the sea, and I was to discover this came from Harry's study, which included a saltwater fish tank along the entire length of one wall.

Everywhere there were books. Bookshelves enclosed the hallway, forming an avenue of literature. It led into a sitting-room with a kitchen off it, and yet more books were packed on every available surface, stacked up on the floor beside the shelves, seemingly waiting to be filed away by a long-retired librarian. It was the same throughout. Every bit of space had books, files, papers and journals piled up in no discernible order.

Frank looked at me apologetically.

'Excuse the chaos,' he said. 'I was under orders not to rearrange anything... says he knew where everything was. Didn't want me to meddle. Never wanted me to have a tidy up.'

I sat in a sunken and decrepit armchair, and, as I waited for Frank to make a pot of coffee, I began paying proper attention to my surroundings.

*

Harry's library was full of academic tomes by his peers, biological encyclopaedias, classical reference books and works by naturalists, with many stretching back to the great eras of the scientist/explorer, when much of the world was uncharted and maps relied on the guesswork and imagination of cartographers.

I noted the huge selection of work on octopuses – but for one who was, according to Frank, so drawn by empirical knowledge, the shelves had a surprising amount of material on sea monsters, sea folklore, and long-forgotten musings by merchant adventurers. I stood and went to the shelves and found a well-thumbed biography of the state-sponsored pirate Sir Joshua Frobisher, knighted by Elizabeth I for hijacking Spanish gold ships on the high seas. He was one of those privateer captains who wanted to raise their standing among their contemporaries and also barter better prices from the venture capitalists who would pay for them to undertake dangerous journeys to the ends of the earth and so wrote memoirs focusing on their personal bravery.

I peered through a door into an untidy bedroom and saw, balanced on top of yet another pile of books by the bed, one called *Sand, Sea And Sawdust: Memoirs Of A Part-Time Boat Builder* by FM Sommerfield. Pictured on its front cover was a sun-bleached fellow with a long straggly beard, leathery skin and a toothy smile. The face looked familiar, and I realised it was Frank.

Other titles in the library stood out and created an evermore intriguing image of the late Dr Zipp. I found a first edition of Silas Buff's *I Survived The Serpents Attack*, a rare 17th-century adventure story that was taken as a true account when first published but later shown to be utter nonsense. For those not familiar with Buff's work, his tale speaks of a circumnavigation of the globe the supposed sailor undertook, while being pursued by a giant saltwater snake with 'fangs the height of Peterborough Cathedral', as the sleeve notes declared. In reality, Buff lived in the attic of a brothel in Margate, from which he penned his famous seafaring memoir.

It occurred to me that the bigger the teeth of the animals who lived in foreign oceans, the more likely the likes of Buff were to get good wages for agreeing to go on trips of discovery and exploration. And flicking through Frobisher's biography – probably paid for by the man himself – it told of long, saline-stiffened battles with giant squids, killer octopus, huge sharks, fierce whales and a creature he called a 'merman', who had such strong arms from swimming through the currents he could squeeze you to death in moments if he were to embrace you.

I found it interesting that Harry bought these rare books on his salary and would later find a payslip among the papers in his bureau which was pretty meagre. It revealed a little more about the man's fascination with the deep blue yonder.

'I greatly admired him, but I have to say I doubt the true worth of Harry's work will ever be properly recognised within his field,' Frank said, coming into the cramped room bearing a tray with mugs, a coffee pot and a plate of custard creams and chocolate bourbons. He precariously balanced it on top of a lopsided stack of the *Fortean Times* magazine.

'I was studying at his university, and he quickly became a friend. A trusted and honest friend, and then, well, we fell in love, and that was that. He helped get me a job as a lab technician at the institute where he worked. I like making things, and so did Harry. Everything from scientific instruments to a gadget that fed his fish each day. It's one of the reasons why we got on so well.

'And Harry was brilliant at this sort of thing. He could build just about anything. He was a superb scientist and a very competent engineer. A remarkable polymath, remarkable.

'For those of us fortunate to have heard him lecture and got to know him over a glass or two afterwards, his contribution to marine biology is unquestionable. But I'd be the first to admit he was damned eccentric. Full of strange ideas. A philosopher as much as anything, a wandering mind, and it could put people off. There are those lab-rat scientists who delve into one field and keep going until they disappear under a pile of theories and theses only of interest to their immediate colleagues. Harry wasn't one of those, and his approach to study would raise the ire of other academics he worked alongside.'

He poured the coffee and stirred a large spoonful of sugar into his mug.

'He wrote over fifty – albeit mostly unpublished – papers. They didn't note this in that court, did they? Harry was awarded accolades from such distinguished groups as the UK's Sealore Investigation Society, France's Guilde Des Anguilles Et Poissons, and the Basque shellfish trade association, Bibalboak Bildumagileak Gizartea. They made my Harry the first non-Basque associate member in their eight-hundred-year history, though that was, sadly, a week after he died. Probably wouldn't have done it if he was still breathing. His unconventional ideas no doubt seem a lot less threatening now he's gone than when he was with us.'

Frank paused and looked at me. I felt he was again weighing me up, working me out – and then he said it: 'He wanted to talk to the octopus.'

I hadn't written anything down yet, wanted to put my subject at ease before I started asking questions and noting answers, but he seemed keen to speak, and I could see that some of this would make nice lines if I did write an obituary. I took my notebook from my bag and opened it up.

Talk to the octopus, I thought. Eccentric to say the least.

'Let me get this down,' I said. 'Let's start from the beginning.'

'Go ahead. And tell me if I'm speaking too fast,' replied Frank.

I flipped open a blank page, and began scribbling.

'I'll tell you about Harry, and I'll also tell you that something doesn't quite fit regarding his death,' Frank said. The words brought a shadow of grief across his face. 'Accidental? Perhaps. But there is a reason why this accident happened, and I think I know what it is. I think he was on the cusp of a rather wonderful discovery, and I believe his death means he has become at most a minor footnote in academic circles in a particularly specialist area, when he could have been the greatest marine scientist of recent generations.'

This rang alarm bells of the 'my-cat's-the-Messiah' variety. Had I just doorstepped someone who would now take up a valuable afternoon of my life with a ridiculous story about his boyfriend, a hero who was going to change the world?

'Interesting,' I replied, as politely as I could. 'How come?'

'I'll come to that in a moment,' he said.

Frank stared at me again and studied my face. He must have noticed the quizzical look I was wearing, as he continued: 'I understand your time is valuable, and I promise I'm not about to sit here and waste it. Simply put, Harry had these ideas. He liked the fact they weren't, well, mainstream. If you really want to cover his life and death, you'll have to hear about his work. He was, you see, interested in communication between animals. Between species. Ground-breaking stuff. Imagine being able to talk to a creature from a different biological branch. Imagine discovering how to truly read another animal and then discovering that their intelligence, while tangibly different in outlook to our own, is advanced enough for us to find a workable bridge over the chasm? Where his theories on language and the octopus are known, his findings are disputed by his peers. I suspect the results of his great scientific work, which he so nearly completed before his death, would have provoked disdain in the common rooms and lecture theatres of esteemed scientific establishments from Plymouth to Waikiki. But I am sure he was on to something.

'It went like this: Harry thought he had discovered a mixture of movements, colour changes and chemical exhalations by the creatures that were a form of communication. He suggested this code could be deciphered and then mimicked, meaning humans could "talk" to them. He built himself a machine that he called an Octo-Com to use to copy the creatures and converse with them.

'He went on and on about how intelligent they were, and from careful study we could tap into such intelligence. Frankly, most of his peers weren't terribly interested, and despite his firm belief it could be proven, he never got the funding required to test his theories.'

I'd once read a line in a preface to a book that would spring to mind when writing up an obituary: 'A biographer works in an unweeded garden.' I wondered what plot was hidden among the remains of Dr Zipp's life. As a layman with no knowledge of marine biology, my interest was piqued because Dr Zipp's body was found washed up in a strange position on a rocky outcrop and in a distressing state. There was the evidence that his cadaver had been badly maltreated either before or after his passing. The coroner had barely touched on his career, only briefly mentioning that the dead man was a scientist. Both facts gave me a top line.

With this in mind, I didn't dismiss Frank. I settled back in the sagging armchair and waited for him to continue.

*

'I first came across the name Dr HJ Zipp as an undergraduate at Plymouth Polytechnic. I was studying oceanography and life sciences, and he had finished his degree and was doing his PhD research with some teaching,' said Frank.

He had a measured, careful way of speaking and it helped me get everything he was saying down.

'In the weeks running up to his death I'd not heard from him much. But this wasn't unusual. He'd often be away on field trips, aboard boats, in the windswept parts of the coast where sending niceties back home was not a priority. It is one of the things that make this all such a shock – I didn't get to say goodbye properly.'

His voice tailed away, and he shuddered.

'Tell me about the early days, when you first met,' I asked, trying to prompt happier memories.

He continued. 'Now that would have been his opening lecture in mid-September of the autumn term. It was 1962. The course was called "On Octopuses".

'When undergrads signed up for his tutorials, they would come armed with plenty of enthusiasm but no real primary knowledge of the subject he was going to teach. As they arrived to hear his lectures, there were many popular misconceptions, half-truths and myths which would raise themselves up in the questions asked. I was no different. His lectures were lively affairs, and he was accompanied by a prop – a tank with an octopus in it. Each year, one undergraduate would raise a hand and waggishly inquire: "What is its name?" to which Harry would reply: "He doesn't have a name, he is an octopus. They are not in the habit, if they have names, of sharing them with us... yet."

'This octopus would perform a feat the students loved. It unscrewed the lid from a jar which contained shrimp and then delicately picked at them, as if it were a bearded professor holding court in front of a crowd of adoring undergraduates at a freshers' week cocktail party. Its precise actions always caused amusement. Harry pointed out that it showed dexterity and problem-solving.

'He would continue with a joke about how, if you see four octopi in one rock pool and another three in the next, how many are there in total? The answer being, of course, none, because octopi do not exist: octopus is singular, and octopuses is plural.

'"There is a mistaken belief that the name comes from Latin, but it doesn't," he would say. "It is Greek. Therefore it is octopuses or, if you prefer, octopodes." Then he would scuttle on to dismantle other popular misconceptions held about the creatures he had become fascinated by.

'"Can anybody here tell me how many tentacles octopuses have?" he'd ask. A barrage of arms would be flung in the air.

'"Eight," a student would offer. I can see it now... the eager undergrads, ready to answer a simple question and impress their new tutor. Harry would carefully take his glasses out of his pocket and put them on, run his hands through his unkempt hair, turn backwards, then forward, and take a few strides across the lecture podium, and then walk up, lean forward, hands clasped behind his back and peer carefully into the tank in front of him.

'"Let us see," he would say and make a show of staring carefully at the creature in front of him. A pencil would appear from a top pocket of the jacket of his grubby suit, and he would tap on the glass gently, attracting the attention of his captive. The pencil would tap again, and again, as if he were counting the limbs of the creature held inside. Then, swiftly, he would spin round to face his audience.

'"None," he would announce. "None at all. I cannot see any tentacles." And then he would glance back to the tank, as if seeking the octopus's agreement in his findings and its permission to continue, before once more facing the lecture hall. A deep breath would be taken and then a furrowed look would be cast at the confused faces in front of him.

'"Octopuses do not have tentacles," he would tell the hall sternly. "They do, however, have arms, and as I am sure we all know, they have eight of them. It is vitally important in marine biology that you get used to using the right terminology. Eight arms. Very handy..." This remark would solicit embarrassed chuckles, as if his students were unsure whether they were expected to laugh at the awful pun.

'"Each has a remarkable ability to work independently of the arm next to it," he would continue. "They are linked by a central nervous system, and what makes this creature exceptional is the incredible dexterity each limb shows on its own and the brain's ability to manipulate these limbs completely separately from the others. It is the equivalent of your right hand playing Schubert on the piano while your left hand creates origami swans."

'He would pause once more for dramatic effect as his class scribbled this down, gathering the first amazing fact of many amazing facts about the creature Harry had fallen in love with.

'Now he had warmed them up, he would increase the pace of fantastic information he had at his disposal. "Did you know," he'd say, "it has been proven that octopuses have dreams? Nerve sensor tests have shown us this, and they have the same type of rapid eye movement while asleep as humans do" – and as he imparted such nuggets he would increase the speed of his walking to and fro, talking without notes, occasionally looking up to the back of the hall to ensure those who had arrived late were getting his attention.'

Frank noticed I'd stopped making notes. While this was good

background stuff, I wasn't writing an essay on the octopus. He asked if I wanted to see some of Harry's work.

'He kept an octopus, one he was quite attached to,' said Frank. 'All of his lecture notes are here, and there is also his prototype of the Octo-Com. He used to delight in showing me how he was "speaking" to his pet, though I was still to be convinced. I'm happy to show you it. I suspect we may find clues here as to why his body was found where it was and what he was doing in such a spot. But let's begin here – you are welcome to look through his bureau, if you'd like. It wasn't his writing desk, that's in the study. He used it to store things... It would be a good place to start.'

The bureau had a flip-top lid and was packed with small drawers and compartments. Its insides were as messy as the rest of the flat. When I opened it, a mass of papers slipped forward. I took an armful to the small kitchen table and began to sort through them.

I found a birth certificate made out by the clerk at St Pancras Town Hall. It stated that Horatio Josiah Zipp was born in 1935 to parents Bernard and Josephine Zipp. Bernard's profession was listed as 'fishmonger', marked neatly in the box under the title 'Father's Occupation'. Josephine was a 'fish curer', someone who prepared fish in a smokehouse.

'I knew that,' said Frank. 'Harry would often talk about his parents and the fish shop they ran.'

The yellowing document bore the seal of the registrar, and the scrawled signature of Bernie Zipp was typically Edwardian – loops and curls, done with a flurry and a sense of pride.

'Harry spoke about his dad – they were close,' said Frank. 'He told me Bernie left school aged fourteen and went straight into the fish trade. It was a family thing. His father – Harry's granddad, Shimon Zipperman – sold smoked salmon, pickled herrings and salted cod.'

Frank got up and went to a corner cupboard.

'Harry showed me these once,' he said and opened the door. It was stacked with large ledgers. 'His dad kept an up-to-date register for his business, and I suspect this drilled into Harry an early understanding of note-taking and its importance and of the joys of methodical work. Harry also had a thing about writing everything down, though filing wasn't a priority, as you can see by the state of this place.'

I took a ledger from the cupboard. The Zipp family fish books were filled out at the beginning and end of each day. One column noted the type of fish bought from the wholesalers, the quantity and cost, and then, perhaps most tellingly for Harry's later profession, sizes and some general comments on its state. As they shut the door and flipped the sign to 'Closed', sales would be totted up, and it enabled Bernie to keep a close hand on the tiller of his fish business as he steered it through the rocky days of the 1930s, the war and then the immediate post-war period.

There was another entry that appeared regularly. 'For Harry', it would say, and then there would be the Latin name for some strange, or hideous, or simply inedible fish that Bernie had brought home for his son to marvel at.

As the ledgers revealed, the shop gave Harry a tantalising glimpse of another world. His father would gather specimens he had found at the market. They rarely sold. Regardless of the price, the fish would sit glassy eyed on a slab during the day. His customers wanted familiarity. They did not want the hairy noses of the dog fish on their plates, or to confront the wonky stare of the megrim, nor to cook the monkfish, with its huge head and horrible jaws.

They wanted cod, haddock, skate, salmon, trout and crab. But Bernie knew how his son would react to unwrapping a damp paper parcel that contained a bottom feeder, a shark or octopus… and as he got older it became a weekly challenge for his father to procure something that would make his son's eyes light up with curiosity and his wife recoil at the bizarre carcass lying on display on the shop's marble-topped display cases. The Billingsgate traders got to know this trait. A few choice scrags, the ugly outcasts left at the bottom of the nets, would find themselves heading for Zipp's Fishmongers instead of the cat-food cannery. Harry clearly had the sea by proxy in his nostrils from the hundreds of boats that still moored up and unloaded their cargoes on the Thames.

'Harry told me that being a fishmonger's boy had the knock-on effect of providing his family with a healthier diet than the bread and margarine so many of his peers lived on,' said Frank as we looked over the files in front of us. 'Refrigeration being what it was back then, they ate plenty of fish that would not last, and it would have given the Zipps an enviable diet for a working-class family during those lean years.

'Zipperman seems to have become Zipp at some point during the First World War to avoid the rampant xenophobia which such a German-sounding name would have attracted,' Frank continued, digging out a rent book dating from the mid-1920s. 'Harry told me his dad had first worked at his grandfather's fishmonger and fish-curing shop as a child and then taken on the business after the war. They moved from the East End to Chapel Market, Islington, when a branch of the Harry Samuel Fishmonger chain was put up for sale.'

A legend on a receipt book saying 'Zipp's Fisheries, formerly Samuel's of Billingsgate' confirmed that Bernie found himself in the position to take on the lease of the small, white-tiled store on the corner of Liverpool Road and Chapel Street, with rooms upstairs. It was here Bernie and Josephine brought their son home from the labour ward of the Royal Free Hospital in Gray's Inn Road in September 1935.

Among the piles of papers in the bureau, we found a school report, and with Frank able to fill in the gaps, a picture of his childhood emerged.

Like his father, Harry left school when he was fourteen. His education was affected by the war, which broke out when he was four.

By then he was known as Harry, as we gleaned from a postcard he had sent to his parents when he was evacuated in September 1939. His school went to Devon, where he and his peers were placed in The Dartmoor Home For The Destitute Children Of Almighty God. Perched on a clifftop overlooking a bend on the River Exe, it was run by husband and wife Thomas and Jeanette Keith, Baptists who, Harry had told Frank, believed they were doing the Lord's work by taking in unfortunate children and whipping them (literally) into God-fearing Christians.

It sounded a cruel regime for homesick youngsters to be foisted into. Isolated, cold, rambling, the Keith house was a dark Victorian pile where food was scarce and love even more so.

'Harry told me that he found solace away from the mean corridors of the Keith's bitter regime by wandering along the estuary of the Exe,' said Frank. 'He soon became a dab hand at fishing, copying the anglers he would see on the riverbank trying to augment their meagre rations.'

Harry was known among the other evacuees for his agility in scampering across the tidal rock pools, skipping from slime-covered outcrop to slime-covered outcrop, knocking mussels, whelks and other edible bivalves from their perches and thus staving off the hunger that the Keiths imposed upon the young bellies they were supposed to be filling. However, his time on the banks of the Exe came to a halt when his mother and father, missing their only offspring and vaguely aware of the vicious Christian upbringing their son was being subjected to, came to collect him in the spring of 1942. He had been away for the best part of three years, and London must have seemed like a strange place for the ruralised youngster as he stepped off the train at Paddington. But his return to the Chapel Street fishmonger's would have an important role to play in his educational development: schooling during the war years was at best patchy but added to in other ways.

His father had not been called up. It must have had something to do with his terrible eyesight – the few pictures of Bernie we found in the bureau show a heavy-set, wiry-haired man whose face is dominated by thick-lensed glasses.

It meant the business was to survive the war years, and Harry worked at his father's side after school and on the weekends. He would, through the gutting of fish, learn rudimentary biology. No doubt the lack of manpower made Harry indispensable – the young men who would have been at Bernie Zipp's side learning the trade in peacetime had been taken away by the demands of the war economy.

Harry liked serving. He liked showing off his knowledge of the fish he had to sell, telling customers where they had come from. He enjoyed skilfully cleaning the purchased fish in front of them, taking pride in the fact that his father trusted him to handle knives.

Harry's childhood, although based around an axis of school and work, also included the usual pursuits of a boy growing up in London. He was keen on football and fishing, playing on the bomb sites and riding a bike with a large wicker basket on the handlebars that they used for deliveries. He would spend weekends, when his father would let him have time off, with a rod dangling bait into the ponds on Hampstead Heath, the Regent's Canal or the tributaries in the Lea Valley.

Frank told me of a conversation he'd had with a childhood friend called Barry Silk, who he met at the funeral, and flicking through Harry's phone book we found Silk's number. I gave him a call and told him I was writing about Harry's life and wondered if he could spare a minute to talk about his childhood. He told me the following story…

'We must have been around twelve years old. I had gone to Zippy's shop, and he told me he was going out for the day and would I like to come, too,' Barry began. 'I took the parcel of whiting I had been sent out for back to my mum. We lived round the corner, and I asked her if it was okay. I remember my mum writing "5.30" on my hand, to make sure I was home in time for my fish tea, which we always had on Saturday. My dad would be back from the football at six, and the dinner would be ready, so I had to be there, hands washed, or the chips would be cold and soggy and the batter on the fish would have gone from crisp to greasy and peeling off the whiting in clumps – something I hated – and so I told Harry I'd come if he could promise me we'd get back in time for my tea. He said something about how he'd borrow his dad's watch so we would know what the time was.

'Looking back, I wonder why I believed his dad would lend him his watch, but it shows the faith I had in him. I remember when we were that age I looked up to Zippy – I believed just about everything he told me.

'We checked our tackle boxes for floats, line and weights in his back yard before we left. I was always impatient to go as quickly as possible, but Zippy was diligent – he hated the thought of getting to the Heath or the canal or wherever it was we were heading and finding he didn't have everything he needed.

'Zippy would get a tin of scraps from his father for bait. I remember recoiling from the fish heads Zippy scooped up. He had no qualms about getting his hands covered in filthy slime, and he'd put the mess into my jar for me. I hated the way they stared at you, those severed heads, and was torn between a feeling of both admiration and disgust for the way Zippy calmly took them from his father's hand, put them in our bait tins and jars, and then wiped his hands down the seat of his shorts. Horrible.

'We caught the number 53 trolley bus up to Parliament Hill Fields and walked with our rods and tackle into the Heath. Zippy was a great one for adventuring, and days out with him were full of fun and laughs and mischief. He thought he was Huckleberry Finn and pretended the banks of the Highgate ponds were the banks of the Mississippi. I hadn't read the book, and I thought he was a genius when he told me tales of Indian Joe and Jim the runaway slave and coasting downstream on rafts... I didn't realise the stories he was telling, as we sat by the ponds with our rods sticking out ahead of us above a silent stretch of water, were actually Mark Twain's. He'd memorised them, pretty much word for word. I didn't realise for years they hadn't sprung from Harry's imagination. It made his company so enjoyable.

'We found a spot on the banks of the Men's Pond, cast off and waited and waited. All the time we sat there, hoping for a bite, Zippy kept up this stream of stories... tall stories, fishermen's stories... stories of the giant pike that lived among the weeds and reeds, a pike that would come out from its murky lair and attack the swimmers and liked to bite their feet. Zippy told me of a champion diver who trained at the pond and had just three toes left. The pike had got the rest... And he told me these elaborate stories in such a matter-of-fact way, always backed up with the statement that he had heard it from his father, so it must be true.'

As I wrote down what Barry was saying, Frank had disappeared into the kitchen and prepared a fresh pot of coffee and made a plate of cheese sandwiches.

'He could make up fantastic tales, but he had this way about him that made them sound as if they were utterly kosher,' Barry continued. 'He once told me about a fisherman at the Hampstead ponds who caught a seal. He must have told me it to keep me interested in watching the float on a particularly slow day for bites.

'The story went like this. There was once a down-and-out who'd spend hours on the banks. He was a poor fisherman and caught nothing, but because he had little else to do he persevered. He would spend his days sitting for hours on a rod that never twitched – waiting, waiting, waiting – until one day he saw some air bubbles surface, and it shook him out of his stupor. It was a cold, damp morning, a time of day where the tall grasses around the edge of the pond had caught the early-morning mist and made it linger.

'He watched the bubbles, and his first thoughts were that they must be some kind of marsh gas. Then, to his surprise, his rod was yanked from its tripod and went scuttling down the bank... He leapt at it, and caught it before it was dragged in... and gave it a tug... and at the end of his line, a bemused and hairy face popped up. It was a freshwater seal.

'So how did it get in to the ponds?

'The fisherman knew – and Zippy also knew – that there was not the fish in the pond to sustain a colony, no matter how small, of such beasts. The idea of a family of seals living there was simply impossible. So where did it come from? Why was it sitting there with a baited hook causing a little irritation on the inside of its cheek? There was only one explanation, and of course Zippy had it all worked out.

'The seal, according to my friend, had come up through culverts that led from the ponds down to outlets dotted along the Victorian-built embankments in Westminster. "Times were tough", said Harry, "for the seals of the Thames Estuary." He explained how the pollution had made them hard-headed and pernickety, the mercury and other heavy metals in the water affecting their behaviour, making them at best grumpy and occasionally loathsome in their habits. One day, a school of equally demented Thames salmon had been teasing the creature, flashing their silvery bellies at him in a display of synchronised swimming, offering themselves up like matadors and then stepping aside as the bull seal came in for the kill. The seal had to avenge their cheek, show the fish who was boss. So, when they tired of their game and headed up a drain that dropped underwater currents into the Thames, the seal swam after them and kept going until it came out into the River Fleet.

'The Fleet, now covered, runs underground through central London, a deep and forgotten river, covered because it had been used as an open sewer, but now running clean and clear and strong again. The seal was able to traverse its tributaries, an underground watery maze, until it came out at its source – the Vale Of Health pond on Hampstead Heath, where it met the tramp fisherman that morning.'

It sounded like the type of folklore that Harry would later become fascinated by, I thought.

'Zippy told me the seal had stayed and made the Heath its home, and if we were patient enough we might well catch a glimpse of the old creature living out its retirement, feeding on ducklings and tiddlers and the bread thrown in for the coots and Canada geese,' said Barry. 'I often wondered, as I saw little arcs of bubbles rise to the surface as we whiled away the hours, whether the old bull seal was about to raise its nostrils, express a snort of derision in the general direction of the non-believers in such tales, before slipping beneath the surface again, content to have propagated its own legend once more with a rare and valued sighting.'

I thanked Barry, hung up, tucked into a fresh cup of coffee and helped myself to the plate of cheese sandwiches Frank had laid in front of me. When I recalled to Frank what Barry had said he smiled: 'That was Harry through and through. He told me plenty of stories like that.'

Frank recounted a walking holiday in Scotland, the year after he graduated. Their itinerary included a fishing trip on the banks of Loch Morar, which is the deepest lake in the British Isles. It reaches over a thousand feet in depth, and Harry and Frank spent their days musing at what creatures could survive so far down and trying to catch examples.

'Harry used long lines and heavy weights,' said Frank. 'He wanted to catch the bottom feeders, the specimens inhabiting a completely dark world, living under immense pressure. "Contacting the aliens," he called it.'

They heard Celtic myths in the local hostelries of the fantastic creatures that lay beneath the calm surface, tales that greatly impressed Harry, although less so Frank, who believed them to be 'Little more than folk stories that were over-egged to attract tourists to this remote area. Low-rent copies of the legend of Loch Ness. But, as you can imagine, like the bull seal on the Heath, such stories were right up Harry's street.

'We heard of the Naddred, a Celtic word meaning "serpent", given to an animal living in Morar, whose appearance forebode something terrible happening. It would be seen when clan members of the hill people that lived beside the loch were about to suffer a mortality... and then we heard the tale of two fisherman who came into contact with this Naddred, around twenty years before we holidayed there.

'Their boat had been rammed at dusk by a serpent-like creature, a monster forty feet in length. Locals told us of the mysterious disappearance of these fishermen, who knew the loch well and were therefore unlikely to be drowned through inexperience. And they also spoke of how sheep were frequently swept from the hills during winter storms into the steep-sided water, which, mused Harry, would provide another rich source of food to supplement a diet of fish for anything that lurked in its depths.

'And as for the monster, Harry pondered on what he was told, and without dismissing completely the idea that it was a drunken cock-and-bull tale told to pass the time, he concluded the Naddred could be an eel of some kind. His reasoning was that the eels that live in Scottish lochs return to the rivers where they came from to spawn, following ancestral paths, and then die after breeding.

'But occasionally a mutation will occur – especially when the lochs are near to farmlands, where fertilisers are washed into the water, as is the case here. The eel becomes sterile. This robs them of the ability, or need, to travel upstream. They stay where they are and grow to enormous sizes and grand old ages.

'Could this be the case? Perhaps not, but that was the thing with Harry. He didn't know, but he did not dismiss the possibility. He came up with a perfectly reasonable, scientific explanation for a well-known myth.'

*

Sifting through another pile of papers, we found a degree certificate stating that Horatio Josiah Zipp had completed an MSc in Marine Biology at the Plymouth Institute Of Maritime Studies And Oceanography. He was an able student. We found a series of end-of-term reports from his tutors stuffed into envelopes in a drawer. They spoke of a questioning mind and an overpowering will to work at what Frank called 'the coal face of scientific classification'. This meant he believed his discipline was best investigated away from the classroom and pursued in the field. His many saltwater-splashed notebooks, stacked along the higher bookshelves in the hallway of his cramped flat, testified to this thirst for first-hand knowledge, gleaned from the natural world and often written in situ.

Judging by the lecture notes we found, he had developed broad interests while a student. There was a dissertation on the peculiarities of animals who thrived around hydro-thermal vents and other chemosynthetic-fuelled eco systems.

This led Frank to tell me about a field trip they had done together that would change the course of Harry's work.

'In the second year of his PhD, Harry was drafted in as a volunteer to help monitor the environmental impact of the disastrous Helm Gorge tanker oil spill,' he recalled.

The Helm Gorge disaster devastated much of the Cornish coast. Whitehall's Marine Management Department used vast amounts of oil dispersants on the slicks. Frank told me Harry thought this was probably more toxic than the oil itself, a belief that was later proved correct, with the dispersants affecting the coasts for fifteen years after the disaster, and the oil itself leaving virtually no trace after three.

According to Frank, this gave Harry the opportunity to look first hand at what effect toxins had on grazers such as limpets. It led to him contributing a chapter to a book on British barnacles and was a formative moment in Harry's career.

Later, I did some research in the newspaper archives at the British Library, and there were many column inches on the Helm Gorge disaster. On a microfiche machine I read the ship was a giant. Built in the United States in 1960, it was designed to carry 60,000 tons of crude oil but was later enlarged to carry double that and was for a time the world's largest supertanker. The sheer scale of the ship is hard to comprehend unless you have stood beneath one of these towering leviathans. They are extremely impressive in terms of riveted steel hulls – however, the usual measure of how many St Paul's Cathedrals you could fit inside the Helm Gorge (ten), or the number of football pitches that would lie end to end (twenty-nine), still fails to portray exactly how incredible these machines are. The fact they move, controlled by a small crew, is not just a testimony to the skill of the designers, engineers and mechanics but to the will of the oil industry. They want to be able to shift their product as far as they can, in as a big a bulk as possible, for as little cost as they can get away with, and this means grand, grand economies of scale, which in turn produces ships like the Helm Gorge.

It also means they are extremely unwieldy. The Gorge's single engine and propeller produced a cruising speed of fifteen knots, and even at such a slow rate it would take a good five nautical miles to stop and around six hundred yards to turn just twenty degrees in either direction. In other words, it was virtually unsteerable.

Its last voyage started in Kuwait, where it was filled to capacity, its hull sloshing about with 120,000 tons of Saudi Arabian crude oil destined for the garage forecourts of Britain. It was heading for the massive oil refinery at Milford Haven in Wales when it tried to make its way through a narrow channel in the Scilly Isles.

The Gorge hit a reef as it attempted to catch a tide into the

Pembrokeshire harbour. The rocks ripped through the galvanised steel hull, biting a chunk out of it, and the sea did the rest. The ship floundered and quickly broke in two as the pressure from the invading water became too much.

Its cargo escaped and spread along the shores of southern England and northern France. A panicking Department Of The Environment had no plans in place to deal with such a catastrophe and decided to call in the Fleet Air Arm to blast the ship into oblivion, using incendiary bombs to set fire to its cargo and burn off the crude oil.

It was a disaster. High tides put out the fire, 75 per cent of the bombs missed and the slick was unaffected, even by the many tons of dispersants and napalm sprayed from the air. For Harry, standing on a Cornish cliff, watching a pall of smoke rise from the wreck, it was a gut-wrenching, hand-wringing, heartbreaking moment, and one that affected him deeply.

'He travelled to the Cornish coast the day after the wreck was reported, and as the first signs became apparent of just how bad the sinking would be,' said Frank. 'Seabirds were already being found coated in the fuel, and we joined volunteers hosing down beaches as a glutinous tarry mess was carried on to the coastline.'

It was while they worked as volunteers that they met a Cornish lobster fisherman and shore-gatherer called Will Rivers. Rivers was known in the county for his distinct home on a cliff near the village of Porthcothan. It had become a museum to flotsam and jetsam, items he had collected from the beaches of Cornwall over the years. Known locally as a wrecker rather than a beachcomber, he had saved everything he had found, spending his days wandering across the shoreline and gathering what the tides left behind. His home had become a shrine to this daily meander, a testimony to the power of the sea. 'We were enchanted by the array of buoys, ropes, driftwood... shaped like carefully turned and chiselled works of art, all stuck on the front of the house,' recalled Frank. 'His vast collection of oddments in the front garden was something else. I thought it a bit of tatty mess, but, of course, Harry loved it.'

When the details of how the government planned to deal with

the emergency emerged, there was uproar, and it was led in the North Cornish region by Rivers. At a hastily convened public meeting, on the quayside of the Porthcothan harbour, he spoke at length and berated the notion that pouring a chemical dispersant from the air – whose toxicity was such that the crews using it would be clad head-to-foot in rubber suits and wearing face masks, and have to be thoroughly hosed down afterwards – was a good idea.

It seemed crazy, Frank said. 'You should remember, too, that the places the oil landed are those that are most exposed, and therefore, by their nature, more likely to clean themselves quicker without outside interference.

'I remember Harry listening with interest and reporting back to his colleagues at the Institute in Plymouth, who, after some debate, which took place while the dispersant was being liberally applied over a thousand square miles of fishing grounds, agreed with Rivers.'

Will Rivers's hobby, which had turned into an obsession, made him more than aware of the power of the ocean to act as a cleanser. He showed Harry his collection of seeds that he had picked up on a beach close to his home. They were diverse: Australian pine cones, monkey pods from East Africa, Java seeds from the Caribbean, Madagascan macadamias, tamarind from Asia, silky oak acorns from the North American seaboard, the Middle Eastern inkberry. The list was huge.

'He told us how, when a southwesterly gale blows, he scooped up artefacts from across the globe, took them home, catalogued his finds, and then put it all on display. Of course, a lot of it is incredibly depressing. Syringes, condoms, plastic crates, petrol cans and oil bottles, a huge number of flip-flops and shoes and the odd plastic duck from a container that held fifty thousand of them and was washed off a ship, doomed, like The Flying Dutchman, to travel the oceans till eternity.

'Did you know conservative estimates say around sixty million manmade items are washed into the sea every single day? When you look at it like that, the global environmental impact is nothing short of astonishing, and Rivers showed this through his collection.

'Harry took the advice of Rivers and recommended to his superiors they construct booms where possible across the most exposed beaches to protect the shoreline, concentrate their efforts on cleaning up the seabirds coated in oil, and hose down the coast with nothing more than high-pressure water jets. His advice fell on deaf ears but was eventually seen as sound. It was not forgotten, and his stock rose among his peers.'

And the Helm Gorge disaster was the first time Harry heard about Will's father John, a Cornish fisherman who became a commando for the Special Boat Service in the Second World War. Will thought Harry would be interested in what his dad had got up to and gave Harry a memoir he had written.

It would change Harry's life.

'It's probably in his study,' said Frank. 'Go and have a poke about and see if you can find it.'

As another pot of coffee steamed on the hob, I took my jacket off, laid it over the back of a chair and went into Harry's work-room. Like the rest of the house, all four walls were covered in shelves, books, equipment and art.

It felt like a grotto. Along one side, bookshelves loaded with box-files contained his own studies. Their spines had the titles of the notes, papers and essays they contained, and revealed further the area in which he was particularly interested, namely animal communication: 'Badgers: Scent Trails And Mating'... 'Compound Chemicals In Cephalopod Blood'... 'Slimy Motorways: Why Slugs Don't Get Lost'... 'Hot Springs: Kickstarting Underwater Societies'... 'Geology, Salt And Deep Trench Exploring'... 'Sight And Colour In Shellfish'... 'Touch, Taste And Smell: How Salt Water Affects The Senses'... 'Eels And The Need To Return – How They Use A Road Map To Their Breeding Grounds'... 'Does Yeast "Talk"?"... 'Frequency Variations In A Cow's Moo'... 'Swallows, Swifts And Starlings: Predicting Movement'... 'The Leader Of The Pack: How Dung Texture Can Predict Who Is Boss'... 'What Your Dog's Urine Says'... 'Baa: How A Herd Communicates'.

On another wall there were more paintings, all of watery bent and with their feet firmly placed in the Naïve School tradition. One particular monstrosity was a sketch of what looked vaguely like the Loch Ness Monster causing havoc among a sturdy bunch of Scottish fishermen. I fortunately kept my views on this sorry attempt to myself, as I later noted Frank's initials in a corner. Other images – which were repeated in nooks and crannies about the room – were engravings, oils, watercolours and prints of the kraken, wrapping slimy arms around schooners, frigates and cutters.

A workbench with a number of microscopes lay on the street side of the room. It included a laptop decorated with a surfboard sticker, a huge number of jam jars, a display case with insects pinned on black velvet and two desk lamps. One was an Anglepoise with a powerful bulb inside – I turned it on and was temporarily blinded by the beam – and another which was the absolute opposite, insofar as it hardly gave off any light at all. It had been designed to look like a candle, flickered sentimentally when it was turned on and was decorated with plastic wax set permanently dripping down its shaft. I mused that the first was probably for when Harry was peering down a microscope or preparing a plate to look at, and the other was for contemplating what he had found.

There were a series of photographs in small frames, leaning haphazardly against each other. On was of a woman, clad in a 1920s-flapper dress, with Greek ringlets framing her face. Another showed a couple wearing starched collars and frills, but instead of the usual stiff poses of Victorians having their images captured in a studio, this pair, sitting in their Sunday best with those heavy draped backgrounds liked by portrait photographers, were laughing their heads off. It was as if the effort and absurdity of keeping a stiff upper lip had just become too much at the moment the shutter opened and closed and the flash went puff.

While much of the desk was littered with those things a scientist may need to have close to hand, a lot of space was taken up by some fairly useless objects. There was an arrangement of squeezy stress-relieving balls, whose logos suggested they had been collected from stalls at conferences on marine issues around the world. They looked like a multicoloured rock garden. In the same part of the desk dedicated to pointless freebies, there was an array of pens, emblazoned with logos of shipping firms and hotels. Next to them, a stack of notebooks, again with logos in the corners, waiting for the free-ranging thoughts of Dr Zipp to be scribbled down. There was a ball made up of rubber bands, a jar stuffed with paperclips, bulldog clips and an old set of tobacco boxes full of random-sized wing nuts. A paperweight, in the form of a snow-scene shaker, sat among this conference detritus – but, as I discovered as I picked it up and shook it, instead of snow it contained miniature plastic goldfish which floated about a sunken wreck. A desktop set of shelves held more jam jars, a number with undeveloped 35mm film inside, and then there were film canisters containing different-sized miniature screws. An array of screwdrivers were clipped to a board, including ones with tips so minuscule I could not at first make out if they were Phillips and/or flat-heads. They were joined by Allen keys, a selection of laser pointers, a jar of marbles, tubes of half-used superglue, ink canisters for refillable fountain pens. It was a sea of junk.

On a section of wall that separated two sash windows, toolboxes had been attached with shelf supports. All looked well-used but well-cared-for, with a neatness that defied some of the chaos on the desk below. I opened the lowest box and saw drill bits arranged in order of size. The next box up had the same arrangement with wood chisels. Clamped at the end of the bench were two large grip vices, with a yard-long brass rule tacked beneath them. There was a series of electronic gadgets, whose uses were a mystery to me. They looked like they may be light meters, voltage measurers, thermometers and microphones. I noted soldering irons and an array of circuit boards, motors and batteries, again all neatly arranged.

But the star of the study was the huge tank that ran along the furthest wall, facing the work bench. Standing four feet deep, four feet wide and at least twelve feet long, it wouldn't have looked out of place in London Zoo's Aquarium house. My first thought was what an enormous struggle it must have been to get it up the stairs, in through the front door, down the crowded passage and then manoeuvred into position in the study.

Mounted on a trestle table, it was a miniature, indoor ocean. It not only provided an eye-catching example of Harry's infatuation with his chosen vocation but a soundtrack, too. A water pump worked away in the corner, its motor providing a monotonous hum while the jets of water that broke the surface tinkled pleasingly. It had a wide variety of pet-shop kitsch on its seabed. Castles, sunken ships, a few pirate figures with wooden legs planted atop of open treasure chests. Water plants created a forest of waving fronds, thriving in the conditions created for them. I peered through the glass of the tank, but could see nothing alive inside. It seemed empty of fish and looked like it was simply an underwater landscape of tacky nautical landmarks.

'He's in there,' said Frank, who had entered the study and found me peering into the tank. 'You just can't see him. But at feeding time he appears, and he is a real sight. A proper brute of an octopus: marvellous camouflage, you know. He'll be right in front of your eyes and you won't know it.'

I tried my hardest to find the rogue creature but had no luck.

'Don't ask me where he is. I'll be damned if I can see him,' said Frank, joining me to stare into the tank. While I was never that interested in the octopus, even after meeting Harry, I can understand why he was so fascinated by them. I sat through his lectures, and some of the things he came up with, well, it is all very extraordinary.'

We both kept fruitlessly searching.

'Did you know their bodies are entirely soft, with no internal skeleton, except for one very rare subspecies, which has only ever been observed in the shallows of one of the distant Kiribati islands in the Pacific?

'This lack of solid calcified tissue allows them to perform extraordinary feats of escapology, a Houdini-like ability to wriggle out of small spaces when lying in wait for prey, and into crevices if a moray eel fancies them for lunch.

'They have a beak, a little like a parrot's, and this bony part is the only piece of the octopus that is skeletal. This is one of the reasons they are so damn hard to catch undamaged for further study, and why Harry did a special field trip every year to teach students how to capture an octopus safely without harming it.

'Harry called them the "royalty of the sea". Their blood is blue in colour, and they boast three hearts, but this does not mean they live three times longer than similar creatures. In fact, an octopus can have quite a short life, and many members of the species only reach six months. Some of the really big ones live for around five years, but there have been reports of others living for much, much longer, although this has always been exceptionally hard to verify. Such information comes from what Harry would call the "fisherman's tales school" of scientific classification.'

Frank ran his fingers along a shelf and pulled out a box-file.

'Rather than hear me tell you what Harry knew, why not let him?' he said. 'Here are some of his notes on the octopus. Have a read through these.'

He passed the box to me, and, forgetting the quest to find the octopus in the tank, I turned on the light that looked like a candle and sat back in Harry's chair. For a brief moment I had an eerie sense that the dead scientist was in the room, that our quest to find out more about his life and demise meant he wasn't truly at rest yet.

I pulled out a sheaf of papers held together by a bulldog clip and sat down. The notes were neatly typed, the sort of handouts tutors give to their students, and the title of the paper was 'Notes On Physiology'.

'Octopus mortality, like so many sea creatures, is tied in with reproduction,' I read.

Some females fail to eat for the month or so that they carry and care for their eggs, while males tend to mate and then die soon after the job has been completed, exhausted by their efforts.

Octopuses have many predators, and in response to the fact that many animals hunt them, they have three main means of defence.

They can disappear in a cloud of ink, a trick where they eject a thick black thunder-cloud plume in the path of their pursuers to disrupt potential attacks and allow them to escape, which will, for most octopuses, be by slipping into a handily located lair. They can also shoot a jet of water from a muscular siphon that propels them extremely quickly over short distances, thereby allowing them to sprint to safety. And another defence is the ability to blend into scenery with the ease of a chameleon. This camouflage stems from skin cells that change colour using light-reflecting and refracting tissue – an ingenious trick.

Each cell is like a tiny mirror, able to reflect its surroundings. It means they can sit still and blend into the background. Octopuses use this ability to change their colour for other reasons as well, such as warning off potential predators. The highly poisonous blue-ringed octopus, whose bite is fatal to everything on the planet, will accentuate its blue rings if it senses danger – like a boxer flexing their muscles in the ring as they limber up before a bout. It is a way of saying: 'Look at me, I'm big, bad and definitely dangerous – you'd do better off searching for grub elsewhere.' This colour change is also accompanied by the expulsion of a colourless chemical-liquid mixture, which has varying degrees of toxicity, depending on the size of the threat. The octopus has a series of pouches containing these chemicals.

Tiny ventricles pump these solutions into tubes where they can be expelled into the sea at varying levels: they can have around ninety of these pouches, and so the potential for combinations of compounds is very, very large indeed. The octopus uses different mixes of this emulsion to 'speak' to other octopuses and other sea creatures. It is part of a three-pronged approach: colour changes, chemical expulsions and then a soft, ultra-low-frequency clicking noise made by its beak. It is similar to the sonar used by dolphins and whales. I have both recorded and mimicked these sounds using ultra-sensitive aqua-microphones.

Octopuses have another trick any southpaw would be happy to be blessed with. The octopus, when under attack, will wave one arm tantalisingly to one side, to draw the attack, to create a diversion – and then, wallop! As soon as the predator's concentration goes that way, the octopus will come in from the other side and either smother the creature with its arms or inject its adversary with poison. And if that doesn't work, one of the arms can be lost with no apparent long-term injury to the body and will grow back. It is the same biological process used by many reptiles, such as lizards, when they shed their tails or other limbs.

Subspecies have other tools in their box. The octopus is such an adaptable creature – and clever. A real problem-solver, it is no wonder they adapt well in terms of the rigours of the environment placed in front of them. One such talent is to mimic the most deadly animal in the vicinity. For example, octopuses who live near the highly poisonous, highly aggressive lionfish in the southern oceans will take on the same hue as them, as if to say: 'We're in the same gang, I'd steer clear if I were you.'

And then there is intelligence. How clever is an octopus? Research has shown them to have a capacity for both long- and short-term memory. They can also solve problems and learn through observation. This fact, and their highly developed physiology, has led me to believe they also have a highly developed system of communication, although my research is still at a primary stage.

They like to play. I have observed an octopus throw shells into the circulating current in a tank and then catch them as they return, rather like a cricketer practising at the slip. They can escape from their tanks to find food, and there are credible reports of octopus boarding ships and breaking into holds to find crab – an astounding feat.

The notes were fascinating. I began to understand a little more why Harry saw the creature as the cornerstone of his professional research. After I'd finished a large sheaf, Frank passed me a slim volume.

'Here you go. I've found it. It's the memoir by Rivers that his son gave to Harry,' he said.

'Harry went on and on about it. I've read it, too, but have to admit I found it not only pretty depressing but also full of drivel. Perhaps you should read it, as I think it contains clues about Harry's final days.'

*

John H Rivers had swapped his fishing jersey and waterproofs for commando khaki in 1939, but his war didn't last long. He was taken prisoner by German forces in 1940. Rivers was captured while leading a three-man reconnaissance mission to Guernsey in the early days of the occupation of the Channel Islands but had managed to escape before the authorities had decided which POW camp in Europe they should ship him to.

Rivers's background as a fisherman before he had signed up to the Royal Navy's Special Boat Services prompted the Admiralty to use his detailed knowledge and experience to scout out the islands off the coast of Occupied France. According to his journal, he had volunteered – although he was probably asked to do so and could not refuse – to lead a team to Guernsey to look at the numbers and classes of the boats the invaders had stationed in the bays of the island. Little is known about why the mission went wrong. In his book, Rivers, perhaps not eager to apportion blame (was it his fault, I wondered), skirts over this. They were rumbled by sentries almost as soon as he and his team approached the shore on a reinforced inflatable boat, and then, despite being skilled sailors, saw their vessel dashed against rocks where it quickly took on water and went down.

Rivers was the sole survivor and was taken into custody by a German unit, from which he promptly escaped.

He was hidden by islanders for four years until the occupying forces were finally driven out. Kept out of sight for so long, he must have had plenty of time to ponder. I could see how Rivers's ramblings attracted Harry. He was also a keen, if amateur, marine biologist and had gathered plenty of knowledge through his daily work at sea and on the quayside. His journal included chapters on such diverse topics as a theory – unproven – of the effect the positioning of stars have on starfish reproduction and the conversational ability of limpets and the common mussel. He believed they were able to 'speak' to each other using invisible chemicals that would flow with messages about food and predators from one colony to another.

Rivers and Harry were interested in very similar topics, and meeting his son through the Helm Gorge disaster was a strange twist of fate that threw like-minded souls together.

In his memoir, Rivers describes these theories alongside his wartime adventures, but what was even more interesting for Harry, I presumed, and what I suspected gave him the idea to go to Guernsey, was his reports of octopus that would appear on the island's shoreline. They were like none other found in cold waters. According to Rivers they grew to huge proportions and, as he put it, 'are devilishly clever buggers'.

These octopuses were rarely, but gratefully, caught by the hungry islanders, and, when they were, the carcasses would be devoured immediately – griddled on driftwood fires on the shoreline, they were an important dietary supplement for people who had to support an army of occupation. This, in turn, meant little evidence of their true size survived, except in reports by the likes of Rivers.

As the memoir revealed, Rivers was occasionally taken out to help fish by those who were sheltering him. This was a risky operation, as soldiers watched the boats going out, partly for security and partly because they wanted to monitor and take the catches.

In the memoir, Rivers talks of the cave system on the southwest flank of the island opposite the Hanois reef, which was particularly rich in an octopus known as the Sarnius, and it was here he believed larger specimens – 'so large they could take down a boat into their lairs with ease' – were found. Rivers returned time and again to this theory of octopuses of monstrous proportions with brains to match, and he had written an unsupported testimony, an eyewitness account, of his own encounter with one.

It was a clear night with a high tide and a full moon. Rivers had been taken from his hideout to help on a fishing trip on a small boat owned by a family called De Garis. It was while bringing in crab pots that the crew spotted 'a creature lolling in the shallows, so large that at first we believed it to be, in the half-light of the moon, a substantial rockfall from one of the precipitous cliffs we were sailing under'.

Rivers turned to the captain, Jean De Garis, and begged him to take the boat closer to the shore so as to ascertain the size and nature of the beast. But De Garis, well-versed in local folklore and knowledgeable of the treacherous nature of the shallows on the southwest of the island, refused.

After the war Rivers returned to thank those who had risked their lives to save his. He stayed for some months and would row a small dinghy to the spot again and again, determined to make a thorough investigation of the caves in the area and find the octopus he was sure lay hidden there. It was partly the hunger of the islanders that drove him on, he said. He imagined paying them back for their years of kindness by bringing home an octopus so big it would feed a village for weeks. No islander would join him on an expedition to see if such a beast truly existed. Normally so brave, and coming from a people who had sailed to the cod banks of Newfoundland across the great Atlantic for centuries in tiny fishing boats, they felt scared enough of the legends to refuse to sail to a stretch of water just off their own coast. It was a fact that made Rivers even more eager to confirm the creature's existence, and, in turn, I surmised, made Harry wish to see the area for himself.

Harry's curiosity was undoubtedly fired by Rivers's writings. Sadly, as his son Will had told Harry, Rivers died a few years after gaining his freedom from a bronchial infection whose symptoms sound very much like a form of tuberculosis, probably aggravated by the months of malnourishment, living a life in hiding, sleeping in damp cellars and exposed barns as he tried to stay one step ahead of the occupying forces.

I wondered how much store I could place on his account.

Perhaps there was something to it. After all, time and again through history there have been mentions of great octopuses living in cold water. Fearsome, clever, deadly – from Victor Hugo's *Toilers Of The Sea*, set in the same archipelago, through to earlier works such as Hubert Laurent De Chavelier's *Book Of Monsters*, published in 1675, which describes cave-dwelling beasts who could survive on land and would sneak into fields in the middle of the night to take livestock. Perhaps this was an excuse given to magistrates for cattle rustling or failing to declare newborn calves.

But maybe it wasn't. The legend of the kraken also comes from this field of work – the terrible, vindictive, always-hungry monster who was under the command of that salty rogue Davy Jones. Perhaps the legends had some basis in fact, Rivers mused.

Will Rivers had told Harry that his father suffered a breakdown soon after the liberation of the Channel Islands. He was treated with electro-convulsive therapy in the months before his death at a hospital in Hammersmith. Again, although there is limited information available, apart from the usual service records (I would later discover at the National Records Office in Kew that he had been given an honourable discharge from the navy after his return at the end of the war), it is probable this mental instability was brought on by a post-traumatic stress due to his ordeal. This meant his musings, when made public, lacked credibility.

But Harry had clearly found enough in the account to warrant a search for the octopus mentioned by Rivers, an octopus so big that it would have a humongous brain capacity – and it was this that Harry wanted to find. He, I reckoned, thought this octopus would have a brain of such large proportions it would be super-intelligent with a clearly developed form of communication. If biologists could just find the right way of deciphering its language, it would lead to a true breakthrough in human/animal linguists.

After I had finished reading and told Frank about my feelings that Harry's trip to Guernsey had something to do with verifying Rivers's theory, he asked if I wanted to have look at the Octo-Com. I had put this to the back of my mind in the excitement of finding out so much about this strange man and wondering how I was going to squeeze it all into a quirky biography for the paper.

Frank fished about beneath the desk that held the tank and brought out a large cardboard box. With some difficulty he dragged it into the centre of the room, moving a chair out of the way, and told me to have a look inside.

'It was Harry's great invention,' he said, opening it up, 'and I think it is linked to what you have said about the Sarnius octopus Rivers reckons he saw.'

Inside sat a contraption with a set of eight opaque fibre-optic cables, studded with what reminded me of the suckers you get on the end of toy arrows from a children's bow-and-arrow set. They stemmed out at regular intervals from a large, round, rubber box. It looked like a toy. I gently took it out, and placed it on the desk.

'This is a project Harry spent years toiling over,' Frank said. 'Here, have a closer look. It was his prototype, the first one he made.'

The Octo-Com had a small catch on one side that allowed you to flip open the top, and inside there was a compartment holding a set of small, flat, silver-coloured batteries. There were twelve test-tube-shaped chambers with rubber stoppers, each with small electric pumps attached. They were operated individually by sluice gates and went into a small hose which then led out at the bottom of the box. There was a radio circuit board and eight air-compressed levers that seemed to operate the eight fibre-optic cables coming out of the main body.

It took no time at all to realise this machine was designed to look like an octopus.

The box also contained a remote-control device, the type of thing you use to steer toy cars or boats, and it included an LCD display and a keyboard. It looked like an old-school Casio calculator with a pair of joysticks added.

I laid the Octo-Com on the bench and flicked a switch on the remote control to 'On'. It did a sort of Mexican wave with the fibre-optic arms and was still. I found the action a trifle unnerving, as if I'd caught sight of a giant spider out of the corner of my eye. Then it was flat, with its arms outspread, and they gradually changed colour until they were the same hue as the wooden top. I looked down at the display on the control, and a legend came up: 'Chambers Empty: Refill', it read, and I wondered what this meant.

I looked inside the box again and found, encased in bubblewrap, twelve test tubes. They were full of coloured liquids, and I remembered Harry's theory that the octopus not only uses colour to 'speak' to the other creatures of the deep but also emits chemical concoctions such as the warning ink. Perhaps these mixtures were Harry's laboratory-made compounds, intended to mimic those created naturally by an octopus?

I called Frank over. We switched off the Octo-Com, flipped its body open again and after unwrapping the test tubes noted they fitted perfectly into the chambers inside the machine. Once they had been inserted, I turned it back on, and the screen told me the chambers were now full and that the Octo-Com was ready to be submerged. I looked at Frank, and both of us agreed we should put it into the water and try it out.

'Will it be okay, you know, with the octopus in there?' I asked.

Frank shrugged his shoulders.

'I don't know, but really, what harm can it do? Harry spent hours mucking about with it, so I'm sure it is fine.'

Frank held the lid open and I rolled up my sleeves. I gripped the Octo-Com and gently placed it in a corner of the tank.

'Here goes nothing,' I said.

I flicked the switch back to 'On', and the machine did the Mexican wave again. Then it settled back down and waited for further instructions.

There was still no sign of the real octopus, so I started wriggling the joysticks and attempted to move the machine. It wasn't easy. You had to press a little accelerator button which sucked water in through a mesh-covered hole at the front, and then whooshed it out the other end to propel it forward. You also had eight arms to control, and I could see it would take some practice to make its movements anything other than a jolty, uncoordinated mess. It looked drunk, not like a graceful sea creature at all.

I tried some of the other buttons on the console, and it was then the real octopus made itself known. The machine's arms had begun to change shades, and as I randomly pressed buttons on the keypad, they went through a whole prism of colours. The octopus, whose living quarters we had invaded, appeared from among a particularly thick patch of fronds and tentatively came to have a look. I carried on playing with the colour scheme, and after hitting on a violet shade with a hint of red, the octopus shot forward and grabbed hold of the Octo-Com.

I was lost for words, and the octopus moved so quickly I hadn't time to manoeuvre.

'Will you look at that!' exclaimed Frank. 'I think it is trying to have sex with it.'

I pressed another button and we saw a milky liquid mixture come shooting out from beneath the machine. The octopus stopped dead in its tracks and turned an even more furious deep red. Then, before my clumsy thumbs could move the Octo-Com out of the way, it shot forward and grappled with the robot, seizing it in a frantic grip and twisting it one way and then the other.

'I don't think that was a good move,' said Frank.

I panicked, and wriggled the joystick to force the creature to unhand it, but it was far too supple and quick limbed. Every time I went one way, the octopus simply found a new place to increase the entanglement, and the wrestling match went on.

'Try another combination of the buttons and see what happens,' suggested Frank, peering in through the top of the tank in the hope of getting a better view. 'Don't worry, I'll step in if needs be. Just try and get the machine away and I'll make a grab for it.'

I did as he said, and this time a greenish liquid was ejaculated. The octopus seemed to dislike this even more, but it made it free its grip – and then, to my horror, I watched the liquid seep through the clear water of the tank and engulf the octopus. Harry's pet swayed woozily, and its limbs went utterly limp. It came to rest on the pebbles at the bottom and took on a pallid shade of grey. It stopped moving.

'Oh dear,' said Frank. 'Oh dear. That is unfortunate. I think you may have killed it.'

*

I met Frank again a couple of weeks later. By then I had made some calls regarding the circumstances of Harry's demise.

I'd managed to track down the name of the police sergeant PC Bougourd had mentioned in court, who was on duty in Guernsey when the body was discovered, and had briefly spoken to the harbour-master overseeing its recovery. Both had been helpful and happy to talk. I had the impression they were as intrigued as I was at to what had happened to Harry.

When I called the St Peter Port central police station, the sergeant said there was a box of 'personal effects' in the basement of the station house and he'd be happy to post them on to a next of kin, and if there wasn't such a person he was sorry to say they'd no doubt be eventually thrown out.

I had decided a weekend in Guernsey could be revealing. I told the officer I would come over and collect the box in person. He mumbled something about making sure I had a letter giving me permission from a relative or the executor of Harry's estate, and I wondered what legal status Frank possessed.

Frank said he would pen me something, as Harry's will put him in sole charge of his effects.

He added that he doubted any of his colleagues knew about the hunt for the Sarnius. It was known, of course, that Dr Zipp had travelled to the island to survey the coast and conduct a census on the ormer, a peculiar shellfish that lives there and almost nowhere else. It meant he got some funding, Frank said, which he almost certainly wouldn't have received if he'd told the Institute he was heading there to find and speak with a giant octopus. He wondered if it would damage Harry's posthumous reputation if such a revelation came out, but he urged me to go anyway, as whatever truths were revealed could be dealt with in good time. I admired his stoicism.

I looked up ferry timetables and booked myself on a boat leaving Poole harbour. It took about four hours to cross the Channel, and I spent the time going over what I already knew about Harry, re-reading Rivers's memoir, sifting through my notes from the inquest and the coroner's report.

As the journey came to an end, I stood on the deck and watched the boat slow and turn from the currents of the Channel into the calmer mouth of the harbour of St Peter Port, Guernsey's civic capital. The captain of the ferry let off two long blasts of his horn as the ship docked alongside the granite of the harbour wall. I watched boys fishing from its end, standing by a statue of a man staring out to sea, and then walked to the bow. I would later discover the statue was a tribute to Rivers. I enjoyed the rhythmic way the wash worked around the edge of the boat. I tasted the fresh salt air. I watched seagulls sit on invisible updraughts and hover, beaks into the wind, above the churning deep blues of the sea. The ferry had slowed as it entered the docks, and I could see the statue clearly. The old man looked angry, his face set in a permanent scowl. The wash of the boat crashed in a slow, rolling gait against the sea wall on which the statue and the boys with their rods were perched. It looked like a great spot to while away a few hours. I wondered if Harry had thought the same and walked along the sea wall to see what they were catching. I was charmed – and for a brief moment, the aching horror of Harry's death, which had sat like a raw sore in the back of my mind since that day in court, eased. Guernsey looked benign – harmless. I found it hard to equate the picture-postcard beauty with the grisly events I had come to investigate.

The port was ringed by granite homes – grey, but riddled with flecks of light-catching silver. The crescent of the bay resonated inland like the rings caused by a stone thrown into a millpond. The buildings looked east, with the setting sun dropping behind their roofs, and the sea twinkled as it caught the rays. Rising from the harbour's edge, snaking up the hill, the houses were tall, the sloping land and view encouraging balconies and terraces to jut out like shelves. They huddled together, sat shoulder to shoulder, with every scrap of land on this sea-battered outcrop utilised. A square-towered church sat opposite a quay at the water's edge. It looked a precarious position for such an important building – naked to the elements – and I could see the sea stains on the base of the granite where peculiarly high tides had kissed it. Narrow and uneven streets converged on the church from all angles.

After passing through the customs shed, I asked for directions to the station house and was told it was a short walk through the mazy streets. Signs were written in the local patois, neither English nor French. It felt otherworldly. Guernsey had done its own thing, and it occurred to me, as I climbed some lopsided steps from the quayside that sat between two buildings, that if a human civilisation could grow in such a unique way, why not a colony of sea-cave-dwelling cephalopods?

*

The St Peter Port police station was a grand Victorian building. Neat and trim, made from the same granite as the rest of the town, double-fronted with white sash windows either side of a set of sweeping steps leading up to a dark-blue front door. There were window boxes with geraniums. Above the steps was an iron archway with a blue police lamp. I'd been to many London nicks, and they always had a depressed air about them – entrances with thousands of fag butts everywhere, fading posters with anonymous Crimestoppers numbers, duty-solicitor information, warnings not to attack the receptionists, yellow lino, yellow walls, yellow strip lights – a gangrenous atmosphere of suspicion, repression and bail conditions. In comparison, St Peter Port's police headquarters looked like a well-kept country cottage.

I stepped inside the quiet foyer and asked a uniformed man behind the desk if I could see Sergeant Rogers.

'That's me,' he said, standing up and straightening his tunic. 'You must be the reporter.'

I got the impression he didn't exactly have a whole heap of crime-fighting to be getting on with.

Sergeant Rogers had closely cropped silver hair, a freshly shaven complexion and a neat uniform that suggested he'd not recently had to tussle with drunks on a late-night beat or chased a suspect through undergrowth. As with the approach to the station, it looked ceremonial. He had a warm smile, too, and I got the impression my arrival had been pleasantly anticipated.

He opened the flip-top gate at the front desk and invited me to come into his office. He asked how my trip was, offered me tea, and I got my notebook out. Sergeant Rogers told me how Harry had been found, the trouble it had been to recover his body and then began to wonder aloud why he was where he was in the first place.

'It has been playing on my mind,' he said. 'He'd hired a holiday chalet out on the west coast to stay in, and, when we'd worked out the body was Dr Zipp's, we went round and had a look through his stuff. We found his notebooks, and they were full of the research he'd done on ormers. You know what an ormer is, yes? You know why he was here?'

I muttered that I knew a little about the ormer, and Sergeant Rogers folded his hands together and leant forward.

'Let me tell you – the ormer is important to us here. Dr Zipp's work mattered. The old ormer isn't just any shellfish. It's unique to these waters. Its only close cousin is found off the reefs in Japan. We're very attached to it – proud of it. They are protected. You can only collect them at certain tides during the year, and they have to be over a specified size. I love them, we all do – like our cows and our tomatoes, they are part of life on the island.'

He fished into a desk drawer and pulled out a shell.

'Have a look at that,' he said. 'Used it as an ashtray when you were allowed to have a smoke indoors.'

It was ear-shaped, and, despite having cigarettes stubbed out on its innards, you could see it had a lovely mother-of-pearl interior.

'Not the most attractive of creatures, despite the shell, to be fair, and it takes a bit of prep to get them edible. Tell you what, all this ormer talk makes me hungry. Let's have some for lunch.' He looked at the clock on the wall and stood up. 'There is a place on the harbour that does a great stew. We'll eat there, then we'll come back and I'll get you what we have of Dr Zipp's things. My treat.'

I had a lot of ground to cover that weekend, but felt I could hardly refuse. Sergeant Rogers called to a colleague in another office that he was off out for some grub. He took a coat off a hook on the back of the office door, led me back through the streets of St Peter Port and down to the harbour. He took me into a café – a place he regularly visited, judging by the reception he got – and we sat down. A waitress greeted him by his first name – Peter – and without opening the menu propped up among the saltcellar and sugar bowl he asked for the 'Fruits De Mer Special' for two.

As we waited for the meal to be served, he told me more: he was an ormer connoisseur, and I discovered he relished the chance to explain all to the uninitiated.

'They don't look much when you get them,' he said. 'They are chewy, fleshy. It's an oddly tough texture for a shellfish. You prise them from their shells and then whack them with a steak mallet. Loosen them up a bit. You can dip them in flour and fry them up with onions, and then you stick them into a stew. Or you can prepare a bouillabaisse with potatoes, onions, seasoning and a pint of stout – that also works nicely. The minimum cooking time is four hours, but some people leave them for twenty-four. They cook them overnight here.'

A steaming tureen appeared with a side plate of fresh bread. The waitress popped back to the serving hatch and brought over two glasses of white wine.

The odour coming from under the lid of the pot was thick, fishy and strong. It smelt like someone had scooped up the contents of a rock pool, thrown in some seagrass and kelp, added half a gallon of Guinness and boiled the daylights out of it. Sergeant Rogers breathed the aroma in with a look of deep satisfaction and scooped out a couple of ladlefuls. He poured a dark-brown, thick sauce with lumps of ormer swimming about into my bowl. It looked meaty rather than fishy, but after my first mouthful I was pleasantly surprised by the soft texture and gentle flavours.

'Cooking them is an art,' he said, 'but collecting them is a trial of strength, persistence and greed. They live in the most awkward places to get to – right out in the inter-tidal. You need to wait for certain spring tides before you can gather them. We used to dive for them, which would make life easier, but that's illegal nowadays, so it means you have to be prepared for a long, cold walk and some heavy lifting. They like to hide beneath the biggest rocks they can find.

'They used to be more plentiful, but a bacterial disease washed through them and near wiped the population out seven years ago. That was the purpose of Dr Zipp's study – to see how they had recovered. It meant that when Dr Zipp arrived we were all interested in what he was doing and what he would find. He was interviewed by our newspaper, the *Guernsey Press*, about the survey. I know he spoke at length with fishermen. I can introduce you to some if you'd like. And I believe you've already telephoned Pete LeConte, the harbour-master? He doubles up as the captain of the lifeboat which eventually recovered Dr Zipp's body for us.'

Sergeant Rogers tucked a napkin into his shirt collar and set about his lunch with vigour. In between great, hulking spoonfuls, he carried on telling me what was known about Harry's final days.

'None of us here could understand why he was found where he was,' he said. 'His notebooks show he had been surveying along the west coast, and it just isn't possible he could have been caught by a tide there or washed out to sea somehow – hit by a wave while rock-hopping, perhaps – and then carried to the reef where we eventually found him laid out on the tide line.'

Sergeant Rogers went on to say he had found among Harry's possessions a receipt for a sea kayak and had contacted the harbour-side chandlers and shipwrights that had sold it to him. They said he had asked for a kayak that could hold some equipment, and they'd suggested a two-seater, which would be fairly unwieldy when crewed by just one person, but had storage space.

'We've never found the kayak,' said Sergeant Rogers. 'But I think it is the most likely reason for him being recovered where he was. He must have been out there in the kayak. But why? There are no accessible ormer beds along that stretch.'

After having our fill of the stew, which included mopping up the remains of the sauce with hunks of bread, Sergeant Rogers took me back to the police station. He led me again behind the front desk and then through a series of doors until we reached a flight of narrow stairs at the back of the building. We went into the basement and through a locked door, which he opened with a large bunch of keys.

'Excuse the gloom,' he said. 'There used to be the cells down here. Haven't been used for a while, not even for the Saturday-night drunks. Now we use it for storage. Too small for prisoners nowadays.'

He found a large cardboard box on a set of gun-metal shelves, and with some difficulty we carried it back upstairs. He sat me at a desk in an interview room and said to take as long as I wanted.

'I wasn't sure what we'd do with it all until you showed up,' he added as he left me with Harry's possessions. 'Not much in there of value, but I suppose his loved ones may want it.'

I opened up the box, and inside were the tools of Harry's trade.

His luggage included wrecking bars of various sizes, used for prising large boulders free from the seabed, a rock hammer and three chisels for fossil hunting. There was a wicker basket with elasticised holders to store pint jars with screw caps and a series of different-sized test tubes.

There were also copies of two very well-thumbed books. One was a treatise called *On Octopus – Giants Of The Sea* by a Dr Jack Percy, and Professor Felicity Gladback's *Cranial Development Of Octopus: Is This The Ocean's Thinker?*

And then there was a collection of mechanical and electric odds and ends which reminded me of the innards of the Octo-Com I had seen.

I sifted through it all and came across a set of Harry's notebooks. These were of real interest, as I hoped to find some evidence that would confirm our theory that he had gone to the island not only to count ormers but to find a Sarnius and test his Octo-Com out on a specimen.

The first notebook I opened outlined his work, but there was no mention of the Sarnius. It detailed how he had chosen to start his survey on the west coast of the island, which faced out to the Atlantic and had beaches that were easy to access. The coast was long, snaking down at an angle from northeast to southwest, and it was dotted with hidden coves cut from the land.

'Guernsey is speckled with smaller islets,' he had written.

They curl into each other, forming beaches like crescent moons, with headlands hollowed out by the tides. A long bay is at the heart of the west coast, protected by rocks and reefs that sit out to sea and have claimed boats and lives.

They are only partially hidden when the tide is in and are a rich site for shellfish. There is a buffer between beach and grasslands, where the dunes are held in place with a wide variety of rushes and the tangled, tough stalks of a grass called marram. It has been used here for a variety of products, ranging from kindling to binding for lobster pots and the thatch for roofs.

It is an exposed stretch of coast, and old windmills on the hills stand like giant stopped clocks, their sail-less arms still in the sea breezes.

Under the sea, running along the shelves and cliffs of the Atlantic bed, are the remains of prehistoric woodland from when the island was still joined to the continent, before northern ices melted and cut the land off.

Flicking through the pages, it was obvious that such geological points were important to Harry. He thought of the island's evolutionary process when he was staring into small rock pools, watching crabs and anemones and crayfish. He knew the world that lay beneath the surface of the waves and the geological history of how the fissures and nicks in the land had been created. It provided a term of reference which he held in the back of his mind as he stared at these creatures.

'I have found myself a playground designed for the curious oceanographer,' he wrote.

When the tide is high, the rocky shoreline is a jagged place, with treacherously slippery rocks surrounding wave-churned craters, a chaotic world enveloped by the power of the Atlantic rollers. As the tide slips away, it seems to become quiet, slow and gentle compared to how it had been when waves crashed in, but beneath the glassy still water there lives an equally hectic world of squirming life.

Life here does not pause between high and low tides. It is all about hunting food and reproduction – constant, twin struggles.

The shore crabs – *Carcinus maenas* – scurry from dark overhang to seaweed forests. Tiny anemones advertise their beauty with gentle waves of their arms, asking passing shrimps to rest a while, luring them in before stinging them, inducing a poisonous coma and digesting their prey with their bitter stomach juices.

A spider crab fights another, and one loses an arm in the struggle. An octopus – not a Sarnius, but a curled octopus (*Eledone cirrhosa*), a more common type – takes an interest in the victor and stalks him with cold intent. A starfish (*Asterias rubens*) feels its way across the rock face and selects a limpet (Patellogastropoda) to prise from the wall and feast on.

The rocks and boulders on this beach are heavy enough to provide shelter for a plethora of creatures from the worst ravages of the incessant motion of the tide, but light enough to be rolled over without too much effort. They are speckled with growths, mottled with lichen and algae, and their rumps sit gently on a bed of yellow and auburn grits.

Higher up the beach lie sands... At first glance barren, but then, on closer inspection containing millions of hoppers and worms, their homes given away by the turban-shaped piles left at the mouth of their burrows... These sands lead down to the shore, past granite sea walls which, at high tide, mark the edge of the ocean.

Harry's diary was detailed. It told of days spent laboriously peering into the small pools where animals, caught by the falling tides, patiently waited for the next one to wash in. He was fastidious with the breadth of life he found. Everything he saw, he logged – no matter how common they were to the neighbourhood or how frequently they occurred.

'Miniature crayfish start and stop and start again. Starfish curl their searching arms out, feeling the wet rocks and, sensing my presence, move slowly away,' he wrote.

At the top end of this stretch of beach is a headland where the currents are unpredictable, and the gentle coves give way to open sea.

But rather than this seemingly inhospitable place being devoid of life, the opposite occurs. The strong churning current brings oxygen and plenty of food. What looks dangerous to us is teeming with sea life. The problems facing the creatures who choose to make this ever-swirling torrent their home and the battles they face – finding a secure foothold and the competition for shelter – creates a vicious trait. They all seemed to be just that more tenacious than their cousins in more shaded areas. I recall the Wellsian theory that where there is little danger, there is little stimulation. In HG's *The*

Time Traveller, his protagonist goes far into the future to find a human race turned into weak sloths by the fact they had conquered all there was to conquer. In this watery furnace on the very edge of the Atlantic Ocean, I have seen tiny creatures battle huge odds – oceanic odds – to stay alive, and it means, whether they be anemones, limpets, crabs, starfish or shrimps, they procreate with an admirable lust and eat with a hearty appetite and fight with the stamina of heavyweights for every advantage. Such danger brought with it life. This is a benevolently hostile planet.

Later in his writing Harry marks a significant find. Stripping down to shorts, he lowered himself into one of the huge tidal pools cleaved into the granite cliffs – a pool that he notes is

at least twenty feet deep and perhaps forty feet wide, tapering off into points at the sea and beach ends and regularly replenished with seawater as the tide rises.

The product of this mixture of shelter and regular incursions from the ocean is a variety of starfish, anemones and sea fronds, swaying in the currents and providing shelter for tiny pink crabs. There was also a successful population of the most delicate of decapod crustacean, the broken-back shrimp, which are impossible to snag. They are almost completely see-through. If you stare long enough you can just about make out a pair of gills, seemingly suspended in mid-water, and then you notice, if you have the patience, a tail and two long antennae, twitching… and then with a flick they are gone. If you manage to hoick one into the palm of your hand, it is like catching a glass marble. They are a creature with no shame of their bodily functions. You can see everything working like the innards of a Swiss clock.

Wearing a snorkel mask and keeping my plimsolls on to protect my feet against the rocks, I climbed into the cold water with a keep-bag which I hoped to fill with limpets and starfish.

But I got more than I bargained for.

At the far end of the pool the crevices seemed to be the entrance to an underwater cave system – I could not get in far enough to see quite how deep they are, but I would be willing to hazard a guess that they stretch a fair distance and are therefore home to a number of those rock-pool dwellers that like their nooks and crannies – eels and, as I discovered, octopuses.

I saw and caught two *Octopus bimaculatus*. They were both young but of a good size, and bringing them close enough to have a good look wore me out. They are extremely devious. Rather than relying on speed and ferocity, this octopus is known for its cunning and guile, and they gave me the runaround. They snuck in and out, hid under cliffs and behind rocks, and when I finally caught the bigger of the two – they strangely did not mind sharing their space with one another – the creature grabbed my hand and then arm with such brutality that it caused blood blisters up to my elbow, and later, as I showered and caught sight of the damage in the mirror, it looked like I had been savaged by a vicious little monkey. I had deep purple welts. They looked hideous, although thankfully did not hurt too much and were worth it for the chance to log another member of the octopus family living in these waters.

So, I thought, he did find octopuses – and if the small ones live in this rich world, then he must have been enthused enough to search for a Sarnius to try his Octo-Com on. But I could find nothing in his notebooks about the Octo-Com, and nothing about a side-line of research or whether he had found a Sarnius with which to test his bizarre machine's language skills.

I had limited time. I had to be back in London by Monday evening, so I put aside the notebooks to be read more thoroughly back home and set out to find harbour-master Captain Pete LeConte. I was curious to discover whether he had any clues to share.

*

The harbour-master's office was in a wooden clapboard shed with peeling white paint at the end of a quay. Small, rust-spotted derricks hung idly like knackered donkeys in the salted winds. The detritus of a fishing industry surrounded the hut. Stacks of weathered lobster pots, thick ropes entangled with seaweed, old anchors, winches, oil drums, pallet crates, buoys and life-saving rings showed this was still very much a working harbour.

The ever-helpful Sergeant Rogers had called ahead to warn of my visit, and, as I approached, Captain LeConte opened the door and stood leaning on the frame with a mug in his hands.

'You must be here to talk about Dr Zipp?' he said. 'Terrible tragedy. Strange events. Wondered if we'd hear any more of it, to be honest. Not wholly surprised you've come.'

He asked me in and offered me a chair.

His office had a picture window with a view out across the Channel in one direction and the harbour in the other. The walls were covered in charts and there was a series of filing cabinets. On his desk he had a computer, three landlines and a short-wave radio that was humming away.

He offered me tea and then made his way to one of the walls.

'We found him here,' he said, pointing to a spot on a chart. 'A tricky place to get to. Dotted with wrecks. There is a shelf here...' he paused and tapped on the wall where the blue of the sea had been shaded a little lighter and interlaid with a crisscross brown pattern... 'and if you don't know the area, you are best to stay clear. Only the smallest fishing boats with the shallowest of drafts go there. There are channels leading to the cliffs here...' he again tapped the chart... 'but not many lay lines of pots there any more. Not worth the grief.

'Takes a lot of time to get there, and what with the cost of diesel it really isn't used as much as other grounds. Sometimes people go on day trips there and do some snorkelling and spear-fishing, but it's not done commercially. A lot of young lads head that way for fun – it has a lot of caves to explore – but it can be dangerous if you don't know what you are doing. Dr Zipp's was not the first fatality we've had there. The place has earned its reputation.'

'So what would Dr Zipp have been doing there?' I asked. 'Did he let you know he was going that way?'

'I just don't know the answer to that,' he said. 'He had come in here a few times, got some charts from us. Seemed like he knew what he was doing. Knowledgeable. Sensible. I didn't worry for him. Some people who come in – the ones on the gin palaces – well, I hardly think they are safe on dry land let alone the sea, and I wince when I watch them go out to the islands for the day, cocktails in hand and a boatload of people under their charge. No, Dr Zipp seemed sensible and showed me where he was working. That was why it was such a shock when I saw it was him that day.'

I asked if Harry had mentioned either octopuses or kayaks.

'Yes, he did,' he replied.

'He asked me lots of questions about a species called the Sarnius. I told them they were found sometimes but were rare. He asked if they were on the south coast, asked how big they got, that type of thing. I have to say, there are so many myths about them that I did find a scientist showing such an active interest odd when we had the state of the ormer to discuss, but I'm a fan of *Moby-Dick* myself, so I suppose I can relate to it.

'As for a kayak – well, yes, I saw him paddling about with it most weekends and was interested to see he had a whole heap of equipment on board, lashed down under a tarpaulin. I assumed it must be some type of sonar device used for depth measurement. I remember thinking it meant his craft didn't look very man-oeuvrable. But I also noted he was wearing a life jacket – something kayakers don't like to do round here as it gets in the way of your arms as you are paddling – so I wasn't overly bothered that the kayak was a two-man craft and quite laden for one person to steer. Let's just say he didn't look like he was going anywhere fast, but I saw no reason to ask what his business was, and he didn't tell me.'

'He was wearing a life jacket, you say?'

'Yes. And I put in a report to the police that I noted there was no life jacket to be seen in the vicinity of his body and that it seemed strange to me that someone who I had seen on a number of times taking all the correct precautions should have chosen one fateful day not to put it on. It struck me as odd. We thoroughly searched the area where he was found and there was no sign of the life jacket anywhere – as if somehow he had slipped out of it or taken it off, perhaps, which again would be strange.

'And there has been no sign of the kayak either. I have had a good look for it. Gone back round that way at different tides. No sign. No sign at all.'

I'd been toying with the idea of telling Captain LeConte the whole story, about my theory of the Octo-Com, of how Harry may have taken off his life jacket to immerse the machine, but I have to admit I felt a little silly. It just seemed so far-fetched. But, then again, even though there had been a lack of physical evidence on Guernsey to prove what Frank and I had surmised in London, this sighting of Harry with a boat, heading to an area he wasn't surveying, taking equipment – well, maybe the captain should at least be asked.

'Would you like to see where we found him?' asked Captain LeConte, as I wondered how to broach the subject of the Octo-Com.

'Yes, if it is no bother.'

'No bother at all. Come on.'

He picked up the radio receiver and spoke briefly over the static to his second in command, telling him to come and hold the fort. He took a couple of life jackets from a cupboard and led me along the quayside to an RIB that was moored in the still harbour waters.

We clambered down a rusted iron ladder sunk into the harbour wall and stepped on board. Captain LeConte fired up the outboard engine and we slowly made our way through the mouth of the harbour, past the lighthouse and statue and into the open sea. As the harbour walls slipped past us, he turned to me, mouthed 'hold tight' over the chugging of the engine, opened up the throttle and we flew forward.

We headed west, and then turned south, plotting a course that kept the coastline around four hundred yards to our left. We travelled at some speed, and I imagined the effort it must have taken for Harry to paddle such a route.

Even though we stayed away from the coast, islets and rocks loomed in front and either side of us. The captain plotted a course through the deeper channels, but I could see in the clear waters a mountainous landscape beneath the prow. It was dramatic and irregular, and the captain had to keep his eyes fixed carefully on the course.

I had quickly lost all concept of where we were in terms of the island. Sheer rock hid the land and I remembered Rivers's precise description of the seascape. The coastal fields were protected from the sea by defensive cliff walls. A mixture of sharp-grey and warm-red rock outcrops became thicker and heavier before moulding into one jagged mass, offering a barrier for the ocean to crash against. As we rounded yet another short headland, I noticed clefts in the cliffs becoming deeper and hiding caves. It was impossible to tell from the craft how far in they went, but from Captain LeConte's launch it looked like they were gaping mouths into another world. And the cliffs were terrific. It seemed as if they had been shot upwards rather than squeezed from the earth's crust over epochs and ages. Surely the land must have shaken and trembled biblically to create such a dramatic landscape. But, of course, it hadn't – it had happened over five hundred million years, then another five hundred million years, and then another, and then another… and the holes and nooks, crannies and gulches were caused by the tidal pull and the corroding sea that created caverns and sinkholes. It was this place Rivers had described, and it seemed probable that it was here that Harry had begun to search.

'Tell me about those caves,' I said.

Captain LeConte slowed the engines and allowed us to gently drift forwards.

'There is an impressive network,' he said. 'Much of it is charted, but there are still a fair number of caves that are simply too dangerous to go into. The currents come down from the coast and push through them and come out further down. It means there are parts where the water flows so quickly it's impossible to enter. There are whirlpools caused by sudden changes in depth and various underwater obstacles caused by the rocks. Experienced divers rarely go far into the caves – and inexperienced divers don't come to this part of the island, so they wouldn't know about them anyway.'

With that, he gunned the engine again and plotted a course for a small collection of partially submerged rocks lying around forty yards off the coastline and directly in front of one canyon that narrowed into a dark, shaded cave, where I could see water rushing in and out at a spectacular rate.

'Dr Zipp's body was washed up on the outcrop there,' he said, stopping next to a reef with a gently sloping rocky incline that came out from the water. 'It looked to me like he had crawled up there, but it can't be the case. He must have drowned first and then been washed up at that point. I've still not understood quite how. And if he had been here in a kayak, which to me is the only reasonable explanation, then where did it go to? And what caused him to abandon ship, if indeed he did?'

We paused at the spot for a while. Captain LeConte had fallen silent, whether out of respect for Harry's memory or the fact the place had a particularly eerie feel to it, I don't know. The sea lapped against the boat, heaved back and forth over the spot where Harry's body had been found. The light of the day had subtly changed as we paused. The caves looked darker, more unwelcoming.

'Let's head back, before we become Sarnius bait,' said the captain and nosed the boat around.

I couldn't tell from his tone whether he was joking, but it seemed telling that he had unconsciously used such a phrase.

*

Later that day, when I was back in St Peter Port, I called Frank to tell him what I had discovered. I felt the reasons behind Harry's death were pretty inconclusive. Without employing a team of skilled divers to head to the caves and undertake a thorough search for his newer version of the Octo-Com, I couldn't see how our theory could ever be proven, but Frank was surprisingly accepting.

I said that all the anecdotal evidence I had come across suggested Harry had made a serious, disastrous error. I concluded that he had taken his latest version of the Octo-Com out to the caves, perhaps searching for a Sarnius, and got into trouble. Frank told me that maybe it was best that the machine had become part of the flotsam of the oceans.

'At least whatever reputation he has in his field won't be affected by this,' he added.

I told him Harry's notes made no mention of his secret project, but there were some bits and bobs that looked like they may have had something to do with an Octo-Com. Frank replied that it was hardly surprising. The Institute wouldn't take kindly to him using the time he should have been counting ormers on chasing outlandish schemes. I told Frank I had found an unfinished letter written in one of the books, and it was addressed to him.

I'd read it earlier that day as I sat with my back to the statue of Rivers on the harbour wall and had posted it on before I left the island.

Harry had written:

I often wonder at the waste of human civilisation – all these discarded items, turning up day after day, day after day on our beaches. It leads me to consider the following conclusion about human development.

Some animals may burrow, or nest, or make homes, but these constructions, from twigs, leaves, earth or their own secretions, make little lasting impression on the world. In fact, they become part of the world, an adjutant to it. But humans scrape, cut, mix, blast, shatter, change, shape the earth all around them. Everywhere you go the mark of humans can be found, from the roads that bisect the grand plains to the paths that snake up the mountains, from the cables that lie across the ocean floor to the satellites in the sky above us and the gases we pump into the air... We leave an awful amount of rubbish behind us, which can never be more apparent than when we are walking along a beach. So why? Do we need these things for our physiological satisfaction? You could build a clear argument that we do not, as many belief systems try to illustrate. But as a species, it is what seems to separate us from the creatures I look at scurrying across the bottom of a sandy rock pool. We are the only animal driven by an external need for products. And these products, so called, become a deeply ingrained part of our being...We measure our fulfilment with the level of products we possess and the power they give us by proxy – and all this in spite of the biological fact that the millionaire and the tramp have the same basic physiological needs.

I gather possessions like anyone else – I fulfil this basic and subconscious human need to collect and collate.

So perhaps this need, this urge, is a step on the ladder of evolution: was the Industrial Revolution, which produced so many of these consumer goods and turned human society into a consumer society, an evolutionary stage, a mutation in human development? If so, isn't this worrying? Shouldn't we consider evolutionary processes as changes for the better? Palaeontologists consider decoration as a signal, a precursor, to extinction... so isn't industrialisation, the creation of an assembly-line world, the mass production of our food with its constant pressure on the natural resources, the raw materials around us, which is bleeding the planet to death... isn't this the evidence of our impending extinction... or will humans be clever enough to subvert what history tells us is inevitable? Will we be clever enough to bail ourselves out through the marvellousness of technological advances?

I hope to find a creature I know to be of comparably extraordinary intelligence as *Homo sapiens*, and see why they have not found it necessary to do what we do. Perhaps we could learn from them.

The letter seemed to sum up this strange man I had only got to know after his death. I wondered if Frank's theory about his partner's work and how it led to his death really was the truth. It didn't change the fact that I would write his obituary. I got up to leave and looked one last time out across the water and then to the inscription on the plinth of John H Rivers's statue. It provided a lovely viewpoint, the perfect summer nook for lovers to lean against, a ledge for young fishermen to leave tins of maggots on while they practised casting off and a launch pad seagulls could perch on before wheeling away to another outcrop.

The statue was imposing, and Rivers's features were that of a craggy face with a natural defiance, his stone beard flowing in the wind, his eyes fixed as they stared out at boats approaching the safety of the port. He was pointing to the horizon with an accusing, weather-beaten finger... His brow had been chiselled into a series of furrows, as if he were lecturing the ocean.

The wash of another ferry crashed against the wall below, and I read on the seaward side of the heavy granite plinth a legend carved deeply in thickset script. It read: 'Where there is life, there is hope.'

I left for home.

The Evening Press And Star, page 8

OBITUARY: DOCTOR HARRY ZIPP, ANIMAL LINGUISTICS EXPERT

Dr Horatio 'Harry' Zipp, who has died aged 56, was a marine biologist whose life's work focused on deciphering signals used in the animal kingdom.

Dr Zipp, who drowned while undertaking a shellfish survey in the Channel Islands for University College London, lived in Blooms-bury for thirty years and taught at both UCL and the Plymouth Institute of Marine Biology. He had grown up in Islington, the son of a fishmonger, and attended Chapel Street Primary School. After failing his 11-Plus, he left school to join his father Bernie behind the counter of their Chapel Market shop.

He would go on to win a scholarship to study marine biology in Plymouth and later lecture at the Institute. He became respected for his forward-thinking approach to oceanography and conservation, believing that monitoring chemical discharges from shellfish and other seabed creatures that feed by filtering water revealed important information as to levels of pollution. His work has been widely used in oceans, seas, lakes and rivers suffering from industrial pollutants.

Colleagues recall a man who, away from the laboratory and fieldwork, provided lively lectures and wrote widely on a number of topics involving animal communication, including studies of octopuses, which he believed provided greater scope for 'language' study than dolphins and whales. Dr Zipp was interested in sea-lore and in his spare time collected maritime artefacts, including a large library of mariners' memoirs and Elizabethan ship logbooks.

He leaves a partner, Frank Asquith.

THE DUSTMAN
AND ROBIN

THAT WINTER WAS long, and it was miserable.

Looking back, I remember it as being relentless, draining, with absolutely no respite. In the same way childhood summers are always sun-kissed, those months at the *Evening Press And Star* appear in my memory as permanently drab. It rained, hailed and sleeted constantly from November through to the end of February. It was icy each morning but without the crispness of a clear winter's sky. We didn't even enjoy a decent snow fall to coat the city in a white sheen, give the kids a day off school and freelance photographers ample subject matter with which to bombard the news desk.

This grey and dreary season matched the news coming in. It was incessantly grim. The country was in the tight grip of the Second Great Depression, and my colleagues and I were swamped with individual stories that were the end game of the downturn and the inability of the government to deal with it.

The misery surrounding us was so complete that we could have filled every news page with sadness and tragedy.

Our patch had been hit by flooding, and the waters forced people from their homes with dead-eyed stares as they watched sewage flow over their photo albums and other irreplaceables, giving us page-lead images that played out like a biblical tale for the collective seasonal affective disorder with which we were unconsciously consumed.

It was described as a natural disaster, but of course it wasn't – it was caused by a plethora of mistakes made collectively, from changes to the weather because of global warming, cuts to the budgets of the Department Of The Environment, intensive farming, no investment in flood defences, the sewers through to people turning front gardens into driveways so rainwater wasn't being soaked up. It seemed to be a symptom of the troubles we all faced.

We felt it was our duty to listen to every person who came to our newspaper's front desk and provide a psychological fillip with a cup of tea and a friendly ear. We patiently heard out stories of rat-infested homes, of blocks with broken lifts, of drug dealing in stairwells and accompanying gang fights over petty turf, of unfair dismissals from low-paid jobs, of long waits for ambulances, of benefits stopped and scores of minor interactions with local authorities and government departments that had gone wrong.

It meant the stock of stories such as 'Missing Moggy: Home After Three Years' and 'Wartime Sweethearts Marry Seven Decades After First Dance' was raised. They acted as antidotes to the heartbreakers we were running.

But, while we felt it our duty to write each tragic tale, we also discussed during our news conferences the need to find stories that could act as political parables, like the floods and how cuts to council budgets meant our city's infrastructure was creaking, to illustrate the state of the nation.

Our thinking went like this. If we found tough-luck yarns that illustrated a wider point, something our readers could either directly relate to or at least feel empathy with, perhaps it would do some public good. And if it didn't, at the very least our readers could say: 'We're not as badly off as that poor sod in this week's *Press And Star*.' We wanted them to shake their heads over their tea and toast at breakfast time, escape from their predicament, feel empowered and angry.

It was, looking back, an attempt to personalise the Depression. We knew what was happening to our readership. We knew the troubles people faced each day, and were worried it was becoming normalised – the general and far-reaching poverty was not creating the outrage it should have done. Standards had been lowered, and the fight to highlight this felt pale and weak, not red-toothed and angry.

As Christmas approached, we discussed finding people to interview who could illustrate this point. We hit on a series of features on those who had work but were still struggling to make ends meet. These were the jobs that in the past would guarantee a living wage and long-term security, involving people who grafted hard doing something vital to keep our city moving but relied on foodbanks and pay-day lenders by the end of the month.

With the incessantly bad weather, I thought it would make for a visually interesting piece if I found someone who worked outside. I had an image of grizzled blue-collar employees tucked up in hats and scarves and gloves, tool belts slung across hips, shovels and pickaxes to lean on, the damp skies providing a suitably gritty backdrop.

It was while I did some background research for this feature that I heard the story of a dustman called Dev Williams.

As I walked to work each day, I'd see the bin lorries on their rounds. It struck me as a particularly tough job. Physically trying, early starts and with a stigma attached. Working with stuff other people believe is valueless made it seem like sub-blue-collar work, Dev told me. It was mucky, dirty and frequently disgusting. The rubbish Dev dealt with created stenches that would linger in the mind long after whatever vile detritus had been turfed from the bins into the depths of the cart and squashed together into a mess of unholy proportions.

Dev was no longer directly employed by the council. A private firm now ran the borough's collection services. They had a Victorian approach to pay and conditions, which meant a lack of job security with their zero-hours' contracts and poor weekly wages, a basic pension scheme and a fairly sloppy approach towards health and safety. With this in mind I decided to speak with dustmen. I knew they'd provide me with interesting copy. I envisaged a photograph of weary and worn men in orange coats, with the rain ripping around them and empty bins by their sides.

And it was while I worked on this feature that I found a story that provided a glimmer of sunshine in those dark months.

Devon Williams had worked on the dust rounds for twenty years. I'd say hello to him when he emptied my bins and see him in the pub on Fridays, and we'd always have a chat. I knew he'd be willing to speak about his work. I thought I'd change his name so he'd get no comeback from his line managers, and this anonymity would give me a reporter's license, a little extra scope, to pluck the readers' heartstrings.

Dev was well-known and well-liked on his beat. Despite his working conditions, he had smiles to share. People would wave at his truck as it went past. They'd stop and say hello if they met him at their front gate, bin bags over the shoulder, lugging their rubbish away. He was the type of person who, if we all still wore hats, would have them tipped in his direction.

Dev was tall. He had been lean and skinny as a child, his frame too hefty for the filling it carried, but not any more. Age had added a thickness to him, piled it on in slabs, around the middle and over once-defined shoulders. His cheekbones now supported extra padding.

I remembered him from younger days. Late adolescence had seen him go through an athletic phase. His body was strong and his limbs articulated and swift. Hard work had at first honed the muscle but then worn it down. A love of greasy fried-chicken dinners and a big biscuit habit had further eroded his natural strength and given his metabolism an enemy impossible to defeat. He had lapsed gently into middle age and had an air about him that people warmed to. Dev was perfect *Evening Press And Star* material.

I saw him one morning on my way into the office and explained that I wanted to do a sketch of someone who works fifty-odd hours a week, takes home a pay packet but still finds themselves struggling at the end of the month.

Dev smiled knowingly and told me to meet him at his flat when his shift finished.

'It has ever been so,' he said in his bassy voice. 'No problem. You can speak to me. We've had trouble.'

Later that day I left the newsroom with my notebook and camera to meet him, a story already forming in my mind. Dev lived in a red-brick 1930s housing-association estate that ran alongside the railway lines in Tufnell Park. He buzzed me in on an intercom, and I climbed four flights to get to his flat. It was his mum's place, and he'd lived there all his life. It had three bedrooms, and Dev told me how he was worried about the bedroom tax. His older sister had moved out, and he'd mentioned it was making things tricky. I thought this could provide an angle for the story.

He led me into the sitting-room, and I sat back on a sofa while Dev put the kettle on. I looked about. The house was pristine. Everything had a place, everything was neat, everything just so. Shelves held books arranged in alphabetical order. DVDs were set out in genres. A picture of a beach with sun-bleached sands and a sparkling blue sea was perfectly positioned in the centre of one of the walls, and a flat-screen TV, hung opposite, was also dead centre. Photographs in silver and gold frames of various family members were arranged in order of height along a highly polished sideboard.

He and his mother, who I noted was called Patricia judging by a thank-you card on a tiled mantelpiece above a gas fire, were house-proud.

Dev came back with two teas and told me his mum was out with friends and that if I waited for her to return she'd tell me her side of things, too.

'Sit tight,' he said. 'Mum'll be back soon, and if she sees we have a guest she'll knock us up one of her curries.'

Slumping on a sofa, placing his mug on a coaster on a side table and offering me a biscuit, he explained they'd been in the flat since the early 1960s. His mum knew all her neighbours, and it was home. She didn't want to move, but it was an increasing struggle to stay put, what with the bedroom tax, cuts in housing benefit and not much of a pension.

I asked him how she was dealing with it.

'She is okay, I suppose,' said Dev. 'She is getting old. The usual ailments for a seventy-year-old. We've had a few worries.'

'And she is still working?'

'Yeah, but only part-time. Two shifts a week at the launderette and then two shifts at the after-school club. She's done them for so long now I can't imagine her ever stopping. It's like a social thing down at the Soft Soap. The customers are her mates. They all get together and do each other's washing. Can't see it outlasting her generation, though, people getting together to wash their smalls. I mean, everyone has a washing-machine nowadays, don't they?

'She's still pretty active when she's not at the launderette or up the school. She has the Circle Club she goes to – plays whist and dominoes on Tuesdays and Thursdays. Goes to the luncheon club on Friday and has a sing at the chapel on a Sunday. She keeps going, but I've noticed something more and more in the last year or so... The fact is, my mum's memory is changing.'

Dev stressed the word 'changing', and it struck me he hadn't said disappearing, losing, becoming patchy. No, just 'changing', and I wondered about his choice of words and whether this was some kind of denial regarding the onset of dementia.

'She has become pretty scatty, especially when it comes to every-day stuff. She keeps her keys around her neck or she'll lose them. She leaves pans of water boiling on the stove and forgets they are there or why she is boiling water in the first place. She asks me the same question three or four times when I've just told her the answer. It's enough for it to be a bit of a worry.

'But get her started on her childhood in Trinidad, and it is as if it all happened yesterday. Her ability to remember has flipped over: old stuff is fresh; new stuff is stale.

'She remembers the general store her dad used to run in a place called Redhead Hill. It overlooked a bay. Lovely spot. She remembers swimming after school – and swimming races – she can recall who beat her and who she beat. She remembers films she watched in the outdoor cinema each summer and who was in them and what they were about. She remembers helping her mother with the cooking and remembers particular occasions and what food she helped prepare for them – christenings, weddings, demobilisation, the May carnival. She remembers singing in the church each Sunday and the sermons that were preached.

'Sermons – now that's something she definitely remembers and will never tire of telling me – the stuff she learnt at Sunday school. My mum loves a bit of the Good Book. Everything I do seems to bring a sermon back to her,' he added and laughed deeply.

I asked him if she ever went back to Trinidad, and a shadow fell across his face.

'She'd love to,' he replied. 'Talks about it all the time, but where she is from has become some posh holiday destination, and the cost of flights are extraordinary. I always thought I'd save something up to pay for her to go back for a holiday so she could show me home, and I could meet some of the cousins, but we just about stagger to the end of the month, and I can't see it ever happening.

'It has become more pressing as she gets older. She is pretty desperate to see her brother Terence. Talks about it a lot. She hasn't seen him for years. There was, you see, a bit of a falling out.'

He paused, and a sadness came across his face. I wondered if I should ask him what happened. Instead, I asked if Terence was older and whether they had any other siblings, hoping it would prompt him to keep talking, allowing Dev to open up if he wanted to.

'Yeah, he is older,' he said. 'My Uncle Terence – came to London, too, back in the late 1950s. He is a proud, clever and industrious man. Done well for himself in Trinidad. I have to say he found London difficult.'

Dev sighed and explained that his uncle couldn't accept the way he was treated in his adopted home. He believed himself to be first and foremost a British Trinidadian, a subject of the Queen whose father had fought for the Mother Country in the war, a man who aspired to a set of British values instilled from an early age as he stood at a wicket with a bat in his hand. He had believed the calypso words of Lord Kitchener, wanted to hear Big Ben chime in person and thought London was the place to be – until he got here.

'As if the homesickness caused by the cold, the horrible food and the poverty he thought he was escaping wasn't enough, he then had people look at him and tell him he was no good, inferior, a sub-human. It was a lot for him to understand, and he never came to terms with it. He persevered, but it was the winter of '62 and '63 that did for him,' Dev said. 'The blizzards and a thermometer that never went above zero made it physically harsh. To cap it all, he was evicted by a landlord for no reason except other tenants who lived in his Paddington boarding-house didn't want him there. He had nowhere to go and ended up sharing a bunk in a YMCA hostel.

'By 1964 he had had enough. He thought why be poor and cold and miserable when I can be warm and proud and happy? He got passage on a ship back to the Caribbean. Walked all the way to Southampton. Couldn't afford the train fare and thought he'd hitch, but, of course, no one picked him up. A tall, proud, black man walking down an A road in Hampshire? It wasn't happening.

'My mum felt he deserted her – he had persuaded her to come here in the first place. By then, she had a steady job, a good job, and had fallen in love with my dad and was starting a family. My uncle wanted her to come, too. He felt betrayed by the British. Saw the promises of a good life in the Mother Country were empty. But she couldn't leave. They fell out over it. She accused him of being stubborn and proud – and he said "Yes, I am", and said it was a good thing to be. Then she called him a quitter, and he didn't like that at all. They didn't speak for many years. Now she speaks about him all the time. She is desperate to see him again. They've finally made up, and she tells me every day how much she wants to step off an aeroplane into the Trinidadian heat and see him waiting on the Tarmac for her.

'Another tea? Let's have a brew, and then I'll show you something. I'd been hoping to use it to send Mum home for a bit, but times are too tough now. Come with me. It's all in the back room.'

I followed Dev down the hall, and he opened a door, stood to one side and waved me through.

I wasn't prepared for what I saw. The room was packed with crates, all neatly labelled: 'Chinaware'; 'Kitchen utensils'; 'Lights, torches, as sorted'; 'Toys, age 0–3'; 'Toys, age 3–10'; 'DVDs'; 'Tapes'; 'VHS'; 'Coats'; 'Scarves, hats, gloves'; 'Cabling (audio)'; 'Cabling (visual)'...

It went on and on. It looked like he was about to move house. I asked him what it was about.

'I can't abide by the waste I see every day,' he said. 'It breaks my heart. When I was a kid there was the fella, Alf The Ragman, who came round with his barrow. He'd recycle everything for you and make a living out of it. I remember there was this pram he had, one of those sprung Silver Cross numbers. He took it round our neighbourhood, oh, for about thirty years. It would be used by one family for six months then passed on to another through Alf. He'd look after it, keep it neat, nice and clean. Once one baby had done with it, it would go on to another.

'When I was younger that was what I wanted to do. He let me ride on his cart with Lucky, his Jack Russell. I'd give him a hand and had this idea that when I was out of school I'd take on his round for him. Times change, though, eh? I found myself on the dust instead, throwing stuff out that Alf would've loved. I remember Alf, and every day on the rounds I wonder what he would have made of the stuff we chuck out. Take this, for example,' he said, picking up a children's tricycle from a corner. Nothing at all wrong with it, except the kid who used it has outgrown it. The people who bunged this couldn't be bothered to find it a new home. There's the Freecycle thing you can do. Couldn't be bothered. You could take it to the dump and leave it by the reuse area for someone to pick up. Couldn't be bothered.

'Perfectly useable – but it got binned.'

'What will you do with it?' I asked. 'Bit small for you, Dev.'

'I don't know,' he replied. 'Might sell it at the car boot I do once a month down Holloway. That's always good for flogging kid's stuff. You get loads of young families down there without a pot to piss in. I wasn't going to let it be thrown away. If it don't sell, I'll probably drop it off at the nursery up the road or give it to the school for their jumble sale. I do that with a lot of the toys I find.'

'What does your mum make of all this?'

'She doesn't mind. In fact, she encourages it. I find stuff I know she'll like, too, and she often gets things from me to give to her friends. You should hear her at the club. She says to her friends when they need something: "Our Dev will have a look out for you." She is from that generation, that war generation, where she can't understand the waste of today. Mum thinks we've ruined ourselves and are like spoilt little children, wrecking the world.

'And she remembers her childhood – they had nothing, really, not when you think of the upbringing she's given me... and she says they were quite well-off. They reused everything. It makes her mad as anything when she thinks of half the world having nothing and the people round this way bunging everything out. Thinks they are mad. Thinks we've got an illness that makes us always want something new, never happy with what we've got. I suppose that's where I get it from, too.'

For a moment, as I looked at his sister's old room, I felt really quite taken aback. I briefly wondered if Dev had that condition that makes people hoard stuff. But it just didn't fit. He didn't seem insecure, depressed, eccentric. Judging by the state of the flat, if he had any type of obsessive compulsive disorder, it was that he didn't like clutter. I reflected on the neatly stacked boxes. Dev didn't show any of the other classic symptoms shared by people we'd occasionally get a good page-three lead out of. He wasn't one of those who'd turn their homes into dangerous rubbish dumps, shout at environmental health officers when neighbours complained, get taken to court and end up being the subject of a headline reading 'Pensioner's 20-Foot Rubbish Mountain'.

No, Dev simply saw usefulness in the items others discarded. And he was right – as we began rifling through the boxes I saw it was all too good for the landfill.

'So what do you do with all this?' I asked.

'Well, the car boot has become vital to us,' he said.

'Since Mum's slowed down with work 'n' all it's been a lifesaver. I'd started doing it as a bit of a saving thing – thought we may one day get enough for that holiday – but now it's putting the food on the table.'

He had six standard lamps in one corner, cables neatly wound around their bases, and a range of Anglepoise lights. I'd have had any of them in my home, I thought. He had a collection of folding chairs, all of different sizes, shapes, designs – each one perfectly useable. There was a collection of amplifiers, tape recorders and CD players stacked up.

'They all work,' Dev said as I fiddled with one of them. 'If you ever need a stereo, I'm your man.' He laughed again. He was enjoying showing off his side-line, and it was clear he was pleased that I got it.

The range was extraordinary. He had a box full of plugs, removed from appliances.

'I take them to the hardware store down the road, and they give me fifteen pounds for every fifty I bring. They sell the fuses, too. It's an easy earner.'

Dev had another box with frames inside, one with pictures and prints. There was a poster with a photo of a gorilla with the legend 'Who says fruit and veg are for wimps?' and a tinted colour shot of the Dunn's River waterfalls in Jamaica. There was a large copy of Jack Vettriano's painting of a couple dancing on a beach with a butler holding a brolly... there was a Constable print and a shot of St Paul's Cathedral swathed in smoke during the Blitz and some tube posters... and there were fifties film stars and eighties pop stars and tour posters from Queen, The Rolling Stones and Black Sabbath. It was like a stockroom in a branch of Athena.

In a fitted wardrobe he showed me yet more boxes, stacked and with more labels – candlesticks, ornaments, figurines, ashtrays, bottles, Tupperware, Lego, shoes...

Among it all, something caught my eye. There was a box marked 'Odds And Nick-Nacks', and considering the room was full of things that could be filed in such a category, I was interested to see what Dev had stored inside.

*

There was a pile of comics at the bottom of the box, and I sat on a rescued folding chair and flicked through them. I loved *Roy Of The Rovers* when I was a kid and pulled a couple of copies out. They dated from the early 1960s. Roy has a neat haircut and baggy shorts, Blackie Gray was smoking a fag and Melchester Rovers were three down in a cup match. Roy had to quell half-time dissent and score four in the next forty-five minutes. There were copies of *The Hotspur* and *Whizzer* and the *Beano* and then a few others from America I didn't recognise. In this pile, one comic caught me eye. It said along the top 'The New Adventures Of Robin – The Gotham City Crime Fighter', and I thought, okay, surely that is Batman not Robin and pulled it out to have a closer look.

The comic was published in July 1958, and the front cover was garish. Red, green and yellow print clashed unashamedly. The spot-pigment printing system used was pronounced – it made Robin's complexion uniformly dotty. Its front-page image had him leaping from a Gotham tenement window. There was a bad guy leaning out, looking distressed and shaking a fist. Below Robin, on the pavement, were admiring onlookers – a pretty young woman in a 1950s bopper's skirt with plimsolls and bobby socks and her hair in a pony-tail and a mother in a mac holding the hand of a rosy-cheeked, blond-haired boy. The legend 'Robin' was picked out in violent yellow and green, and then, in a different font, a serious black, it said 'In His First Solo Adventure'.

It looked like it had never been read. I wondered about the schoolboy who had gone to a newsagent's and run his eyes along the rack. He'd seen *Superman* and *Green Lantern* and *The Hotspur* and *The Boy's Own Paper*... looked at his pocket money in his little palm and wondered what he should go for... then he'd been sold by this front cover, wanted to see how Robin would fare without Bruce Wayne alongside him.

'His First Solo Adventure...' The words suddenly leapt off the page, and I looked at Dev and then back at the comic. It definitely said in the top corner 'Issue Number One', and it was in as good a condition as the day it rolled off the press.

'You may have something worth a few bob here,' I said.

'Oh really?' Dev nonchalantly asked. 'What is it?'

I held the comic up and clean forgot the reason I had gone to Dev's house in the first place.

Dev, however, didn't look pleased with the find. I asked why it bothered him, and he replied that he didn't think any good would come of it.

'You don't understand,' he said. 'They don't just frown on us taking stuff that has been chucked out. It's against the rules. A sackable offence. My boss turns a blind eye mostly because he thinks I'm crazy and doesn't know how much I collect, but if he were to know I'd got something like this... well, I know he'd not be happy. And I bet he'd demand a piece of it...'

I scowled and told him his manager could do one. 'How on earth will he know?' I asked.

'Yeah, well, that's fair enough, maybe he wouldn't find out, but it ain't worth the risk. And it's not just that,' he continued. 'Someone out there is cursing. They've thrown out something they cherished. They've lost something worth a fortune. Actually, you know what? We've got to go and give it back.'

I admired Dev's honesty. I'm sure the vast majority of people I know would have thought ker-ching, thank you very much, re-e-e-sult. Instead, the idea of some quick riches via the sale of this comic was giving him a rough time.

'Well, do you remember where it came from?' I asked.

He looked thoughtful. 'I think so. In fact, I'm sure. The day I found it stands out,' he said. 'The amount of stuff they were bunging out – there were boxes and boxes and boxes. I think they were moving house. It was about a month ago, and I don't know if they will still be there. I suppose if that's the case, you could help, couldn't you? We could find a forwarding address, ask the estate agent. There is still a board outside. Or if that doesn't work, then perhaps you could put something in the *Press And Star*?'

I told him he'd get scores of people claiming it was theirs if I did that, and he'd be best going to the house first and even then holding his cards close to his chest when he knocked on the door.

Dev told me he'd got the comics from outside a five-storey Victorian home in one of the wide, tree-lined streets around the back of Kentish Town.

He had watched a woman bring out the boxes, and instead of doing what she should have done – taken the stuff to be recycled or put it in a dump – she stacked them up, load after load, by the bins.

'She was having a right old huff and a puff and a curse,' he said. 'I remember thinking it was proper selfish, throwing out all that stuff and leaving us to deal with it.

'Paul, the round manager, said we should just leave it all there and let them get a bloody skip. He said something to her about it, and she shouted back about making a complaint if it wasn't gone that day. She said to us that it had to all go, and now. She had people coming round to see the house, and we'd better get a bloody move on.

'I thought, you stuck up cow, but I couldn't help having a quick look at what she was bunging out, and it was then I saw a box of comics. I'd been pretty annoyed at Paul for getting uppity at her, too, as I knew we'd end up shoving it in the back of the cart anyway, and I'd fancied having a good squiz through the clobber.'

It transpired the woman had thrown out a load of her husband's possessions and had also systematically chucked away everything in the house that wasn't directly hers. She didn't want anything coming to a new home that would remind her of a broken relationship. She'd paid two men to come over and carry it down the flights of stairs, and, following her instructions not to leave anything behind, they'd gone into the loft and cleared out stuff that had been up there for years, from way before she moved in.

It was in one of those boxes that Dev found a heap of old Marvel comics. He shoved them to the back of the bin store and made a mental note to walk back that way after the round was over and pick them up.

'I didn't think they'd be worth anything. I just like that sort of thing,' he told me. 'Always been keen on Batman.'

*

Dev went to the house the following week. There was a sold sign outside, but the woman was still there. The place was nearly empty and her bins now only used to discard ready-meal containers. Her kitchen utensils had already been taken to the new house.

Dev played it cool. He didn't want to go up to the door and say: 'Oi, have you thrown out a valuable comic?' He just rang the bell, said he was her dustman and asked if she had lost anything.

'You should have seen how she reacted,' he said. 'What a mouth on her. She thought I was "being funny". She must have remembered Paul telling her we weren't happy taking away everything she was bunging out.

'Before I had a chance to say "No, no, I'm not", she started shouting and swearing and threatening all sorts. Said something about how the house was a tip when they bought it and most of the crap she'd thrown out wasn't her problem anyway… I told her there was no need to be like that and walked off. I'll not be going back there any time soon.'

*

I met Dev again a few days later. I had hoped he'd had a think about things and decided to hang on to the comic, but he hadn't changed his tune. He was insistent we find the owner. He'd checked online and saw that the comic was exceptionally rare. Dealers in America were touting them for four-figure sums.

I wanted to see for myself, so I spent an afternoon researching the market. eBay had similar things for sale for big money. I called an organiser of a comic-book convention I'd once interviewed about their own graphic novel – a story, I recalled, about a dog that made sculptures – and popped into Mega City Comics in Camden Town. Here I bought a coffee-table-style guide to collecting rare comics, packed with pictures and potted histories by a bloke called Alan Thompson, a comic-book expert who knew his first editions and rare releases. I flicked through the index, and there it was, a page, including an image of its front cover, on the story behind Robin's big day out. It was rare – very rare indeed. I tracked down Alan via his publisher and called him. I said I was writing a feature on buying comic books as an investment. He was more than happy to talk about his area of expertise, and he explained in detail how prices continue to rise each year but often go through spikes. This was based on how much the superhero was in the zeitgeist. If a new Batman film was released, for example, the comics would leap in price.

'It's worth looking at studio schedules for the next two years,' he told me. 'If there is a new superhero film in production, hoover up the comics before a release date is announced then sell them when the studio marketing kicks in. You'd be surprised how simple it is. Guaranteed, 100 per cent, a good profit.'

I asked him about the Robin comic, and he confirmed what we had seen online – it would be worth a few grand.

I wondered how I was going to help Dev out. I knew that if I told him its value it would just make his fretting worse. He was still tortured by the idea that he'd come across something worth a few bob at someone else's expense. Dev had imagined them frantically searching over and over for their prized first edition, their nest-egg, their treasure.

'I heard what you said,' he explained. 'I did what you said. If she'd known what she had thrown out she would have been relieved to see me. Instead, she might as well have chased me up the garden path with a bloody pitchfork.'

'Look, why don't I have a go?' I said, hoping that would give him some peace of mind. 'If it's not hers then it must be the person who lived there before. They shouldn't be too hard to track down.'

The records of searches done by solicitors each time the home was sold would give me something to go on, but before I delved into land-registry records I headed into the offices of the estate agent's whose name was on the 'For Sale' sign outside the house. I thought they would have some answers regarding the building's history.

They told me the house was once split into flats but five years ago, at great expense, it had been bought with sitting tenants by a couple. After various wrangles over planning permission, and a fairly large payout to the people living there already, its new owners had turned it back into one dwelling.

The couple wanted to settle in and have a family, but it didn't work out like that. Maliciously delivered gossip from one of the estate agents, who was gleeful to have got a commission on such a place twice in just five years, revealed things didn't turn out well for them. Soon after they had spent a heap of money on converting the place to satisfy their whims – a big, open-plan kitchen and dining area in the basement, oak floors and gallons of Farrow & Ball paint everywhere, a new terrace leading down into the back garden, a top-floor bedroom turned into an en-suite bathroom – and the house was back on the market. The couple were divorcing.

'Domestic strife is very lucrative for us,' the agent told me, with a leer and a grin.

It made things a little clearer, so I thought I'd try the house again.

Dev texted me the address, so I went around there and knocked on the door, hoping I'd get a different response.

The owner wasn't in. Instead, the door was opened by a cleaner and she took my details and a message. Unsurprisingly, I never received a call, so I returned a few days later. This time the woman who owned the place answered and asked me with a frown what I wanted. I explained I was from the *Evening Press And Star* and was doing a story about recycling in the area. I asked her if she wouldn't mind answering a couple of questions and if she was happy with the services the council provided, and she tartly told me she was.

'I had a clear-out the other day,' she said. 'The stuff I threw out is not there now, so yes, I suppose I am happy,' and with that she closed the door firmly in my face.

It was revealing. I imagined that if she had lost a valued comic she'd have said so. She would have made a song and dance about it, and she certainly did not appear to be a superhero-comic geek.

I checked the Land Registry for the previous owner of the top flat, who would have had access to the loft. It was logged in the name of a company called Ideal Management, which, I noticed, had a portfolio of properties in the neighbourhood. I took the details of the office address for the firm and then turned to the electoral register. The previous name was O'Neill. It was little help. I suspected that the flat would have had a high turnover of tenants – probably students, young couples, staying a year or two – and when I cross-checked the registers with council-tax logs at the Town Hall going back over the past twenty-five years the names changed almost every eighteen months.

I had a decision to make. I suspected that if I told Dev how unlikely it was we could track down the rightful beneficiary, he would not alter his belief that he had no rightful claim to the windfall.

I came to the conclusion that whoever the original owner was hadn't been a comic collector. The box the comics had been stuffed in had an Express Dairy logo on it. A search on the internet of the company's trademarks dated it from the early 1970s. And it wasn't as if they had bought Robin's 'First Solo Adventure' at vast expense.

It had cost 6d from a newsagent the week it was printed and had eventually been put in the box, shoved up a ladder, through a hatch and left under the eaves to linger and gain in value. I decided to tell Dev the search was fruitless, and he could either give it to someone who clearly wasn't the owner to salve his conscience or keep it for himself.

We met at The Bell for a pint, and I went through what I had done.

Dev thanked me for my time. He couldn't hide his disappointment.

'It's giving me sleepless nights,' he confessed. 'I've just been warned by the guv'nor about taking stuff. He caught me last week nabbing a Scalextric set someone had bunged, and he wasn't happy about it. I just don't know what to do.'

I told him to give the comic to me, and I'd come up with an answer.

We met back at The Bell for a pint a fortnight later, and I told him I needed to discuss what we were going to do with the comic. I'd brought it with me in a brown envelope, and I placed it on the table. He groaned and said he'd rather leave it, if I didn't mind, and pushed it back towards me.

'Mate, we're not going to find the owner,' I insisted. 'That means it is essentially yours.'

'I just don't know if I want it,' he said. 'It's not worth risking the monthly cash I get from the stuff no one cares about for a little windfall like this. What if someone sees it up for sale and comes forward? I'd be up shit creek. I could lose my job. I don't want to lose my job.'

And then he looked at me.

'You have it. Sell it and give the money away. I'd never be able to explain where it came from. I'm not good at keeping secrets, and if this got out, well... they'd sack me. Instant dismissal. Gone. They're always looking for reasons to get rid of people.'

I wanted to tell him to stop being ridiculous, that we could wing it, the chances were tiny, but I really didn't have the heart. His scrupulous honesty was unnerving. I'd have leapt ten feet and bought champagne all round. But it suddenly became clear what was holding Dev back when he drained his beer, looked me in the eye and said: 'What on earth would my mum say?'

*

A few weeks later a letter arrived at Dev's home. Inside were two flights to Trinidad and four weeks' stay in a hotel on the central street of Redhead. There were some travellers' cheques to spend and a letter thanking Dev for his lengthy public service on the bins from a 'philanthropic well-wisher who wants to celebrate the unsung heroes of civic life'. He had given me a present, a pristine copy of a superhero's crime-fighting adventure, so I gave him one back.

The Evening Press And Star, page 5

BINNED COMIC SETS NEW RECORD AT AUCTION

A piece of superhero history went under the hammer this week after a long-lost first edition of a rare comic was sold for more than £4,500.

The comic, which was the first of a short-lived series featuring Robin of Batman fame, was sold at the Charing Cross Art Auction for a record-breaking figure.

The owner, who did not want to be named, said they had found the rare first edition among a box of discarded comics dating from the 1950s and 1960s in a house clearance from a property in Kentish Town. Despite attempts to find the owner, no one came forward. It is believed the Robin comic was probably left in the home from the day it was bought and not seen since the early sixties – when it would have been valueless.

Comic expert Alan Thompson told the *Evening Press And Star*: 'This is an important find. Few have survived, and the publishing house's print run was limited as they feared Robin on his own would not be too much of a draw. They were right – his solo adventures were discontinued after twelve editions. This copy was in immaculate condition and is an excellent example of 1950s comic-book storytelling and the graphic art of the period.'

WE'LL MEET AGAIN

THE KWANTLEN TRIBE of Aboriginal Americans made their home in the northern Pacific territories of the Canadian outback.

They'd lived nomadically for centuries, moving across the valleys, mountains, forests and plains, but by the 1930s a different world had seeped into their communities, and they had settled into the towns that dotted the coastlines, making their homes in settlements and reservations near Vancouver. They found jobs in the district's large foundries and in the construction and engineering industries. When war broke out against Germany, many joined the Canadian armed forces and went abroad to fight.

The Canadian troops, who swore allegiance to King George VI, were sent to Britain.

They prepared for D-Day among the gentle hills and woods of southern England, living under canvas, a long way from home, and played a significant part in the liberation of France.

There were 18,444 Canadian casualties in the Normandy Campaign, and a fairly sizeable minority were of Canadian Aboriginal descent. They were at the forefront of the invasion on the beach code-named Juno. Canadian paratroopers were dropped into the countryside near the coast the night before the main attack. They were sent to secure bridges and take out heavily fortified encampments that held through-routes and observation posts, clearing obstacles for their comrades who were at that moment boarding ships and landing craft, heading to assault the beaches of northern France.

Treated as second-class citizens at home, being posted to Europe brought with it mixed fortunes. Their social status transferred itself to the pyramidal structures of the forces. They were at the bottom of the heap, expendable manpower to be sacrificed for the greater good. Yet among the rank and file they found camaraderie, a sense that they had a common enemy to take on and that was best done through teamwork. They were also admired for their various skills. Many were excellent engineers. They were considered to be particularly tough, combining a knowledge of bushcraft survival that other soldiers envied and an acceptance of the conditions war brought. Life on reservations back home was hard. To many the offer of three square meals a day was difficult to turn down.

Added to this, the people living in the English towns and villages where the units containing these young men were billeted considered them a bulwark against the German foe across the Channel, and the majority of hosts went out of their way to make them feel wanted. This didn't ring true everywhere, but from what I'd read for a feature I was working on, many testimonies from the Canadian Aboriginal troops were positive about their time in Britain.

*

In 1944 a second German Blitz hit London. This time it was through the random lobbing of 'doodlebug' V-1 and V-2 rockets across the Channel rather than attacks by the Luftwaffe, and this led to a fresh migration of youngsters into the countryside.

Bob Sixsmith was nine years old. He was a slight cockney lad whose father Ralph had been abroad since the early months of the war with the Eighth Army. His mother Janey had made the hard decision to part with her boy for a second time during his childhood. She realised the war was heading towards a conclusion, but no one knew how long it would last. With the threat from the flying bombs, Janey Sixsmith wanted to ensure her husband had a son to come home to.

Bob was packed off to the Gloucestershire town of Tewkesbury around the same time as the Third Canadian Parachute Squadron arrived to prepare for the liberation of Europe. This quirk of fate threw three very different people together, and seventy years later I came to hear their story and in a small way became involved in its conclusion.

*

The wine was pretty dire. Even such a basic action as chilling it – an oversight on the part of the caterers meant this had not been done – would not have improved the experience. It tasted cheap and nasty. The fact that it was served in a small plastic cup – 'We've run out of glasses,' said the waiter cheerfully – seemed fitting.

Perhaps the organisers hadn't quite realised how many people would show up when they said they were throwing a retirement party for Bob. The amount of effort they had made was in direct contrast to the number of people who had come to show their appreciation. The place was packed out, and they'd clearly been unprepared.

The horrible drinks were matched in their turgidity by the nibbles on offer. A tray of sandwiches passed me. Normally I like to tuck into a free buffet on these types of jobs, happy to station myself by the food and work my way through what's on offer. But the sandwiches here were made with cheap white bread, and the standard of fillings inside were no better. As I ran a disparaging eye over the silver foil trays, I pictured a cold warehouse on an industrial estate in Wembley with scores of zero-hour workers scooping cheese, onion and mayo balls from a giant vat before methodically spreading it on a slice of bread, slamming another one on top, and passing it down the line for the slicer to chop the sandwich into a triangle and a packager to push it into a plastic carton. This would have a sticker put on it proclaiming it was handmade, and into a crate it would go, ready for delivery to corner-shop fridges across London.

It was early evening, and I knew I wouldn't be home for a while yet, so such grim fare would have to do. I remember thinking it was disrespectful to Bob for the council to lay on such a rubbish spread as its way of saying 'Thanks for your long service', but I supposed it was the nature of these things. I was hungry, so I loaded up a paper plate with the least curly edged sandwiches on a tray and tried to balance it as I searched vainly for a shelf or table to loiter next to so I could put my wine glass down and work my way through the grub.

I'd known Bob for a long time. Our paths would cross regularly.

We'd find ourselves at the same civic events. I had stood around outside town halls, community centres, libraries and churches, gossiping with him while the mayor did his duties. Bob was a kind man, always remembered the name of my son and had a cheer about him. He had a big smile and enjoyed his work, liked the cap and suit, the flag on the bonnet and meeting the drivers from other councils at the larger civic affairs he took dignitaries to. His shoes were always well-polished, as was the car. He had a nervous habit of giving the old Rover a rub down with a chamois he kept in the glove compartment as he waited for the mayor to reappear, sweeping away minute specks of grime picked up on route and admiring the shine.

As he flesh-pressed the room, Bob stopped and shook my hand and gave me one of his grins.

'So what will you do now?' I asked him. 'The world is your oyster.'

While I was hoping he'd say something to give me a top line for a picture story I had to write on his life and times – 'Chauffeur hangs up cap to concentrate on building a full-scale model of a Lincoln from matchsticks' – I expected a stock-in-trade reply: a holiday, clearing out the shed, doing up the bathroom, hanging out with the grandchildren, some gardening, sort the lawn out.

Instead, he looked at me with steel in his eyes. 'I've something rather important I need to do,' he said. 'I have been thinking about it for a very, very long time. Something I've needed to do for virtually all my life but never been able to. And, come to think of it, I wonder if you may be able to help me.'

I was intrigued. 'So, what is it?' I asked. 'How can I help?'

'Now is not the time to explain. Let's meet next week, and I'll tell you all about it,' he added with a whisper, before moving on to shake more hands and accept the good wishes of more ex-colleagues.

In the following days I didn't have a minute to think about what Bob had said to me that night. I'd been chasing an odd story about a spate of thefts from churches where statues of Jesus were targeted, apparently being nicked to order.

I'd then spent two days catching up on a double murder at the

Old Bailey, a case that had been running for months and was providing me with regular page leads as gory evidence was read out by the prosecuting barrister, seemingly with half an eye on the press bench as well as the jury. It was a horrible case. Someone had found the thumb of a missing man in Dagenham. It had fallen from the sky and landed at his feet on a high street. It appeared to have been in the beak of a seagull and was once connected to the hand of a waiter called Ali Ramalh who worked at a Bengali restaurant in Euston. I'd been there lots of times – their lunchtime all-you-can-eat for £6.99 was legendary – and I vaguely knew the bloke and his family, which made it even worse. The police had not found the rest of his body but gathered enough evidence to charge a cousin and friend with his abduction and murder. The motive was related to an argument over a failed curry house on the North Circular Road.

With this story and the hunt for the missing Christs, after writing a picture caption 'Driver Bob hangs up his cap' I had not thought too much about his plans for the future.

*

When Bob rang and asked if I wanted a bite to eat, I was slightly reluctant. I'd only just made it home and fancied an evening in. But there was something insistent about his voice and there was nothing I liked the look of in the fridge for supper, so when he offered to treat me to a meal at Maria's Fish Bar And Grill up the road from my house, I said yes.

Maria's was a lovely, old-school fish-and-chip restaurant with a typically north-London twist. While she was of Italian origin, Maria unconsciously drew on eastern Mediterranean cuisine as well as solid British fare. Her menu featured the usual chips, battered fish (cod, plaice, haddock), pickled eggs and onions, gherkins, mushy peas, pies and battered sausages, but she also did Greek salads, grilled lamb chops, roast chicken, a minced-beef moussaka and halloumi-and-falafel wraps – probably in response to the good trade the kebab shop next door enjoyed.

Matriarch Maria kept a close eye and a firm hand on the happenings at the restaurant. Her station was by a triple fat fryer with a griddle pan behind her. The fryers had heated shelves above, with glass fronts so customers could come in and select something already cooked and ready to go.

It was a compact enough work area for her to be able to spin around and punch the keys of the till, slam its drawer closed and place greasy piles of change on a small stainless-steel saucer in the hope it may be left as a tip. She saw to it that she not only knew exactly what food was going out in the white paper squares for the takeaways, or served on the oval china plates with the blue rims for those taking a booth, but also how much was being paid in. It was a form of mental stock control. She ran a tight ship, and her staff were very much considered minor assistants. This was no co-operative team. Three nephews – her brothers' sons – worked with her. They had pallid complexions and wore squashed expressions. This was the result of continual, daily exposure to the noxious airs given off by the vats of cheap boiling oil, while the look on their faces was the result of years of Maria's no-nonsense management.

Maria extended this attitude to her customers, and I was surprised Bob was a regular and by the warm greeting he commanded. I'd always found her scary, but Bob had been going there for years and liked her approach.

I spotted Bob in one of the booths at the back, with a large Coke in front of him, which he sipped through a straw. It was another of Maria's idiosyncrasies. She'd always pour your drink into one of her tall glasses and always give you a straw, no matter your age. After exchanging 'hellos' and 'how are yous', 'enjoying the lie-ins' and 'yes thank yous', we scanned the menu, and Bob went off to order chicken and chips with a side of beans for himself, while I had chips, a steak-and-kidney pie and mushy peas.

As I settled back, wondering what it could possibly be that was eating away at this genial old pensioner and why he had bought me a meal, he began to unbutton his shirt. As he reached halfway down his chest, he scooped out a worn wooden trinket that hung on a piece of leather around his neck.

'Have a look at this, will you?' he said, holding it gently in the palm of his hand.

I was a bit taken back. It looked like the sort of thing boho trendies would buy from a street stall in Thailand during a gap-year trip, not the type of adornment an elderly man from Kentish Town might have swinging close to his chest.

He slipped it from around his neck, laid it gently on the table in front of me and said: 'I want to tell you about this. I need your help returning it.'

*

Bob gave me a stern look, as if to say listen carefully and take me seriously. He began by telling me how he had grown up in Kentish Town during the war and was old enough to remember bombs falling on the railway lines and hitting the nearby streets.

He recalled how Parliament Hill Fields had been dug up for trench-building practice by the Home Guard and then used to grow vegetables as part of the Dig For Victory campaign. He remembered the sirens in the darkness as bombers flew overhead and the searchlights and gun batteries. He told me about the fire watches, nights in cold shelters or hiding under the stairs, collecting shrapnel the following morning and the sound of broken glass underfoot all the way up Kentish Town Road. He remembered collecting a cardboard box with a gas mask inside from an ARP centre and the overpowering smell of the rubber lining that made his head swim when he put it on.

'I was evacuated, twice,' he said. 'Both times I went on my own. In 1939 my school had left three weeks earlier, but I didn't go with the others. I'd had pneumonia that year, and in the months running up to the war I'd been in the Konstam Children's Hospital. I had recovered by the time the Germans marched into Poland, mind – but I was still off school, convalescing at home.

'It was a right shock to find all your peers, your schoolmates, your pals you'd play with in the street, here one minute and gone the next. I was sent to Gloucestershire instead, but after the Battle Of Britain my mum came back and fetched me. Couldn't stand being parted.'

His school would stay at a place in Bedford for the duration, with a few stragglers like Bob gradually returning after the first Blitz was over.

His mum Janey then took the difficult decision to send him out of London for a second time later in the war. He told me how a doodlebug fell on the railway that ran along the back of the terrace in which they lived.

'Shook the bugs out the walls,' he said with a smile.

A family conference was called, and his mum informed Bob that he was going to be sent away, back to the countryside, until it was safe to return once more.

'There wasn't room at the place in Bedford my companions had been sent to, so I went to Gloucestershire again. This is where my story really starts.'

He was placed on a train at Paddington Station, smothered by his mother's kisses, packed off with his gas mask, a tag around a battered suitcase containing all he owned and a packet of sandwiches shoved into his grubby hands.

'I was that much older, and I remember it vividly,' he told me. 'I was met at the station by a couple called the Holbrooks.

'They lived in a village called Ashchurch, near Tewkesbury, and Mr Holbrook was a dairyman, someone who worked processing the milk and butter from farms in the area. They didn't have any children and were quite old. In my young eyes, they were truly ancient.

'I was all on my own. There were other families with evacuees, but perhaps they were full up, maybe that was why the Holbrooks had volunteered to give up a bed. Anyhow, the Holbrooks had offered to take one London mite in – and that London mite hap-pened to be me.'

Bob recalled those stock-in-trade evacuee stories – of the extra-ordinary feeling of seeing an endless horizon, a sky not framed by roofs and chimneys nor coloured dirty-yellow by the city smog... of a new and strange diet, which included plenty of golden butter instead of the dripping or marge Bob was used to having. It sounded very much a rural idyll, and yet I sensed Bob spoke of this new experience with a genuine sadness. I could hear it in his voice and see it in the furrows on his brow.

Bob had finished his Coke, so I left him at the table and went and asked Maria for two more. She brought them with our meals, and we both fell silent as we tucked into the mounds of chips in front of us. I had a fairly early start the following morning, and I wondered how I could get Bob to skip the reminiscences, which I didn't think would make a story, and find out how this odd trinket was connected to his wartime childhood and how I fitted into it.

Without prompting, he continued talking between mouthfuls of chicken and chips.

'Of course, I missed my mum and dad more than anything, but the Holbrooks were decent people,' he said. 'I hear of how some evacuees were treated – abused in different ways – beaten, made to work all hours, used as free labour. Not me. No, the Holbrooks looked out for me, as best they could. I was a skinny little thing, and they fed me well. But I did have some troubles.'

Bob recalled how he was sent to Ashchurch school, a single-storey, solid-stone building in the middle of the village. Children came from miles around to fill the two classrooms. With his London accent and scruffy clothes, he was immediately singled out for long, painful and systematic bullying. A gang of children did not like the sound of his voice – 'I spoke pure cockney' – nor that the school had mixed ages in the classes, and his English and Maths were not up to the same standard as his peers.

'I was a shy, meek child,' he said. 'I had a wheezy chest. I wasn't much to look at, and I found it hard to speak to my classmates. I had no clue what they were going on about half the time – and the teacher, an evil woman called Miss Thompson, made sure everyone knew it. She'd scold me ferociously.

'What with being an outsider, a stranger, living in an old house with old guardians – well, they singled me out from the start, from the moment I walked in.'

It was pretty hard to hear of the cruelty inflicted on this poor sparrow. Even seventy-odd years later, you could sense how much it hurt Bob. He told me how every day children would wait for him at the school gates, and as he made his way home – it was a two-mile walk – he would be subjected to all sorts of ambushes and beatings.

'There was a gang led by this bloody great bruiser of a kid, a proper regular, pink-faced agricultural type, built like a brick shit house and raised on six eggs for breakfast. He made me look like a soot-covered little weed, and he'd thrash me whenever he had the chance.

'I was thrown in a pond a few times, beaten black and blue, made to fight them one at a time, one after another. I was chased into fields where they knew a bull would be waiting... I had my only pair of boots ripped off me and thrown in the upper branches of a tree, where they dangled by their laces, taunting me.

'I hated it, I hated the school, I hated the countryside. I missed my folks, my friends, I missed the streets of London and, above all, I truly hated Hitler and his war. If it wasn't for bloody Hitler, I'd tell myself, none of this would be happening.

'And it was because I bloody hated Hitler that I watched with extra special interest the preparations being made by the soldiers coming in. Gloucestershire was teeming with soldiers – teeming. And they were on my side, out to get the man who had made me leave my mum behind, leave the familiar surroundings of my house and lose my mates and get beaten up every day. It was bloody Hitler's fault, and I saw the soldiers traipsing down the lanes and over the fields as my saviours.'

*

After one particularly savage beating, which left him with a bloody nose and two black eyes, Bob was stopped by a pair of soldiers standing guard at a five-bar gate which led into a field where rows of khaki tents had been set up.

'"Hey, little soldier," one said to me. "What happened to you, little soldier?"

'They were huge. Everything about them was towering. They had big brown eyes, coal-black hair and dark, oily skin. They looked like brothers.

'I lied,' said Bob. 'It was a default thing – never tell an adult, no matter what. That's what I'd learnt. I thought telling this soldier that I was getting a pasting was almost as bad as the pasting itself.

'I said it was nothing, that I'd taken a tumble, but, of course, they knew this wasn't true. One of them asked if I was in trouble or making trouble, and I got all tongue-tied. He lifted me up on to the top of the dry-stone wall around the field and looked at me carefully. Then he gave me a bar of chocolate and asked my name. Asked me where I lived and who I was.

'I remember him saying they were on the lookout for spies and asking me if I had any credentials.

'I told this soldier where I lived and that I was an evacuee. He asked me where my folks were, and I said my dad was serving in the army, that he'd helped smash Rommel in Libya. I remember how kind the man was – I'd only known violence and beatings and bullying from the other children – and this adult, well, he was just so gentle. He said: "Well then, your dad is my comrade", and added that if I didn't belong in that village, neither did he.

'"We're family, me and you, both travelling spirits, a long way from our homes and our parents. We've got to stick together, me and you," and he gave me another bar of chocolate from the depths of his tunic.

'I was astonished. Two bars in one meeting when I'd not seen proper chocolate for years.'

The soldier had a manner that suggested a wisdom his age belied. Bob told me his new friends came from Canada, and that they were two Aboriginals in a unit posted to this little corner of England.

'I asked him his name, and he laughed, said his fellow troopers called him Skylark, and his mate was known as Wolfie. "Nicknames," he admitted, "not our tribal names. I suppose they think it sounds Indian, and we don't mind too much."'

Bob described how he had thought his friends would live in tepees, track deer, chase the buffalo and go to war armed with bows, arrows and tomahawks.

'Of course, it wasn't like that,' said Bob. 'They lived in Vancouver, in regular houses, and worked in the steel industry. But they looked like the people I had seen in the cowboy films. They explained they still had their own ways, the knowledge passed down through generations, the folklore stuff and the skills a Native American would need in the old days. I was charmed, and it had a practical application, this knowledge, in a way that would change my life.'

Wolfie and Skylark started looking out for him. While the village boys and girls had shown him nothing but contempt, these adults, a long way from home and facing racism as outsiders in a white man's army fighting a European war, could identify with little Bob.

'They said I was an outsider, too, and they gave me tins of powdered egg with a Mountie on the label, which we'd turn into delicious scrambled eggs or use for making drop scones, an almost unheard of luxury in the war, even out in the countryside. They always had food spare and, more importantly, they always had time for me.'

That spring, as preparations for the invasion of Europe geared up and Britain became a giant troop carrier as the New World came to the rescue of the Old, Bob spent plenty of time with Wolfie and Skylark. The two soldiers taught him rudimentary bushcraft, such as how to identify tracks and lay traps, and taught him how to swim in the River Avon. They showed Bob how to defend himself from the bullies who had made his life a misery – 'Never go down... always stay on your feet... Lead with your left, and strike with your right... Find the higher ground and let them come to you...'

Their self-defence lessons didn't just show him how to physically fend off the attacks. It gave him a newfound self-confidence that was even more valuable. The school bullies knew he had back-up and soon tired of waiting for him after school. Wolfie and Skylark made sure he got home safely each night.

Then, one day in May, they had the news Bob knew was coming.

'We'll be moving soon,' said Skylark, as Bob sat on the five-bar gate where he'd find them on sentry duty.

'Things are happening,' added Wolfie. 'We're getting ourselves ready for the big one.'

The kindly soldiers did not explicitly make it clear, but everyone in England knew it was on the cards – the big invasion to rid the continent of the despots, the battle to end all battles. Even in Bob's young mind, he knew what this meant.

'Don't be down, soldier, we'll be back,' said Skylark. 'We'll go and bash up Hitler and be back in time for tea, or at least Christmas, and then it'll be home again for good, back over the water. You'll have to come and see us. We'll show you real open country.'

Bob, whose life had been transformed by these two surrogate fathers, recalled the tears that fell and the bitter realisation that their friendship was due to be interrupted.

Seeing this sadness on their young friend's face, Wolfie pulled something from beneath his tunic. Hanging around his neck was a small piece of carved redwood, a keepsake his mother and father had given him as a baby and that his tribe's tradition stated he would wear throughout his life and eventually be buried with.

'He explained the importance of this symbol in his culture,' Bob said. 'He told me he could never be parted from it but asked me to look after it, keep it safe, until he returned. "That way you know I'll be back,"' Bob recalled him saying. 'He said that it was unheard of for his tribesmen to be buried without this trinket, so he knew he'd be safe over there, as nothing could happen if he didn't have it around his neck. Looking back, I'm not sure how true any of this was, but it helped me face the prospect of not having my friends near me. I put it on around my neck and there it has stayed.'

Bob fingered the wooden medallion. It had been rubbed and polished over the years and gave off a warm red hue.

'You see, this is what I want to do with my retirement. Skylark and Wolfie never returned. I know they were among the first wave of Allied troops who attacked the Normandy beaches. I've kept this safe all my life, and now I've not got work to fill my days, I'd like to return it to him, wherever he is. If he is alive, he'll be well into his eighties. I could go on a trip to Canada and meet him. And if he is dead, I'd like to find his grave. But I'm not sure where to start the search, and I thought you could help. Might make a nice story for you.'

I was charmed and intrigued by Bob's tale. I loved the sound of these two lonely soldiers in their early twenties, thousands of miles from home, facing a terrible job, to kill or be killed, but who had confronted it with a stoicism that allowed them to see past their troubles, notice this poor little boy and look after him for a short but crucial time in his childhood.

After dinner I went home and did some reading up about the tribes of the Pacific coast. I found images online of their cultural artefacts, and they were similar to the object Bob had treasured for more than six decades. His small piece of wood was a Kwantlen birth talisman, which had particular significance within the tribe's culture and was something that would not have been handed over lightly.

The first problem I faced was that Bob did not know the names the soldiers had enlisted under. Neither would have been able to give their native monikers at the recruitment office. Instead, like scores of other Canadian Aboriginal soldiers, they were likely to have at first been registered under Anglicised versions, which meant there were an awful lot of troops called John Brown. But Bob knew the village he had been evacuated to, and so I began researching the story of D-Day, and, using the Canadian War Department's records, I looked for units that had made temporary homes for themselves in the fields of south Gloucestershire in late 1943 and early 1944.

I found that the Library And Archives Canada had a database with this type of information, but an online search came up with nothing. You had to be specific with your request, so I emailed an information officer with what I knew and, while I waited for a reply, told Bob I was going to take a couple of days off work and see if I could dig up anything in Tewkesbury.

He thanked me and admitted he hoped Skylark was waiting somewhere over the Atlantic for the wooden icon to be returned before he could rest. This spurred me on, and I drove westwards along the M40 and then up through country lanes into Gloucestershire. I followed the signs to Tewkesbury and pulled up in the high street. I found Tewkesbury Library, and here there was an extensive local-studies archive and a helpful librarian who had an active interest in the area's past. She told me she had been born in the town and recalled vaguely the events of the time.

'I know there were soldiers stationed here,' she said. 'They were up at Lykenham Farm.'

I asked if she recalled any evacuees living there, but she looked blank. 'I was too young to have noticed,' she said and turned back to her cataloguing.

But the files had plenty of information on the basic encampments that farmers whose fields had been requisitioned hosted, and I noted the Third Canadian Parachute Squadron had arrived in January 1944 and stayed put until 7th May. This was the vital piece of missing information I needed. I now had a definite regiment, and I could go back to the Canadian archives and find the names of the servicemen in this unit. Hopefully, two would be the Aboriginal soldiers I was looking for.

Before leaving the county, I decided I'd head out to Lykenham Farm on the off-chance someone there recalled the events of that time. I got directions and drove through the outskirts of the town, past ribbon developments that were slowly eating up agricultural land and into the countryside. I soon turned off an A road into smaller lanes and edged the car through a couple of hamlets until I came across a sign for Ashchurch. I saw the old schoolhouse and took a couple of snaps to show Bob and soaked up the rural atmosphere of the Cotswold stone and the red earth of the surrounding fields.

I imagined Bob walking home from school along this lane, with its high-banked edges and twists that followed the contours of the Gloucestershire weald, warily looking over his shoulder as he was followed by the bullies until he reached the five-bar gate that marked the farm.

Lykenham Farm looked run down, but I suppose it was just the fact that it was a place of work and bore the scars of the agricultural industry. I pulled into a farmyard, concrete drive with tin sheds and barns on one side, cattle pens ahead and then a much older stable block and farmhouse opposite. Rusting equipment lay stacked up against a wall, a gleaming tractor was parked to one side next to an aged Land Rover. There was a dilapidated caravan with peeling paint, broken windows and moss on its roof. I could hear a dog barking at my arrival from within the house. No one came out to greet me, so I gingerly approached the front door and knocked.

Eventually, after more barking, it swung open and the farmer stood there in a grubby checked shirt with the sleeves rolled up, jeans tucked into hiking boots and a cigarette dangling from reddened lips.

'I'm sorry to disturb you, but I've come up from London,' I said, and before I could explain any further, he'd invited me into a large kitchen, cleared a space at a table, and asked if I wanted a cup of tea.

'It's my family's place,' said the farmer, who'd shaken my hand and told me he was called William. 'We've been here for decades. My grandfather worked it during the war, and yes, I know we had troops stationed in the upper fields. It wasn't actually that bad, you know. We got paid for the space they took up, and they helped get the harvest in. The extra manpower must have been a good help for the old boy, considering so many men had been taken away to fight. You only have to look at the war memorial in town to see how many from round here were lost.'

He poured me a strong cup of tea through a strainer from a tin teapot.

'I was born after the war, so I don't remember it, of course, but my mum did,' he said. 'We've got some pictures somewhere.' He stood up and fished around in a cupboard, eventually finding a tatty-edged photo album. 'Here you go. Have a look through this.'

He lay out the old scrapbook, and inside were a series of faded, well-thumbed photographs. They showed the farm and the family, haystacks being made in fields, lots of collie dogs, women in printed dresses with flowers in their hair, picnics by millponds. He turned the pages, talking me through the various relations he recognised until he reached a series of images that were taken during the billeting of troops in pastures.

And there, taken like a football team photograph, was a picture of three rows of Canadian paratroopers, sporting self-conscious smiles for the camera.

I looked closely, and among the white faces were two that stood out. They had high, proud cheekbones and jutting noses. Their eyes were melancholy and knowing, shrewd and dark. They had straight black hair and smooth copper skin. I was enthralled: surely these two must be the pair Bob recalled? One was tall, handsome, slender, smiling an impossibly cheerful smile for a man so far from home and immersed in learning the art of killing. The other was more thickset, chunky. He boasted impressive neck muscles, a natural prizefighter, with a uniform that struggled to contain him. I used my phone to take a series of shots, thanked the farmer and started for home, eager to share my find with Bob.

*

On my return, I found a note emailed from the Canadian archivist who was looking into my enquiry. They apologised but said they could not easily cross reference the files by searching for a name of a small town where a unit had stayed briefly, and did I have any more I could go on? I replied with the details of the unit and asked if they could send me service lists with the names, ranks and other details of those who'd served in it, and then I waited for a reply.

*

In the meantime, I found a collection of articles in the archives of a Canadian newspaper called *The Hamilton Spectator*, and here it reported the work done by the Canadian forces.

Written by a reporter called Ross Munro, whose byline revealed that he had been given embedded access under the guise of working for the Combined Press Of Canada, he told his readership how a group of Canadian paratroopers had been dropped into an area near the beach codenamed Juno – three miles from the abbey town of Caen – the night before the main invasion and how they had cleared the way for a larger body of their countrymen.

The report said that Canadian paratroopers were taken by gliders at 3.30am across the Channel and captured several important bridges, which they held while landing crafts zigzagged their way over the dark sea.

'The Canadians won and established their beachhead in two hours of fighting and pushed inland,' he wrote. 'There was stiff street fighting in the little coastal hamlets of the area, and the

Canadians met some considerable enemy fire on the beaches. As they worked their way into the German defences that they had to overcome, numerous steel and wooden obstacles...'

Among the news reports lay the testimony of a John Anderson, who in 1943 went from Sandy Hook, Manitoba, to Europe with the Third Canadian Parachute Squadron. He was dropped into France at midnight on June 5th 1944, to establish a special zone of safety for the rest of his battalion, who would be coming in the next twelve hours, and I could safely assume that he was in Skylark and Wolfie's unit.

'I was picked for this job because I was Metis (a First Nation tribe) and they thought my bush skills would be very valuable in enemy territory,' he wrote. 'It helped me make it, but I'm afraid to say, such was the resistance from the Germans, many of my friends did not. The slaughter of the parachutists was heavy. We were the first wave, and in my platoon, I was just one of seven who survived out of eighty.'

It didn't sound hopeful, and I dreaded the idea that Bob's friends would be among the seventy-three who had met violent ends as their boots hit the soil.

I pictured them in the heat of the battle, using their bushcraft to take cover, their powerful physiques and fierce wills to hold their own. And I hoped so, so much they had made it. I knew they were set and ready for this moment, had spent those months of training in preparation. They would have known in those hot early June days that their operational level of preparedness was being cranked up a notch. They'd know that soon they would be leaving the safe havens of their green canvas tents and taking trucks to an airfield near the coast and then boarding gliders to fly silently into enemy territory.

Bob would be oblivious that their hearty 'Cheerio, young man' and 'See you soon, little soldier' were to be final. I imagined their nerves as they said these cautious goodbyes, knowing they mustn't let on that they wouldn't be seeing Bob again for some time. I pictured the impulsive handing over of the trinket to him for safekeeping as his eyes filled with tears.

*

Later that week I received another reply from Canada, and it had the information I needed. An attachment contained the service records of the unit, and with a sense of excitement I scanned down the list and there they were. The names stood out, as they were both Johns – one Armstrong, the other Armfair – with the names Two Rivers and Good Leaf in brackets.

They were from the same small town near Vancouver, and under the column stating their religious denomination there were simply dashes. There was one other name that stood out – John Anderson – while no other names in the unit seemed to be of Aboriginal origin, and all other troopers clearly had a Christian denomination noted. I concluded it had to be them.

The columns included a service number. I took a deep breath as I checked online with the Canadian War Office for their war records, and I'm sad to say it brought me the news I dreaded.

Their numbers revealed they had both been killed in action on the morning of June 6th.

*

I met Bob at Maria's for lunch later that week and handed over the papers I'd printed off, with the war records of his friends and the news that they hadn't made it. Grief fell across his face, and he fingered the trinket as he peered through his glasses and checked the simple sentences that confirmed their mortality.

I hated being the bearer of such news, so I had held back the photographs I'd found at Lykenham until he had digested the information. Then I showed him the pictures I had taken at the Farm, and his eyes lit up.

'That is definitely them,' he said. 'And now, at least, I know what happened. Now I know where we can find them. It is time to return Wolfie's treasure.'

*

The Commonwealth War Graves Commission has lists of all those who died overseas serving their country and have done a comprehensive job of logging the whereabouts of hundreds of thousands of people who gave up their lives during the world wars of the 20th century. I'd called a clerk at their London office, and they were refreshingly helpful. As a reporter you are used to the gatekeepers of archives guarding their records like the crown jewels, wary of journalists digging for things they unconsciously feel are best left to rot quietly in dusty filing cabinets. It is as if they have a default position that the keys to the drawers are best left unused.

Not so with the WGC. Perhaps it is a mixture of respect for the sacrifice made by the people behind the lists they hold, the understanding that their legacy remains active if the living show an interest, and the sheer logistical nightmare of cataloguing the remains of those blown to pieces on foreign fields meaning such information has innate value to the clerk responsible. It is there to be shared.

I explained what I wanted and was told they'd have the information ready for me in a day or so. Good to their word, I got a phone call forty-eight hours later and scribbled in my notebook the address of a cemetery in northern France that contained the mortal remains of Bob's friends. A few weeks after our first meal at Maria's, I found myself on a wind- and wave-battered ferry, peering over a barrier as the white cliffs of the South Coast rescinded and France beckoned, with Bob, well-wrapped-up in a heavy overcoat, standing next to me.

I could sense his anticipation, mingled with a sadness that he wasn't heading to Canada to meet the now-aged pair.

'Did you know the navy wouldn't accept Native Americans because they didn't think they would mix well with whites in the tight, confined conditions on the boats,' he told me. 'Funny to think they wanted their muscle and flesh but had so many hang-ups as to how they'd use them. Also, they still dished out a grog ration and didn't think the Indians could handle it. There was terrible alcoholism among the First Nations, and the navy brass used that as an excuse.

'Not many flew, either,' he continued. 'The air force had a high entry test that required much more than the basic schooling the Aborigines were given. It was skewed towards those who had a traditional English education, and that worked very well as a colour bar. But as the war progressed and they needed the manpower, this slackened and both these services started to enlist Aboriginals, but it took time. The army, of course, was less choosy, but the population was riddled with poor health and that meant many were simply not able to pass the fitness test. There were huge numbers of cases of tuberculosis, for example. Skylark and Wolfie's good health was their downfall, I suppose.'

*

After arriving at Dieppe, we took a taxi to an Allied cemetery a few miles out of town. Stuck on a hillside overlooking the beaches where so many had fallen, I tried to imagine what it must have been like for the soldiers, tried to conjure up an image of the first few hours of D-Day as this peaceful, contemplative spot became, for a time, the most dangerous place in the world, where modern history twisted and shook under earth-shattering bombardments, where the sky turned black from the high explosives and flesh was beaten raw by bullet and bomb. We said little, and I could see the tiredness and sense of grief in Bob's slumped shoulders and long face.

Having consulted a ledger in a well-kept, pebble-dashed gatehouse, we made our way through the rows, rows and more rows of white crosses.

In one corner of the cemetery was an area for soldiers who were not Christian, and the headstones switched from crosses to simple plinths, with names and ranks etched across them. I stood back as Bob walked timidly through the grass avenues, stopping occasionally, until he found what he was looking for.

There, lying next to each other for eternity, were the two graves of Bob's friends.

Without a word, he took the talisman from around his neck and hung it on one of the gravestones. He paused and mumbled a prayer under his breath. He looked at the ground, and then up into the darkening skies, and crossed himself.

I didn't want to intrude, but needed a picture for the *Evening*

Press And Star. Bob stood glumly with the graves behind him, and after I'd got him to look into my lens, he managed a smile.

'Let's go home,' he said and turned, leaving the Kwantlen talisman where its original owner would have wanted it placed.

The Evening Press And Star, centre-page lead

CHAUFFEUR BOB'S WAR HERO QUEST – HOW THE MAYOR'S DRIVER LAID A SEVENTY-YEAR-OLD GHOST TO REST

It all started for Bob Sixsmith when he was a lad, a small boy ripped from the bosom of his family in Kentish Town to avoid Hitler's deadly Blitz.

Mr Sixsmith, now in his seventies, retired in the summer from his job as the Town Hall's chief chauffeur, a position that saw him ferry more than thirty mayors to and from civic events. And all his working life he carried a secret with him dating from those war-torn days as a child.

This week, he travelled to a cemetery in northern France to return a small talisman a soldier had given him as a keepsake – and honoured a promise he made to himself throughout his working life.

Mr Sixsmith said: 'I was evacuated from my home in 1944, and while I was staying in Gloucestershire, I met two First Nation Canadian paratroopers.'

Homesick and bullied by country children who laughed at his London accent, he was protected by the soldiers who took him under their wing.

He continued: 'They looked after me, and before they went to play their part in the invasion of Europe, they gave me a Native Canadian talisman known as a Kwantlen neckpiece.'

The trinket, carved from Redwood, is presented to a new-born child by tribal elders and hangs around their neck. It is, according to custom, eventually buried with its owner.

Mr Sixsmith added: 'The soldiers, who I only knew as Wolfie and Skylark, handed me this item in the days before they embarked for D-Day. I never saw them again, and it has been my wish to find out what happened to them.'

With *The Press And Star's* help, Mr Sixsmith tracked down the soldiers' war records and discovered that the pair – real names John Two Rivers and John Good Leaf – had played a heroic role in the battle to take Caen from the Germans. Tragically, they both lost their lives in this crucial part of the conflict in northern France.

Mr Sixsmith travelled to an Allied cemetery near Dieppe last week to find their graves and pay his respects – and return the gift he had been given nearly seventy years ago.

He said: 'They were two important people to me during my childhood, two father figures who I looked up to and took the place of my dad, who at that time was fighting in Italy. To be able to return their talisman was important to me, and it is important in their culture that it should be laid down at their last resting place. I feel I have now honoured the memory of two very special, very brave men.'

A FISHERMAN'S TALE

'POLYESTER...' SAID PROFESSOR Barr, 'does not rot. That is why it is widely used in the manufacture of maritime rope. It is a formidable fibre. It was invented in 1951, and for a time it became a must-use fabric for menswear. Cheap to make, it lent itself readily to mass production. Versatile, hardy and easy to style and to dye.

'In the 1970s, people loved their drip-dry polyester shirts. Horrible things, when you think about it, but it was an era of clothing technology that seemed to think anything man-made – and polyester was linked with the space suits that took Aldrin and Armstrong to the surface of the moon – was simply better than raw cotton. It also meant people didn't have to worry about ironing, a unique selling point in the eyes of the clothing industry. In a time where housework was no longer seen to be the preserve of women staying at home, the attraction of a shirt that just did not crease after washing was immense. It was seen as a selling point, something the tailoring profession and clothing companies could peddle.

'Problem was, of course, it is not the most comfortable material and eventually got found out. Our skin breathes, and such a waterproof material meant, essentially, when you wear a 100-percent polyester shirt, you are slowly drowning your pores...'

I wrote all this down into my notebook, hoping to be able to read back 'polyester' in my garbled shorthand. But it was a very enlightening interview, and I thanked Professor Barr. His knowledge provided a vital clue for a story I was working on.

Professor Barr, who I found via the Fashion And Textile Museum, had no idea why I was quizzing him on the staying power of shop-bought shirt fabrics from the 1970s. I'd told him I was a reporter on *The Evening Press And Star* and wanted some information on how long a shirt would last if completely submerged under water.

'Hard to say,' he'd told me. 'It depends, of course, on whether it was pure polyester. Sometimes they would make clothing that included a rayon or nylon mix. It also partly depends on the type of water. If it was saline, I'd expect that to have an accelerating effect on decomposition. Fresh water less so. Water temperature would potentially affect any dyes and colourants in the material, too, and that, in turn, could leech into the fibres and speed up the process of forming a microscopic mildew. But polyester was particularly designed to be water-resistant, and research shows it has remarkable capabilities and the ability to survive some pretty harsh conditions. Tough stuff. I'd say a polyester shirt, especially a pure one, submerged in the conditions you described, could still be recognisable as such forty-odd years later.'

This was the answer I was looking for. It gave me a fighting chance of proving, perhaps not beyond reasonable doubt but enough for a good page lead, that I had the answer to a mystery which had tickled our readers one summer.

A couple of days later I was standing on the banks of a pond on Hampstead Heath, watching a large yellow digger gently roll up a short grassy slope. Attached to it was one end of a towrope, and on the other was a semi-submerged, mud-coated and rust-covered car, which was gradually being dragged from its resting place.

When it finally reached dry land, I moved forward. As the digger operator and some parkies looked on with a cool bemusement, I forced open the boot and peered inside. I was looking for a vital clue in the shape of a tatty, soggy piece of polyester.

*

Highgate Number 2 Pond, or the Men's Pond, as the expanse of water is known locally, is about twenty-feet deep in the middle. It's hemmed in by bushes and trees on two sides and then has two banks with pathways snaking around them. It is here where people stand to throw bread at the swans and moorhens, and anglers sit on stools and camping chairs, staring at floats that rarely twitch.

It's not a natural lake. It dates from the late 1700s and was dug out to catch the springs that sent clean streams twinkling through the coarse heathland from the heights of Hampstead down through the valley. These little tributaries eventually gathered their strength and formed the River Fleet. They were a natural resource for a city with an unquenchable thirst.

With London expanding rapidly and the need for fresh, clean drinking water putting a huge amount of pressure on its piecemeal infrastructure, the north-London parish councils decided that a series of reservoirs to catch the Bagshot Sands filtered springs would make the most of this pleasant quirk of geology.

Over the years, the ponds' original use became redundant. The big Victorian waterworks, prompted by the Metropolitan Water Act of 1852, saw private firms invest in creating brick-lined sub-terranean lakes hidden beneath mounds of earth. One was built just a quarter of a mile away from the Heath in Highgate Village, and another in Dartmouth Park Hill. Both offered plenty of capacity and put paid to the Heath ponds' short lives as reservoirs. They gently slipped into being considered natural features on common land. As swimming became popular, they had a new lease of life, providing a place to paddle, practise dives and perfect strokes. They are still an attraction for those who like a refreshing dip in natural waters. The ponds are tranquil spots in a hectic, dirty city. I had swum in them, knew the lifeguards and regulars and would pick up the odd story from changing-area gossips.

It meant I was intrigued when I answered a call from Bill MacDonald, the Superintendent of the Heath. He asked me to come to see him for a cup of tea and a chat at the tail end of an afternoon. My interest was piqued when he said it was about the Men's Pond.

*

Swimming for leisure became a popular pastime in the Victorian period, and Captain Matthew Webb, born in Coalbrookdale, Shropshire, in 1848, was a key figure in its rise.

He'd become known when he dived into the Atlantic while working as a merchant seaman in an attempt to save a crew member who had fallen overboard. Later, he would repeat the feat by rescuing his own brother, who was drowning in the River Severn.

In 1873, the sea captain read of a failed attempt to swim the Channel, and suddenly he had a new purpose: he would be the first to go from Dover to Calais under his own power. He eventually conquered the challenge and became a national hero. He knew Hampstead well and showed off his prowess at special exhibitions in the ponds on the Heath. He'd give diving displays to crowds gathered along the banks and provide public lectures on the importance of learning to swim and staying safe in the water.

Webb died in tragic circumstances, attempting to go over the Niagara Falls in a barrel – a crazy stunt that went disastrously wrong – but by then his effect on the British public had been telling. Swimming became a pastime. The Heath had, by Webb's day, started to shift from being an economic to a leisure resource. It was already used for sports and recreation, with Londoners coming up there on bank holidays for its fairs, using its slopes for sledging in the winter months, and, as swimming became popular, leaping into the ponds from the banks and splashing around in the water was another draw.

Gradually, the use of the ponds became more organised. Ladies-only and men-only ponds, for reasons of modesty, were established. Changing areas were created, fences put up, jetties built and the Men's Pond had a thirty-foot diving platform constructed. Following Captain Webb's example, a diving troupe called the Magnificent Martinelle Mariners were formed from Heath swimmers. They tumbled, spun and somersaulted. They twisted through the air together, performed graceful swallow dives, japed about and brought both gasps of 'How did they do that?' admiration and guffaws of giggles to the boys watching along the banks, inspiring copycat displays among the youngsters. The platform used by the MMMs was demolished in the 1970s after an accident, but swimmers today still enjoy the use of a springboard from a concrete walkway.

And it was this springboard that indirectly brought me into a small office on the Heath, smelling faintly of damp welly boots, to hear what the superintendent had to say.

I settled down in a comfortable chair opposite Bill with my notebook and pen at the ready. He was a large bloke with a face mottled with broken veins, the product of his outdoor life and post-work drinking with staff.

He'd always struck me as a straight talker and had previously been a good source of stories about the land he managed. I liked his company. He was interested in the soil, which he carried beneath his fingernails, and all that grew in it. He had a thorough knowledge of every tree, bush and bit of scrub and grass on the eight-hundred-odd acres he tramped across each day.

'We're going to have to close the Men's Pond,' he said. 'Thought you'd like to know first.'

Having enjoyed both refreshing leaps into the waters and story-producing gossip I'd regularly hear from the austere concrete-floored changing area after I had wrapped myself shivering into a towel, I knew how important this was to people who use the Heath and could see a great story for *The Evening Press And Star*. As Bill spoke, I remembered how a year before a swimmer had got into trouble after diving in and injuring themselves. While the Heath Corporation had been absolved of any responsibility, in a subsequent report by the Health And Safety Executive, the facts stood that the swimmer had struck something on the pond bed and gashed his head open. He'd passed out, and if it hadn't been for the quick actions of the lifeguards it could have been much worse. I wondered aloud if this closure had anything to do with the incident the previous year.

'I thought you may think that, and that's why I wanted to speak to you in person,' replied Bill. 'The answer, officially, is, of course, "no". The investigation absolved us of any blame, remember. I can't tell you on the record anything about that, but let's just say we both know that the pond isn't as deep as it used to be, and there are certain items underwater that shouldn't be there. I don't want to sit in a court again and hear that my lifeguards had to save a man's life. This means we need to act, and the time to do so is now, before something else happens and the outcome is much worse.'

'Okay,' I said. 'So what are we talking about here? How long? How much will it cost? How's it going to work?'

'This closure will be temporary, and we'll do the work as quickly as we possibly can,' he continued.

'It should take a few months. The thing is, we've a problem with silt. It's just never been cleared out before. It's affecting the water quality, and it's also making swimming in some parts dangerous. It's getting too shallow to dive in safely, and there are some spots where swimmers think they can stand as they touch the bottom, but it's just ten feet of squidgy muck. Easy to get your foot caught up in it and be slowly sucked downwards. Not a nice situation to find yourself in.

'We're going to drain it, use a giant hoover to suck up the silt and then get excavators in there and scoop out what's left on the bed till we get back to the London clay. It will increase the depth in parts by at least twenty-five feet, we'll clear out any underwater obstructions. We won't have to worry about this for another hundred years, minimum. It's going to cost north of one million pounds, but it needs to be done, so it's a price we'll have to grin and bear.'

He told me that while they did the work they'd use the opportunity to plant new reed beds around the edges, spruce up the changing area and reinstall a diving platform.

'It won't be thirty-odd feet high this time,' he said. 'More like six, but we're sure the swimmers will like it. While it's closed, they'll have to go to the Mixed Ponds, but it has to be done.'

Spring was fighting its way through the murk of winter when work started. The early blossoms had begun to announce that the worst was over. Snowdrops poked up through patches of grass and early cherry had skeletal branches dusted with pink. It was still getting dark at 5pm, but February was rapidly slipping past, and the Heath was shaking off the torpor of a cold winter.

I'd gone to the pond to take some pictures of how they planned to drain the 22 million gallons of water. It was an intriguing project. They'd closed the sluice gates that let water in from above and opened the ones below. You could hear the water rushing through submerged pipes downstream, an unfathomable amount of water disappearing while the surface lay still. The engineers told me that once the lip of the sluice gates had been reached, they'd use giant pipes to suck out the remaining water, and then turn them on the silt. As this happened, they'd stick an electric current in to stun the fish, scoop them out and then bring them back to life by putting them in tanks of highly oxygenated water before moving them to a new home upstream.

The draining would take about a week. For a photo story for our centre pages, I went up every day before heading into the office to take a fresh picture as the water levels dropped bit by bit.

Finally, the long-hidden pond bed emerged. When work began to remove the mud, I got another call from the superintendent, and he said to me: 'You may want to come up here. We've found some interesting stuff at the bottom of that pond.'

Laid out on his desk on top of sodden towels, were a motley collection of items.

There was a fair amount of rubbish that had gone straight into a skip – a few bikes, a surprising number of wire shopping baskets and other bits and pieces that made you despair at the lack of respect people had paid the pond down the years. It had been used like a municipal rubbish dump. Bill knew I wasn't interested in this detritus but instead, laid out on a table, were some more newsworthy bits and pieces.

There was a large chain and anchor, which dated from the mid-1800s, a twenty-four-inch stone lion and what looked like a brass sceptre. Here was a javelin, a grandfather clock in surprisingly good condition and an electric wheelchair.

More sinisterly, the work had uncovered instruments favoured by armed criminals and murderers over the past three hundred years, emerging from hiding places their previous owners had considered to be pretty foolproof. This included a short broadsword and the barrel of a flint-lock pistol.

Handling them, Bill said: 'The silt preserved much. Incredible. There used to be duels on the Heath, and I'd not be surprised if this piece of metal was used to run someone through and thrown, bloody-bladed, into the water.'

More recently, the pond had received a sawn-off shotgun and two pistols, one dating from the 1950s, while the other was only ten years old.

'The police will take that one away,' he said, 'and the rest will go to the Museum Of London for further analysis.' He also showed me a Second World War hand grenade, which I suspected was linked to the Home Guard drills on Parliament Hill Fields when dummy bombs had been used for practice.

I took pictures of the superintendent holding up the pistols, trying hard not to capture him in a gangsta pose and looking suitably serious, and wrote up an entertaining page-three lead for the paper.

I thought that was it for finds in the pond, but a couple of days after we'd published the story I got another call from Bill.

'You'll never guess what else has emerged,' he said. 'There's only a bloody car, too. God knows how it got there. Between us, it must be what the poor bloke smashed into when he dived in. It's about forty years old. The police say they aren't interested, but we're all scratching our heads over it. How does a Ford Escort end up in the Men's Pond? And why?'

*

My first port of call was a retired police officer who had worked on the Heath. Today it has its own team of constables, but this was a fairly new service. The open space never used to have its own, dedicated constabulary. In the 1970s it was managed by the Greater London Council, and the Met would be called if a copper was needed. When the GLC closed in the late 1980s, a new patrol was established and called the Heath Constabulary.

My source, Sergeant Stone, had been a beat copper in the neighbourhood, based at the Hampstead police station. When the Corporation of London took over, he moved from being a regular officer stationed nearby to managing the small team that would patrol the fields and hills during the day. His job was basically to scare teenagers smoking dope in the bushes, tactfully suggest lovers put their clothes back on before they got done for indecency, stopping cyclists tearing down paths and scaring walkers and frowning at dog owners who did not pick up their pets' shit.

He had an encyclopaedic knowledge of happenings up there, a

well-stocked memory of events that had taken place, and over the years I'd learnt that he loved to show this off over a cup of tea.

We met at the Dog Café on Parliament Hill Fields and, sipping steaming hot brews, I quizzed him about the car.

I'd taken a series of pictures of what was left of it and had managed to confirm from the shape of what remained of its chassis that it was a Ford Escort. The sloping back window and the two-door design suggested it was a Mark I, the most popular type of the vehicle they made. It first rolled off the Dagenham plant production lines in 1968, and that gave me a date from when it could have been put in the water.

Before I met Stone, I'd taken a walk around the pond and tried to work out where the car could have been shoved in. One side had a steep slope leading down the bank, the other a steep slope going up. It was found on the far north side, so I imagined that was where it must have entered, unless it floated fifty-odd yards before sinking slowly downwards. There was a copse of fairly dense sycamores along this stretch, but it was possible they were mere saplings around the time the car was sunk.

In our newsroom, we had a shelf full of local history books. The Heath had been well-covered over the years, and one fairly recent publication called *Hampstead Heath In Pictures* was full of images of the ponds.

Looking at old photographs, trying to judge where trees were now and how quickly they had grown, I noticed that in the earlier part of the 1970s there were no barriers around the pond. I then found another photograph, taken in 1977, and there was a fence. I asked Stone if he recalled it going up and he said that after the heat-wave of 1976 the GLC had become so concerned with people swimming from the banks that they'd secured them and put up warning signs saying 'Deep Water'. This meant I could safely assume the car was shoved in there between 1968 and 1976.

'Do you recall anything untoward happening around these years?' I asked Stone. 'Do you remember an incident involving a car – a Ford Escort?'

I imagined it must have some criminal connection. Surely it was dumped there by a gang who robbed a Post Office or held up an armoured van, which in my mind was the kind of crimes robbers committed back then. A *Sweeney*-type blag, I thought. It must have been.

'It was all rather tragic,' he said. 'In 1973 – '74 perhaps – we found a body in the pond. It was a woman who had gone missing, and we'd been told that she liked to swim after hours in the moonlight. Police divers went in and found her, and I remember one of them telling me there was a car in there, too. As far as I know it was never removed, and I did wonder why. Find out what year that death occurred – the coroner's report will tell you, or your own newspaper archives probably – and that will narrow the years down even more.'

It wasn't conclusive, but it was information I could use, so I went through some back issues of the paper that night. They were in a bit of a jumble, yellowed and musty, and I got distracted reading the penny-dreadful-style crime capers that were prominent in our paper back then.

Eventually, I found a small report by a court agency that noted the nocturnal swimmer's passing. It was dated September 1973, which meant I could further narrow down the years when the car must have been dumped.

Stone had told me to consider all the possible reasons someone might want to hide a car from view in such a manner that made retrieving it impossible. It could be a way to get rid of fingerprints – DNA swabs for serious crime were not in use in the period between May 1968, when the first Mark I was sold, and September 1973, but this didn't seem plausible. Surely you'd find some wasteland and torch it, or wash it down and leave it in a back street, or shove it in a car crusher, said Stone. Going to the bother of driving a car on to Hampstead Heath, and the inherent risks of being caught doing so, then getting it safely on to the bank and pushing it over the lip and into the pond, was not the easiest way to dispose of a vehicle.

Because of the texture and depth of the silt, there was no way I could safely get close enough to have a look around inside and see if any clues had survived the forty-odd years it had spent in the water, so I had to wait for it to be removed. At the very least, I thought, watching a digger drag it from its resting place would make a picture for a fairly decent page-five lead.

Over the coming days, the newspaper received a lot of calls about the car. There was a thirst among our readers for more information, so I didn't want to admit defeat.

I contacted the Men's Pond swimming club, and asked some of the older members if they recalled any incident with a car. None of them knew anything to further my search and all seemed surprised that it had lain there undiscovered for so long.

'You'd think someone wearing a pair of goggles would've spotted it at some point,' one had said. 'The water is murky but not that murky.'

I thought I would wait until it was taken from the pond bed, and I could see if a chassis number was intact then contact Ford and find out if it could link that with a dealership. Perhaps there would be a record of who it was sold to, but it felt like a long shot. This type of information would only be stored on a piece of paper in a filing cabinet in the office of a Ford showroom, and the chances of it still existing more than forty years after the sale seemed pretty minute.

*

It was some weeks later that I finally discovered the most plausible explanation, and it gave me a nice page lead.

I'd been told the car was finally going to be dragged out in the coming few days, and we'd discussed in the newsroom what had really happened and whether we would ever clear up the mystery. I felt I'd pretty much exhausted every avenue I could think of and was annoyed nothing had come from my various enquiries.

But, as is often the way with stories like this, something pops up when you don't expect it, and a little chink in a mystery's armour opens.

It was a Friday, heading towards pub time, and I'd had enough for the week. I went for a shave and trim at the College Street Barbers before going for a pint. It was always a good place for a chat, with its proprietor, an elderly Turkish bloke called Muz, playing host. He saw it as a social club where various Camden Town faces mixed, a haven where customers could come and spout forth on the news and sport of the day, drink one of his coffees and feel a sense of camaraderie among the powder, soap and lotion. I liked going in there and having a cheap short, back and sides and listening to the natter above the buzz of the razor. I liked the way customers read my newspaper. It was a bit of an ego trip, the fact these old boys thought you had the inside dope on what was going on locally, and it provided them with various topics of conversation.

I sat down in the faded red-leather barber's chair and, as Muz lathered up a cake of soap, I gazed around, listening to the chit-chat, the talk of gardening and holidays, wayward children and delightful grandchildren. Muz and his customers had various passions – football, politics, cigars and coffee – but the overriding thing they all loved was fishing. On the walls of the barber's were scores of photographs. There were snaps taken on boats during trips in Florida showing portly men, tummies tucked in, chests puffed out, holding rays and tuna and marlins on quaysides. There were postcards from Ireland, images from Scottish rivers, a man in tweeds and waders with a hat casting a shadow over his face, a fly line flicking at the surface. Posters with humourless legends such as 'Gone Fishing' across them filled space, and there was a Billy Bass The Singing Fish above a sink.

It was one set of pictures that started a conversation which would open some doors to the Escort mystery.

Pinned on the wall were pictures of Muz and others clutching a mirror carp, taken on Hampstead Heath. They'd been cut out of *The Evening Press And Star*, and as I lay back in the chair, my chin being covered in warm soap, I asked Muz what had happened to the fish in the picture. It was a bit of a legend, that fish. Every season we'd get a call from an angler who had reeled in the same thirty-two-pound mirror carp that had long lived in the murky depths. This poor creature had been caught so many times he'd been nicknamed Old Iron Jaw due to the number of hooks he'd snagged. I asked Muz if anyone had caught it recently, and I wondered aloud how it was faring, what with the pond drained.

'Nah,' he said. 'The old bugger must be finally dead. They say there are mirrors that live for fifty years and Iron Jaw must have been well into his third decade. I heard that when they took the fish out to drain the place when they were doing that work he was nowhere to be seen. Maybe he was wily enough to swim down the pipes into the lower pond before he got stunned – although he wasn't that wily if you consider how often he was caught. Or perhaps he was, and he liked an annual picture of himself in your rag?'

Those waiting for a trim giggled like a Greek chorus at the host's joke.

'Maybe he was in the boot of the car they found, choking his breath away like something out of *Goodfellas*,' I suggested.

'What, Flynn's old Ford?' Muz said. 'Doubt it. We'd have heard.'

I'd never heard the car referred to as Flynn's Ford, and it took me a moment to register the comment.

'Why do you call it that?' I asked, as he stretched the skin on my face and drew the warm razor across it.

'What, Flynn? It was his, Paul Flynn's Mark I,' he replied, with a conspiratorial smile in the mirror.

'Go on...' I said, intrigued, between swipes of the blade.

'You don't know, do you? I did wonder if you'd run something in the paper and I'd missed it.'

'Do you know how that car got up there? The old Escort they found?'

'As a matter of fact, I do – and I don't suppose there's any harm in telling you now. The old girl responsible is long gone, and I bet Paul wouldn't mind me revealing all anyway – it was a pretty funny thing. All about revenge...'

He said 'revenge' with a sinister glee, and I instantly imagined some kind of blag gone wrong, just as I'd hoped. It sounded like a pitch for a film that would star a young Michael Caine, or perhaps, if it was a little less classy, Dennis Waterman.

'Keep still now,' he ordered. Muz wiped the razor off on a towel and continued scraping away at my face.

'In the early 1970s there was a gang of us who used to go up the Heath on the weekends and stay there overnight to fish,' he recalled as he ran the blade along my jaw and under my chin. 'We didn't catch much. Not much better than the canal, to be honest, but it was a social thing. We'd sit back on our camp beds, cast our lines, drink beer, have a smoke and chat. It was a good excuse to get out the house.

'There was a bloke who'd come up with us, a mate of mine, Paul Flynn. He worked on the post. Used to live off the Crescent. Nice bloke. Handsome as anything. I still cut his hair, and it's as thick as it was back then. A bit of a ladies' man. Terrible angler, though.

'Now, he was married to Evie Driscoll. Big family, the Driscolls. You must have heard of them. The dad was a scaffolder. She had four sisters and three brothers, and poor Paul got a rough time from them. Hell of a family to marry into. Suspect it may have been a shotgun do.

'Anyway, he'd come up on the Saturday after the football with us, set up his rod and tackle and disappear off to meet another woman. He had a girlfriend up the Newtown, and he'd use the fishing as an excuse to have a few hours with her. We'd cover for him.

'So, it must have been the summer of 1972, and Paul goes and buys himself a new Ford Escort. Loved it more than anything. Spent every Sunday polishing the bloody thing. His wife was a nightmare – hated him coming up the Heath instead of going to the pub with her and her family, hated the fact that he'd then spend half a Sunday wiping down and polishing up his bloody car. I remember only too well – brute of a woman, you'd not mess with her, or her bloody sisters for that matter. Terrors, all of them – absolute terrors.

'Anyway, one night Paul gets royally rumbled. I remember him telling me later he'd make the mistake of wearing his favourite shirt out on the Saturday night, and Evie must have been suspicious anyway, but it was this horrible loud shirt he'd wear that made her sure he was up to no good. We used to laugh at him. I remember it clear as yesterday. Shiny purple-and-white thing it was, with proper big collars. Hardly what you'd wear to go fishing in. One day she comes up, sees his stuff but no sign of him, and all hell breaks loose. She'd suspected, of course, but wanted to catch him. Came and gave us all what for. Shrieked the place down, effing and blinding, telling us all what degree of murder waited for poor Paul when she got her hands on him. I didn't see him again for weeks. She had him under strict orders, and I heard that the family were on his case as well.

'Then, one day, I see him, ask him how it's going, and I could see in his face he was broken. They weren't going to get a divorce, old man Driscoll wouldn't be having any of that, but they were making his life a total bloody misery.

'And, to cap it all, he told me his beloved car had been nicked. He was heartbroken. Gone, disappeared – and slightly fortunate he wasn't in it at the time, I thought to myself. The police never found it.'

Muz paused for dramatic effect and then lent closer to me. I could smell the hair lotion he used, and he whispered in my ear, holding the razor at arm's length theatrically. He was clearly relishing the memory of Paul and his Escort.

'Now, years and years later, I was cutting the hair of Sean Driscoll, Evie's brother, and old Paul's brother-in-law. He asked how the fishing was going, did I still spend my days up the Heath, you know, we got chatting, small talk and stuff. Nice bloke, Sean.

'Then he tells me all about what happened. After Evie found out her husband was up to no good, she and sisters got his clothes, shoved them in the boot of his car and drove it up the Heath. They took it to the edge of the pond, took off the handbrake, gave it an almighty shove, and away it went.

'And that, my friend, is how that car ended up at the bottom of the lake. Nothing to do with bank robbers, kidnappers or joyriders, I'm afraid. Just a lesson to be learnt – never double cross your woman if she has a big gaggle of sisters to egg her on to avenge your behaviour.'

He laughed, and the other customers sitting around his barbershop laughed, too, on cue. He wiped my face down with a steaming towel, splashed some lotion across my cheeks, spun the chair around and said: 'Who's a pretty boy then?' I thanked him, handed over a tenner and rushed back to work, eager to scribble down what he'd said before I forgot any of the funnier details.

*

A few days after my shave, I received a call from a parkie who told me the engineers were dragging the car out that day, and if I wanted a closer look I should head up there. Muz had told me Paul's clothes went the same way as his car, so I waited with a sense of expectation as the digger strained and dragged the old Ford slowly through a few feet of mud towards the bank. It left a glutinous trail in the sludge, and someone joked about it looking like a mechanical missing link, creeping out of the primordial swamp on to dry land. It finally reached the bank, and we stood about as the last gunk and water oozed out from the rotten chassis.

'Mind if I have a closer look?' I asked the Rangers, and they said I could do what I wanted.

'Let's try and open the boot,' I said.

'Reckon there may be a body in there?' one replied sarcastically.

'Nah. Just a smoking gun,' I said, smiling.

The boot wasn't locked, but it was so rusty the hinges no longer worked. I borrowed a pair of gloves and gradually managed to wriggle it open.

There was a gooey mess of fabric inside. I found a stick and swished it carefully out. It was a pile of polyester rags, slowly deteriorating, covered in slime. I laid it out on the ground. I nudged gingerly with the toe of my boot and could just make out the shape of two fly-away collars, the type of thing a dashing young lothario might sport in the early 1970s.

The Evening Press And Star, page 5

A FISHY TALE?
THE MYSTERY OF THE FORD ESCORT

The rusting Ford Escort found in the dredged waters of the Men's Pond was dumped there by a furious wife who caught her fisherman husband cheating, *The Evening Press And Star* can reveal.

New evidence uncovered by *The Evening Press And Star* seems to finally lay bare the truth behind a mystery that Hampstead Heath walkers have mused on for months.

As we reported earlier this summer, engineers found the car when they began draining water to clear silt and debris from the pond bed.

The Evening Press And Star has investigated various theories as to how the car met its watery grave. Now a Heath fisherman, who was a regular on the grassy banks during the 1970s, has provided a new lead that has unlocked the mystery – and it involves anglers, an affair and revenge.

Our research has shown that up until 1976 there were no fences running along the edges of the pond, meaning the car must have found its way into the water before the summer famous for its heatwave. With the vehicle being identified as a Mark I Escort, which dates from 1968, the rusted two-door saloon must have been submerged sometime during five years in the mid 1970s.

The angler, now in his seventies and who did not want to be named, said: 'Me and my mates would spend every summer up there. I had a friend who came night after night, but it was really an excuse for him to visit a lover.

'He'd tell his wife he'd be up the Heath, and we'd cover for him. He would spend a few hours setting up his tackle, then slip off for a bit of time with his girlfriend.'

According to our source, this fishing-rod lothario had another passion: his new Ford.

He added: 'His wife wasn't happy with him always being out the house, and then he'd make matters worse by spending his Sundays polishing up his car.'

Things went wrong one evening when she visited the pond looking for her husband.

'His game was up,' said the fisherman. 'We tried to cover for our friend, but it was because he would go fishing wearing his best shirt that made her suspicious.'

A few days later, the man's car was stolen and never found.

Police say they are not investigating whether the vehicle is linked to a historic crime, while Heath manager, the Corporation of London, add that it has no idea how long the car has been beneath the surface. It will be scrapped without any forensic study taking place.

Our source concluded: 'Years later, his brother-in-law told me the man's wife, who was part of a big extended family in Kentish Town, had stolen the car with the help of her sisters. They had driven it up to the Heath, trashed it and then rolled it into the pond.'

The cleaning work has also revealed a host of weapons, dumped in the water over the decades. These include a sword, seven knives, a hand grenade, a sawn-off shotgun and four pistols.